About the A

Melanie Barrin is a primary school teacher in London. A French national, she has lived in the UK most of her life and spends her summer holidays in Royan, a small seaside resort where her mother's family is from. This idyllic backdrop inspired the setting and plot of her first book.

L'APERITIF

Melanie Barrin

L'APERITIF

Vanguard Press

VANGUARD PAPERBACK

© Copyright 2025
Melanie Barrin

The right of Melanie Barrin to be identified as author of
this work has been asserted by her in accordance with the
Copyright, Designs and Patents Act 1988.

A CIP catalogue record for this title is available from the British Library.

ISBN 978-1-83794-306-7

This is a work of fiction. Names, characters, businesses, places, events and
incidents are either the products of the author's imagination or used in a fictitious
manner. Any resemblance to actual persons, living or dead, or actual events is
purely coincidental.

Vanguard Press is an imprint of
Pegasus Elliot Mackenzie Publishers Ltd.
www.pegasuspublishers.com

First Published in 2025
Vanguard Press
Sheraton House Castle Park
Cambridge England
Printed & Bound in Great Britain

CHAPTER 1
SUMMER 2022

Anne

I open the door to our holiday home. It has been almost a year since we were last in France, and the inside of the house is dark and stuffy. I make my way to the windows and open all the blinds, letting the hot summer air breeze through the open-planned kitchen and living room. I repeat the process in all the other rooms. Thomas' and mine, Alex's, Katie's and finally the two rooms we keep for occasional guests. When they were in primary school, the kids liked to use these rooms to invite friends for a summer getaway. Now, friendships have become more complicated, tangled in drama, petty fights and high school gossip, all of which I am no longer privy to. Katie does not talk to me as openly as she used to. She is seventeen and she has outgrown the need for her mother's advice. As for Alex... I suppose he is a grown man now. Although I still think of him as a little boy. That is the problem when you have a child as young as Thomas and I had Alex. You are not ready to let go of them when they become adults. It feels too soon. Alex does not like it when I mother him. It antagonises him when I treat him like a child. Which he definitely is not anymore. I might be his mother, but I am not blind. He has grown into a gorgeous man. A few hours ago, I noticed a group of young girls eyeing him up and down as we stopped in a café to break up the drive from Paris. And I have definitely noticed Diana, Louise's teenage daughter, casting him side glances whenever our two families meet up. It is somewhat adorable, she reminds me of myself when I was a teenager and infatuated with older boys. I was too shy to ever speak to them and Diana is just as innocent. Lately, whenever Alex speaks to her, her cheeks go bright red and she stumbles on her words. We are actually expecting Louise and Victor and their children, Diana and Marco, or the Munroes as we like to call them, for *l'apéritif* later this evening.

I glance around me; there is a thin layer of dust on most of the furniture. There is no escaping it, I need to do some light cleaning before they arrive.

However, before I start tidying up, I grant myself a moment of respite. After all, the summer holidays have just started. I head to the terrace and lean against the brick wall, taking in the unobstructed view of the beach which is bordered by multicoloured *carrelets*, small fishing huts typical of the south-west of France. A view Thomas and I have worked very hard to afford.

A few years ago, when Thomas and I were starting to become somewhat successful in the finance world of London, we bought this beautiful 1920's home in Royan, a small holiday destination in the south-west of France. The kind of place that only comes alive during the summer. French and European tourists flock to Royan's sandy beaches for two months and just as fast as they arrived, they disappear, taking with them the sun, late-night parties and seasonal festivals. While tourists greet the start of the new school year with regret and long for days spent lounging on the beach, the residents of Royan, most of whom are retired, sigh with relief when it gets to September. Finally, they are able to move freely in their own city without having to navigate through a crowd of loud, and sometimes aggravating, tourists.

Louise's family is from Royan. This is how we all came to know the place. When we were all studying in Durham, it became a summer tradition to spend a few weeks here in her family home. At the start, it was just the four of us; Thomas, Victor, Louise and I. But then Louise moved in with Liliane and she became part of our group. Sasha, her now husband, came into the picture a few years later, after a series of disastrous boyfriends. Eventually, Louise inherited her parents' house and we kept our summer tradition going throughout early adulthood. At the time, we were all struggling to make ends meet in London and every summer, it was a relief to escape our tiny, overpriced flats for a three-week rent-free holiday. Our first holidays as newly married couples and as young parents were also spent in Royan. Therefore, when we finally started to make money, getting the gorgeous castle-like house on the other side of the promenade from Louise's seemed like the natural thing to do.

Thomas walks out onto the terrace, interrupting my train of thoughts. He has just finished unloading the car and his flannel shirt is sticking to his chest with sweat.

'Anne,' he calls, 'Alex and Katie have just offered to go to the wine shop and to the butcher to pick up wine and nibbles for tonight. That would give the two of us some time to do some quick vacuuming and dusting before the Munroes arrive.'

'That's helpful of them,' I shout towards the kitchen. 'Alex, darling, can you please make sure to get a case of that rosé we had last year, you know the one with the lighthouse on the front of the bottle? And some beers. Any will do.' I look at Thomas mockingly. 'You know what Victor is like.' Victor does not drink any alcohol that is not beer nor whiskey.

'A true Brit!' he laughs.

'No,' I protest, 'a true Scot!'

Alex's voice travels from the depths of the house, 'Sure, Mum, no problem. We'll be back soon.' His tone is sulky. I raise my eyebrows questioningly at Thomas.

'Why does he sound annoyed?' I ask my husband.

'Well, when I say Alex offered to go shopping for us…' He pauses. 'Really, Katie is the one who offered and I had to force Alex to go with her,' he whispers back. 'She needs an adult with her to buy the wine.'

I shrug, slightly irritated. Ever since we left London yesterday afternoon, Alex has been making it clear that he does not want to be here with us this summer. I am frustrated. We have not spent much time together as a family in the past year and I have been looking forward to this holiday for months. I do not want my son to spoil the mood. Furthermore, I cannot help but find Alex ungrateful. We are paying for him to spend a three-week holiday in the south-west of France, right next to the beach, and he cannot show a tiny bit of appreciation? I am disappointed by his attitude. I do not recognise my son. My emotions must be written all over my face as Thomas pulls me close and kisses me on the cheek.

'Don't worry, Anne, he is probably still thinking about work,' he tries to reassure me. 'Soon, his brain will switch off from his problems in London and he'll be in a much better mood.'

I hope he is right. Before I have time to answer, Thomas turns around and strides purposefully towards our suitcases. His body language screams, 'things to do, places to be'. I sigh and turn my back to the ocean. I suppose I should get the house ready before our guests arrive.

CHAPTER 2
SUMMER 2022

Louise

I am sitting on the terrace, sipping a strong coffee and looking at the Villa Grand Large. The blinds have been pushed open for the first time since last summer. Anne, Thomas and their family have arrived. I tap my sandal nervously against the leg of my chair. I have barely seen them over the past year. The last time we got together was in March, when I was back in London for a week before flying back to Germany. I could barely bring myself to look at either of them straight in the eye. It is late July now and those five months are the longest time we have spent without seeing each other since we met at university twenty-five years ago. Unfortunately, there was no getting out of our annual summer reunion. I did scrap my brains for a valid excuse not to come, but Anne would have never allowed it. She has spent the last ten months moaning about how little we have seen of each other since I accepted to move to Berlin for work last September. When I last got her on the phone two weeks ago, she could not stop talking about how excited she was to spend some quality time together. Apparently, lots has happened in London during my absence and I need to catch up with our friends' most recent scandals. Obviously, her enthusiasm made me feel guilty. One of the reasons I accepted this one-year sabbatical was because it had become increasingly difficult for me to be in the same room as her since last summer. Her presence reminded me of what I had done. I could not cope with the shame so I took the coward's way out. I ran away. But Anne knows none of that.

To this day, I remember Anne's incomprehension when I phoned her last September to let her know I was leaving London for a year.

'Anne, I have something very important to tell you!' I recall exactly how I faked my voice into sounding thrilled and excited. 'I've got some very, very big news!'

'Go on then, you are being very mysterious! Oh my god, are you pregnant?'

I remember thinking, *Urgh... That would be such a disaster.*

'Nothing like that,' I answered instead. 'No, something exciting has come up at work!'

'Like a promotion?'

'Not quite. I've been offered to go on a one-year sabbatical in Germany. I am going to be teaching French at this university in Berlin. I would be working there until next summer.' I soldiered on bravely, working hard to come across as enthusiastic, grateful she could not see my face. I have never been a convincing liar. 'And the man who usually works there is going to take on my undergraduate course.'

'You are moving to Berlin for a year?' asked Anne, completely bewildered.

'Well, not a full year... Only ten months.'

'I mean, that's practically the same. What about Victor? And the children?'

'Yes, well...' I launched into a well-rehearsed speech. 'Victor and I have spent a lot of time talking logistics in the past few days. Victor decided that this sabbatical is an incredible opportunity for me, he doesn't want me to miss out on it.' I struggled to get those last few words out. As I said, I have always been a poor liar. 'We talked about the four of us moving to Berlin, but neither of us wants to disrupt the children's education. And there's just no point uprooting them just for a year. I mean, ten months. On top of that, Diana is going to be taking her A levels soon, she needs to be in a supportive school and I'm worried a sudden change might affect her academic performance. In the end, we decided the best solution was for Victor to stay in London with Diana and Marco so we can keep them in Chelsea's School for Boys and Lady Cecilia. I will go to Berlin on my own. It's not ideal, and it is going to be hard not being able to see the kids every day, but it is relatively easy to fly between Berlin and London. I can come up for a long weekend once in a while, they can visit me during the school holidays... It will take some adjusting, but we will make it work. And it's only for a year... Plus, the job is good money, the German uni is offering to cover some of my travel expenses and it's an incredible opportunity!' My monologue was met with a confused silence.

'Honey,' replied Anne eventually, 'I had no idea you wanted to go on a sabbatical! I mean this is great news! I am very happy for you. It's just... surprising. I thought you were dead set on teaching that post-grad course this year. You've been fighting tooth and nail for your department to hand that course over to you for months. That German university must be offering some amazing opportunities for you to give it up. Would that sabbatical fast track a promotion to professor? Is that why it's so important to you?'

'*Ummh.*' I hesitated. 'Yes, it's always an advantage to be able to show that you can teach in a range of different environments. It's not a prerequisite, but most professors will have gone on a sabbatical or two.'

'Ah… I see,' Anne replied.

My answer sounded flimsy and Anne knew it. I could tell by the tone of her voice that she was not convinced. I kept repeating I had been offered an amazing opportunity, but I was struggling to explain what exactly was so amazing about it. I was not fooling anybody, Anne suspected I was not being honest about the reasons that pushed me to accept that sabbatical and she was right.

A movement in the Villa Grand Large's front garden snaps me out of my reverie. I can see a silhouette stepping onto the terrace, shortly followed by another. Probably Anne and Thomas. I wonder if Anne has ever suspected that the reason I decided to move to Berlin was to avoid her and her husband. And now, to be reunited for three weeks, in the same place it all started last summer… A knot of anxiety twists in my stomach. I look away from the villa and reflect on all the lies I have told in the past year. My phone chimes. I flip it over and skim over the text message I have just received.

CHAPTER 3
SUMMER 2022

Willow

'Oh my goodness, what is that guy doing, is he insane? Cannot believe he cut in front of me like that! If I hadn't slammed on the breaks, I would have driven straight into him! Bloody French people, where do these guys learn how to drive?'

I roll my eyes from the back seat of the car. We have been driving for hours since we left London this morning and Dad's temper is getting shorter and shorter by the minute. I cannot wait to finally arrive in Royan. I feel bloated from sitting in the car for so long and I desperately need a shower. It feels like the temperature has risen by ten degrees since we crossed the Eurotunnel into France and my t-shirt is clinging uncomfortably to my back and underneath my armpits. Furthermore, I need to get away from my family. Spending the last ten hours in a confined space with the three of them has not been easy. I have had to endure Mum's lame country music and Leo's incessant shouting as he tries to complete the latest level of his video game. What a geek. I stare out the window and plug my earphones into my phone. Pop music drowns the sound of the car's speakers and I sigh in relief. I turn my mind towards the weeks ahead. I have got high hopes for this summer.

When I found out we were staying at the Villa Grand Large with the Daltons this year instead of in a rental house, I was ecstatic. Not only because their villa is so much nicer than any of the places we have ever stayed in, but mostly because that means I am going to be able to spend most of my time with Katie. I cannot wait. We can go to the beach together every day, maybe have sleepovers, drink wine in our rooms without our parents knowing about it and just spend lots of one-on-one quality time. I like Diana, she is nice and all, but if I am completely honest with myself, I prefer it when it is just Katie and I. I feel more comfortable when it is just the two of us. I feel like I can be myself. Diana intimidates me a little, plus I am not one hundred percent sure if I can trust her. Ever since we started secondary school at Lady Cecilia, she has become obsessed with being popular and I am worried she can be a little bit fake sometimes.

'For the love of god, use your indicator before you switch lanes, you moron!' Dad's outraged scream snaps me out of my reverie.

'Sasha, honey, please stay calm,' Mum whispers softly. She reaches over from the passenger seat and gently squeezes his arm. 'We've passed La Rochelle, we only have just over an hour of driving left. Do you want me to take over? I don't mind driving again, I have had a good rest since we swapped at Tours.'

'No, don't worry about it, Liliane, I'll be fine. We're going to come off the motorway soon anyway so there should be less crazy French drivers on the road. Hopefully…' Dad answers.

Mum smiles at Dad and turns around to check on Leo and I. I smile at her and turn back to the rolling landscape that is flashing past the window. Once again, my thoughts trail back to the Daltons and Katie. I cannot wait to spend all summer with her.

CHAPTER 4
LAST SUMMER, 2021

Louise

Louise is running along the ocean front. The sun is beaming down on her, adding to the physical exertion. She can hear herself inhaling and exhaling loudly. She has been running three days a week since the start of the summer holiday (she is determined to get back in shape), but unfortunately, despite being consistent, every run still feels just as hard as her first.

How does Anne genuinely enjoy this? Louise wonders for the millionth time as she painfully drags herself along the coastal path. She looks at the small row of houses at the end of the road. These houses are her goal. Another five hundred meters and she will allow herself a break. To distract herself, she listens to the sound of the waves crashing against the white rocks below her. Despite the effort taking over most of her thoughts, the scenery reminds Louise of how lucky she is to be able to call Royan her childhood home. Finally, she makes it. She comes to a sudden halt and bends over, forearms pressed against her thighs, head down, desperately trying to catch her breath.

Gosh, I really hate exercising! she thinks to herself. *Why am I doing this to myself?* she wonders not for the first time. She knows exactly why. It is because for the past two months, she has been suffering from a sudden excess of vanity. Wanting to look her best. Wanting to catch his eye, entice his gaze to linger on her body for a little while longer than necessary… Louise straightens up and starts walking towards the promenade. She passes a group of tourists strolling in the opposite direction. They look uncomfortable in the heat, some of them sporting unfortunate tan lines. Louise has always found it amusing to try and guess people's nationality based on the shade of their tan. Lobster red usually means British. Or German. That is Victor's shade. Golden usually stands for the French, Spanish and continental Europeans.

It is late afternoon, families and groups of friends are starting to leave the beach. Most of them will be heading back to their holiday rentals for a quick shower, *l'apéritif* and then they will probably have dinner at one of the ocean-view restaurants situated along the harbour or the beach front.

Louise herself has got exciting evening plans to look forward to. Cédric, their local French friend, is hosting a *soirée* on the rooftop of his bar-brasserie, which he unoriginally named Cédric's, after himself. Even though she only comes here during the summer holidays, Louise likes to regard herself as more than a tourist. Not quite a local, but a regular enough member of the Royannaise community to be invited to such events. And of course, *he* is going to be there.

Louise has reached level with the street she lives on but decides to continue walking towards the promenade in order to allow her sore muscles to cool down. She passes the *Villa Grand Large* and covertly glances up at one of the house's multiple bedroom windows. Her thoughts flash back to the previous night, an evening spent drinking on the terrace of Le Parasol until one in the morning. Being able to sit outside until the late hours of the night without getting cold is one of the many things she loves about summers in France. She cannot bear to stay inside when she is in Royan, probably because she spends most of her time indoors during the rest of the year in London.

She was out with her friends from university, Anne and Liliane and their three respective husbands; Thomas, Sasha and Victor. Diana, Marco, Kate, Alex, Leo and Willow – their children – were out doing their own thing with some friends they had met at the surf club earlier that week. That was another of her summer pleasures: children-free evenings. None of them would ever allow the children to go off on their own in the evening in London. After all, apart from Alex who is twenty-one, Katie and Diana, the oldest of their five other children, have only just turned 16. However, Royan is such a small town, and a family holiday destination, they knew their children would be safe. Furthermore, they are a very sensible bunch; they were home by eleven p.m. that night and even came to see them at Le Parasol to wish them goodnight. Willow sported that slightly judgemental and embarrassed look children sometimes get on their faces when they see their parents drunk.

What a serious girl, Louise thought. Willow had a point, though. The parents were getting a little bit too wild and feeling a little bit too free, wanting to relive their university time with their old friends and insisting on 'moving this party along to the Bodega', the only club in Royan. Louise felt out of place the moment she set foot in the club. She was a mother of two, back in the same club she used to spend most of her evenings almost three decades ago. She was too old for this. To her greatest embarrassment, the six of them bumped into Alex, Anne and Thomas' oldest son and his friends, which made her feel even more ridiculous. Louise decided that at 42, she did not have to get drunk on overpriced vodka and engage in superficial conversations with random strangers if she did not want to. So, she left early under an avalanche of protests and accusations of being a 'killjoy'. She did not care, she felt happy, free, and definitely tipsy. Discreetly, he left with her. They flirted all the way back from the Bodega. She cannot remember what they talked about, the alcohol and sexual tension clouded her thoughts at the time. However, she clearly recalls finding him incredibly sexy. She could not take her eyes away from his arms and the firm muscles that rippled underneath his t-shirt. Eventually, she gave into temptation and stroked the outline of his bicep with the tip of her index finger. She remembers the electric current that passed between them as they touched. She remembers how she reached out for him with her whole hand and her enjoyment at the fact that her fingers were not able to fully close around his bicep. It made her feel dainty and petite. Almost precious.

Louise walks past the villa's garden gate in front of which they stopped inches away from each other the previous night. She knew she was about to make a bad decision from which there would be no coming back. She also knew she would not be able to resist.

'I should go home,' she said, inching herself closer to him, her body language contradicting her words. He gasped.

'Do you want to come in for a drink?' he asked.

'I shouldn't… I can't do this to Anne.'

He did not look convinced. He knew that in this exact moment in time, she did not care about Anne's feelings. Nevertheless, the rational part of her brain was ringing in alarm. She was, without a shred of doubt, about to make the worst decision of her life. 42 and pursuing adultery. Not just pursuing. Encouraging. He gave her that piercing, lustful stare they had gradually developed between each other throughout the summer. He opened the gate and held it open for her, challenging her resolve further than she could endure. She carefully stepped into the garden and followed him up the stairs. He opened the front door and made his way to the kitchen where he grabbed a bottle of that rosé Anne had recently become so found of. The one with the lighthouse on the front of the label. He poured some wine and

I reply apologetically, 'I'm not sure... My parents' family friends are arriving today and Mum is expecting me to come and have *l'apéritif* with everyone.'

'You mean Katie and Alex's family?' asks Tala. 'They should come! Katie is lovely.'

Nora raises her eyebrows. 'Yeah, sure, Katie is the one you want to see.'

I look away, uncomfortable. Tala has been swooning over Alex ever since we ran into him and his friends at the Bistro de Cordouan, our favourite bar, last year. To be honest, Tala is constantly swooning over lots of different boys. After all, two seconds ago, we were talking about Bastien. She is constantly seeking validation from boys and I find it incredibly frustrating. Tala is a shameless flirt and the ease with which she slips from one personality to another to seduce is unnerving. Three years later, I am still not too sure who the real Tala is. Sometimes, when I see her behaviour radically transform from one interlocutor to the other, I catch myself wondering how genuine our friendship truly is. On more than one occasion, she has completely ditched Nora and I for some random bloke she had just met that night. I remember that one time when she did not hesitate to throw Nora under the bus with some embarrassing story to get another guy's attention. Yes, there is no doubt about it, Tala's obsession with boys does not always bring out the best in her.

I dig my feet in the sand and sigh. 'To be honest, girls, I don't really want to spend time with Alex and Katie. Willow, Leo and Marco are also going to be there, but I don't really fancy seeing them either. It's weird, I used to go to primary school with all of them, we were close actually, probably because our parents have been friends since university and forced us to spend lots of time together when we were little. But we have kind of lost touch since secondary school. I can't be bothered seeing all of them tonight. It's going to be awkward... I'd rather meet you guys at Cédric's on my own. I'll try and leave without anybody noticing, I reckon I can probably be there around ten-ish.' I feel dishonest badmouthing Willow, Marco, Leo and Katie. Especially Katie and Willow. The truth is, they are lovely girls. We get on really well when we are in France, but we do not spend much time together in London even though we go to the same school. Our friendship groups are very different. I remember Mum constantly nagging me about Katie and Willow when I first started at Lady Cecilia. She did not understand why they suddenly stopped coming over after school and why I did not invite them for sleepovers any more. I tried to explain that we had made new friends at Lady Cecilia and that these new friends did not really get on with each other, but Mum would not understand. She could not comprehend a world in which her own daughter and her best friends' daughters had drifted apart. On the contrary, she was convinced that since she, Liliane and Anne were best friends, Katie, Willow and I had to be close as well.

'If you say so, Diana,' Tala pouts. 'I personally think it's always more fun to go out with a bigger group.' I knew Tala would not give up on the idea of seeing Alex this easily.

'But whatever you prefer,' adds Nora. 'If you do not want to see them, we'll just have a girls' night, the three of us. Will still be lots of fun!'

I smile gratefully at Nora. Thankfully, she has always been a little bit more considerate of other people's feelings than Tala.

'Fine,' sighs Tala. 'Just a girls' night then!'

'There will still be lots of other boys there,' Nora reassures Tala. 'Like Bastien, remember?'

'You're right; after all, I can't leave France without French kissing a French boy,' replies Tala.

'Exactly!' agrees Nora. 'That would be absolutely and utterly unacceptable!'

Tala does not pick up on Nora's sarcastic tone. Covertly, Nora shoots me a mocking smile. I grin back, it is hard not to make fun of Tala when she comes up with cringy statements like this. Nevertheless, I am relieved the topic of Alex has finally been dropped. It is still so painful. So embarrassing seeing him. Hot shame flushes across my chest, spreading into an unattractive red rash. Thankfully, Nora and Tala do not notice my discomfort. Knowing that I am going to be in the same room as Alex in a few hours' time fills me with dread. I would give anything for tonight's reunion to fall through. Maybe by some miracle, the Daltons' flight got delayed and Katie, Alex, Anne and Thomas are stuck in London. And Sasha, Liliane, Leo and Willow, or the Brandsons for short, who are driving down from London got stuck in a humongous traffic jam and neither family will make to Royan by tonight. I know I am being delusional but just to make sure, I spin my head around to look at the Villa Grand Large. Confirming my fears, I notice that the blinds have been thrown wide open. The villa, which has been abandoned and inhabited for the first part of the summer, has suddenly sprung back to life.

CHAPTER 6
SUMMER 2022

Katie

It's boiling. Like every year, the first day in Royan as a Londoner comes as a shock to the system. Alex and I have been walking for less than five minutes along the narrow, pedestrian cobbled streets of Royan and a thin stream of sweat is trickling from the middle of my shoulder blades all the way down to the small of my back. The heat is unbearable, my whole body feels sticky and my thighs are chafing uncomfortably against each other. I am suffocated by my thin strap dress and the soles of my open toe sandals are burning against the bottom of my feet. My brother Alex is walking silently next to me, also struggling with the heat. We pass a few cafés; and all their terraces are empty. Everyone is either inside or swimming at the beach. We walk past our local *boulangerie*, the smell of freshly baked *croissants* tickling my appetite. I feel bad for the poor bakers who have to deal with the heat of the ovens on top of this inferno. Finally, we make it to La Cave à Jules and it is with relief that I step inside the temperature-controlled room of the wine shop.

'*Ahhhh, mes petits Britanniques préférés !*' exclaims Jules. He strides from behind a shelf of *vin rouge* and smacks us an enthusiastic *bise* on each cheek.

'*Désolé*, Jules, I am all sweaty,' I apologise, looking at the fat beads of sweat I have imprinted on the left side of his face.

Although I said so, I am not really that *désolé*. Maybe that will refrain him from kissing me hello and goodbye every time he sees me from now on. I am all about adopting the customs of our host country, but the French *bise* is something I just cannot get on board with. It involves too much physical contact with a man who is essentially barely more than a vague (although Mum and Dad are probably amongst some of his most loyal customers) acquaintance. And I always worry the day will come when Jules misses his target and his bise lands a little bit too close to my lips for comfort. Confirming my fears, Jules and Alex are saying hello and I watch my brother hastily turn his face further towards the door to avoid their lips touching. I giggle. Jules is one of these salespeople who love their product a little bit too much for their own good. Messes with his appreciation of distances.

'Don't worry about it!' he replies good-heartedly. 'How long have you been in Royan?'

'We drove in about an hour ago,' replies Alex. 'Mum and Dad have a sense of priorities so we are here to stock up the cave.'

'*Ah oui, très bien, très* important! So, we have rosé over there, I know it's your parents' favourite...'

'Yes, actually, there is a specific one they have in mind...'

I watch Alex and Jules weave away through the aisles and I trail behind. I walk along a shelf of white wine, absent-mindedly deciphering the different labels, practicing my French pronunciation. I have spent most of my summer holidays in France since I was a child, and even though I can get around in shops and restaurants and hold my ground through basic conversations, I am not half as fluent as I would like to be. It is not surprising though when you spend all your holidays in France with your family friends from London.

I am looking forward to seeing Diana, Marco, Willow and Leo. Well... One of them in particular. I know Marco and Diana have been in Royan for a few weeks already. They always stay here longer than us. As a freelance journalist and a university lecturer, their parents can take longer holidays. And this is Louise's home town, it must feel good for her to come back to her French roots for a couple of months every year. I was messaging Willow earlier today when she was in the car. They were stuck in traffic somewhere around Tours, but they cannot be far away any more. Usually, Willow, Leo and their parents Sasha and Liliane, or the Brandson family as my parents like to call them, rent a beach house not far away from the promenade. However, by the time her parents got around to looking for a place to stay this year, everywhere was already fully booked.

'This is crazy!' I remember Liliane saying to Louise a few months ago during Mum and Dad's annual Easter barbecue party. 'I am trying to book somewhere to stay in Royan this summer, but everywhere has already been rented out! I don't understand how that's possible, it's only March! I thought I was being very proactive and organising our plans for the summer holidays ages in advance, but apparently not!'

'That's such a shame,' answered Louise. 'I'm not surprised though,' she added, 'Royan is becoming an increasingly popular tourist destination and more and more people are finding out about it. And obviously, the more people know about Royan, the more people are going to come here on holiday. And the busier Royan gets, the earlier everyone is going to start booking to make sure they have somewhere to stay. And let's not forget, the more touristy Royan becomes, the more expensive restaurants and bars and… And everything really is going to become. If it continues that way, soon we are going to have to start booking restaurants weeks in advance like we have to do in London if we want to get a table during peak summer time. You remember last year?' Louise asked Liliane. 'Impossible to find anywhere to eat for the fifteenth of August! Oh gosh, and don't even get me started on finding a parking space for the market. Worse than parking in central London!'

Louise went on like that for a while. Every year without fail, she rants about how busy Royan has become compared to what it was like when she was a child. She thinks Royan is slowly losing its authenticity and charm because of the rising influx of tourists. I suppose she is right. Over the years, more and more family-owned businesses and traditional restaurants have been replaced by chains in order to cater for mainstream tourism. On the other hand, small shops like La Cave à Jules have become very successful because there is still a vast majority of tourists who prefer to shop locally when they are on holiday. Furthermore, the moment you step out of the city centre of Royan and venture inland away from the beach, it is not hard to stumble across small, quaint little establishments that serve culinary specialities from the south-west most people have never heard about.

'I agree with you,' Liliane had eventually cut Louise off. 'I also wish Royan was less touristy as it used to be! But the issue remains, I don't know what we are going to do this summer! I'm not sure we are going to be able to find a place to stay!'

For a scary moment, I had been worried I would not be able to see Willow and Leo, Liliane and Sasha's children, both roughly my age and with whom I get on really well, this summer. But thankfully, Mum overheard the end of Liliane and Louise's conversation and could not help but step in to save the day.

'What's that?' Mum asked and Liliane quickly filled her in on her dilemma. Naturally, Mum came up with a solution right away, 'Oh, Liliane, if you can't find your own place, why don't you come and stay with us this summer?'

'I wouldn't want to impose,' replied Liliane, 'I appreciate you and Thomas might want some privacy, and the children probably as well.'

'Oh nonsense, it's a huge house, you'll have a whole floor to yourselves, we'll have a whole floor to ourselves and we will barely have to see or talk to each other if we don't want to. I won't take no for an answer,' insisted Mum as she saw Liliane hesitating. 'A summer in Royan is not a summer in Royan if you are not there!'

Eventually, Liliane gave in. Mum always gets her way.

The Brandsons drove out of London this morning a few hours before our flight took off, so they should be arriving at the villa anytime now. I absentmindedly look at the row of wine bottles in front of me and wonder if they would have already arrived by the time Alex and I come back from the wine shop. I cannot wait.

CHAPTER 7
SUMMER 2022

Liliane

Finally, my husband Sasha turns into Rue de la Plage and brakes in front of a pair of tall, green metal gates. Almost immediately, the gates start to slowly open. I messaged Anne ten minutes ago to let her know we were driving through Saint-George and that they should be expecting us any minute. I sigh in relief. The drive has been long and my husband increasingly irritable. I cannot wait to unpack and finally sit down with Anne and a glass of rosé. Hopefully, we can have some time to catch up before the Munroes arrive. I wonder if Anne is apprehensive about seeing Louise again. I certainly am. She has almost disappeared from our lives since moving to Berlin last September and I have this uneasy feeling in the pit of my stomach that there is another reason behind her sudden departure than meets the eye. An unsavoury reason. Sasha slowly drives our SUV up the Daltons' driveway and a tall, slim figure comes bobbing down towards us.

'Guuuyyss, you made it!' Anne exclaims. She is wearing flowy linen trousers, a light green tank top and a pair of brown sandals. She takes her French designer sunglasses off and pins them back into her hair. 'How was the drive?'

'Long! How long ago did you get here?' I ask as I embrace my oldest friend. As I let Anne go, I can see Katie and Alex walking through the metal gates. They are carrying shopping bags. I can hear glass bottles clanging against each other which makes me think the bags are full of wine. Upon closer inspection, I recognise the logo of our favourite wine shop, La Cave à Jules. Katie squeals and run towards my daughter Willow, wrapping her in a warm embrace. I smile. I am happy our children are as close as their parents are.

'Thank you so much for letting us stay with you this year,' says Sasha as he steps out of the driver's seat and hugs Anne.

'Don't worry about it, I'm just glad we are all able to spend the summer together,' replies Anne. 'It's been too long since we have all been together.'

'Since Easter,' I interject.

'Yeah, and we were only able to spend Easter Sunday together before Louise had to leave for Berlin again,' says Anne. 'This time, we are finally going to be able to spend some proper time together. There's so much we need to catch up on!' Anne grabs me by the arm. 'What do you think about a little glass of rosé before everybody else arrives?'

'You cannot already be offering our guests alcohol,' laughs Thomas as he makes his way down the driveway. He greets Sasha and I with a big smile and a friendly embrace. I cringe slightly when he fist-bumps Leo and Willow. The gesture does not look natural on him.

'I don't see why not,' Anne replies with a cheeky smile. 'They are on holiday after all and they've just had a long drive. They deserve a bit of rest.'

'I wouldn't mind a glass of rosé,' I say. 'I'll just help Sasha carry our bags to our room and I'll meet you in the kitchen.'

'Oh, don't you worry about that,' Anne dismisses me with a swat of her manicured hand. Her engagement ring and wedding band glisten in the sun. I have grown used to Thomas and Anne's wealth along the years, but once in a while, I cannot help but feel bewildered by the difference of lifestyle between both our families. 'The boys can take care of it. Alex,' she calls to her son, 'would you mind carrying Liliane and Sasha's bags upstairs? I've put them in the sea-front bedroom and Willow and Leo are sharing the smaller guest room.'

'Yeah, that's fine.' Alex shrugs.

'Don't be ridiculous,' I interject, 'I can carry my own bag.'

'Don't worry about it, Liliane.' Alex smiles at me.

I cannot help but notice he has grown into a handsome young man since he has left university. He has abandoned his long hair for a more shaven look and his muscles ripple underneath the thin fabric of his t-shirt as he picks up my red suitcase from the trunk of our car. His jaw clenches as shifts the heavy weight of my luggage and I cannot help but linger on the virile frame of his body. I snap myself back to reality. Youth will forever remain irresistibly attractive, especially when you have reached your forties.

'I'm going upstairs anyway,' Alex continues. 'I was thinking of going for a quick swim before everybody arrives,' he tells Anne.

'That's not a problem, sweety.' She smiles at him. 'Just make sure you are ready for seven, that's when we are expecting the Munroes.'

'Yep, that's fine,' he replies over his shoulder as he makes his way into the massive villa.

'I'll carry the rest of our stuff,' my husband calls after him. It does not look quite as effortless as he lifts his suitcase from the trunk of the car, but I cannot help but sigh fondly at my husband. He might have lost the chiselled physique of his youth, but he is still the kindest and most loving person I have ever met. When he is not driving, that is.

'I'll give you a hand,' adds Thomas. 'And then let me show you the latest toy I just bought myself,' he adds excitedly like a child. Anne rolls her eyes playfully at me. 'A pool table for the game room! We might have time to squeeze in a game before *l'apéro!*'

I watch Thomas and Sasha disappear in the house and by the time I have turn back around, Katie and Willow are already walking off arm under arm, whispering and giggling to each other. They are probably gossiping about boys and people they know from school. Leo finds himself suddenly on his own and looks around awkwardly.

'I think I'm gonna take a nap or something,' he tells me.

'That's fine, honey, but you heard what Anne said, we need to be ready for seven p.m.'

'Yeah, yeah, don't worry, I heard her,' he replies distractedly as he scrolls through his phone. 'Gosh the Wi-Fi is rubbish out here, I hope I get better signal inside,' I hear him murmur as he trails off towards the house.

Anne grabs me by the arm and leads me towards the garden. The sea suddenly comes into view and I take in the scenic landscape.

'The Wi-Fi is pretty rubbish out here,' she admits, 'but who needs a phone when you have all of this on your door step?' she adds, gesturing at the beach and the shimmering blue water. 'But enough of that, how have you been?' she asks me. 'What's new with you?'

I stare at the blue water in front of me and I sigh in contentment. I have been going on holiday in Royan for years now, but the scenery never gets old. Every time I come here, I feel like I am transported into a different universe. A different universe full of familiar sights, noises and smell. A universe that soothes me. In the distance, I can I can hear families on the promenade speaking French. I can smell the faint aroma of the pine trees shading us from the punishing July sun. It is almost six p.m., but the heat is still pretty intense. I can see lazy waves crashing onto the shore and children splashing around in the water. I recognise Alex's silhouette as he walks past the tall hedges that partially obstruct the villa's garden from view. He keeps his flip-flops on as he walks onto the beach, the sand must be too hot to walk on barefoot.

'Oh, I'm fabulous,' I reply enthusiastically, 'I am just so happy we are back in Royan again! I have missed this place so much. I just can't wait to spend a relaxing summer together. Just like old times.'

'Me too,' agrees Anne. She pauses. She does not want to spoil the mood, but it is clear something is on her mind.

'Come on,' I urge her on. 'I know something's bothering you. You might as well tell me what it is.'

'You know me too well, Liliane.' Anne laughs.

'I know, that's what happens when you've been friends with someone for over twenty years,' I reply. 'So come on, spill it. What's on your mind?'

'Well, I just hope that you are right, that we can have a nice, relaxing few weeks all together just like old times.' She pauses and hesitates. 'I feel like things have changed a bit over the last year and it would be nice for them to revert back to normal.'

'What do you think has changed?' I ask my old friend. I wonder if she is thinking what I am thinking.

'Things have been a bit awkward with Louise, don't you think?' she asks me.

'You know what,' I reply, 'I am glad you said that. I've been thinking that for a while, but I wasn't sure if I was just making it all up in my head. It's nice to know that you have also noticed something is up with her.'

'It's since she moved to Berlin—' Anne says.

'Yes, exactly, since Berlin,' I cut her off. 'I don't understand why she suddenly decided to do that. It makes no sense to me.'

'Me neither,' Anne replies, 'and she was acting weird every time she came to visit in London. I feel like she's been trying to avoid us. Do you remember Easter? She couldn't have left the barbecue any earlier had she wanted to.'

'I agree... I wish she would just talk to us about whatever is bothering her.'

'I tried to broach the subject a few times over the past few months, but every time I mentioned Berlin or asked if she and Victor were OK, she sent me packing.'

'Do you think she and Victor might be going through a rough patch?' I ask.

'I don't know, it's hard to say...' Anne pauses. 'She won't tell me anything anymore. Has Sasha ever said anything about Victor confiding in him? Has Victor ever mentioned any problems between Louise and him?'

'Not that I know of,' I reply. 'But to be honest, I think that Victor would be more likely to confide in Thomas than in Sasha. Victor and Thomas have known each other since first year of uni, whereas Sasha still feels like he is relatively new addition to the group,' I admit.

'What do you mean?' exclaims Anne in surprise. 'We have known Sasha for years now! What has it been? Like fifteen years since you first introduced us to him?'

'Sixteen,' I correct her. 'We met in 2006, just after you and Thomas had Katie.'

'See, we've known him for even longer than I thought! How can he possibly still see himself as an outsider to the group after all this time?'

'I guess sixteen years doesn't feel like a very long time when the rest of us have known each other since university. To be honest, I get how he feels, I used to feel that way. I met you, Louise, Victor and Thomas after the four of you had already spent two years together at uni. For a very long time, I used to feel like the group's fifth wheel. It's only when Louise and I finished our masters and moved down to London with you guys that I really started to feel like a part of the group.' I pause. I have never admitted this to Anne and Louise, but I have always felt like the two of them are closer with each other than they are with me. I suspect there have been many secrets and confidences that I have not been included in over the years. That has stopped bothering me a long time ago. I like to stay away from drama and it does sound like the two of them, especially Anne with her tumultuous relationship with Thomas and an unexpected pregnancy at twenty one, had a very dramatic time during their undergraduate degree.

'Really?' replies Anne, surprised. 'I never realised you felt that way,' she adds.

'I don't any more,' I say. 'As you've said, we've known each other for so long now. Two years' difference doesn't feel like much in the grand scheme of things.'

'I definitely don't feel as close to Louise as I used to,' Anne admits to me. 'She's been so distant since she's moved to Berlin, I barely recognise

which slopes down towards the seafront. Louise looks up towards the front door and a mixture of dread and excitement pulsate through her veins as she spots him. Dread of being caught. Excitement of what might potentially happen. He looks striking. Square-jawed, tanned skin, muscly build and sun-bleached hair. Anne appears in the background, bag in hand, looking purposeful in a classic but very elegant black dress.

'Louise, Victor, what perfect timing!' she shouts from across the distance. All of a sudden, the whole Dalton clan is making its way down the narrow and winding path that cuts through their front yard. They form a neat line, walking casually one behind the other. Anne, Thomas, Alex and Katie.

'Hi, Anne, you look fabulous,' says Louise.

'That's sweet, thank you! I'm glad we don't have far to walk, these shoes are already starting to hurt my feet,' replies Anne, waving impatiently at a pair of gorgeous, but deadly looking black stilettos. Everyone starts chatting casually. Anne, Thomas and Louise talk about the soirée they are heading to; Victor and Alex, as they usually do, start talking passionately about Formula 1 and Katie trails behind everyone in silence.

'Have you watched qualifying today, Alex?' inquires Victor. The two of them are big F1 fans. Leo and Marco also share their interest for the sport but not to the same degree. Only Alex and Victor are passionate enough to forgo a day lying on the beach to watch the Grand Prix. As a result, Alex has become Victor's surrogate child when it comes to F1. Behind Victor and Alex, Louise, Thomas and Anne question Katie about her plans for the evening.

'Where are you off to tonight, Katie?' inquires Louise.

'I'm going to Nora and Tala's for dinner. Then probably the Bistro de Cordouan...'

'Ah, that should be fun,' answers Louise. 'Diana mentioned she might be there. And Marco.'

'Yes, they said earlier they would meet up with us. Leo and Willow will probably come as well.'

'One party for the children, one party for the adults,' laughs Thomas.

'Alex is going to Cédric's as well and he is technically a child,' interjects Katie.

Thomas roars with laughter. 'Don't let him hear that! He's already frustrated enough with your mum because according to him, she treats him like he's still sixteen like you are. Always asking where he is going, who he is seeing, what he's been doing out so late...' His eyes twinkle in amusement and he catches Louise's gaze. She averts her eyes.

'You make me sound like an overbearing and nosy mother!' Anne smiles. The tone of the conversation remains playful. 'Did I tell you he got through to the third round of interviews for one of the graduate scheme jobs he applies for?'

'You didn't! That's great news!' replies Louise.

The two women drop further back. 'Just between the two of us, I really hope he gets this one. It would be so nice to have him living in London again. I've missed him for the past four years he's been at university. St Andrews is so far away, we haven't been able to visit much. Hopefully, if he gets this job, we'll be able to see more of him. Of course, I haven't said any of this to Alex. If I did, he would be worried about me dropping by his flat every day. Thomas would probably think I would do that as well. As if I have time for that!' Anne laughs.

As a personal financial advisor for a big bank, Anne runs a tight schedule. This annual summer holiday in France is the only time she ever takes off work.

Finally, their little group arrives in front of Cédric's restaurant. Katie waves goodbye and heads towards Nora and Tala's, whose parents own a small holiday apartment located a few streets off the beach. Alex breaks away from their group and mingles with a younger crowd. Adopting local customs, he makes his way around a group of six or seven people, kissing each of them on both cheeks before accepting a glass of rosé poured by one of his friends. The restaurant is filling up rapidly. The terrace, which is located on the promenade, is overflowing with clients. There are no empty tables left, leaving the people who are still arriving to stand on the pavement with their drink in hand. Everybody is admiring the sunset over the ocean. Anne, Louise and both of their husbands walk inside the restaurant and climb the stairs to the rooftop terrace. For a short moment, it is completely silent around them. No one wants to sit inside in this weather. The noise of their footsteps echoes amongst the deserted tables and chairs. The four of them are relieved when they emerge back outside, greeted by the animated buzz of countless conversations.

'It's easier being silent with each other when there are other people around us to do most of the talking,' muses Louise.

Anne shouts out enthusiastically, 'Liliane, Sasha, amazing! You guys are already here!'

'We got a bottle of rosé. Hope that's OK.' Sasha, the life of the party of their little group, greets them with a big smile.

'Well done, mate,' answers Thomas.

Sasha starts pouring four glasses. 'Victor, is rosé good for you? Can always get a beer instead.'

'Of course, you know me, I'm not fussy,' Victor answers. He would prefer a beer, but it is also against his nature to refuse a drink when it is right in front of him. 'You know what's really frustrating about pints in France?' he asks Thomas. 'The size of the head they pour on it! By the time it foams down, the alcohol level barely reached the 500ml line on the glass.'

'Not worth seven euros then,' answers Liliane, sipping her drink.

'Definitely not.'

'Anne, Louise, there you go. Ladies first,' says Sasha, handing them two full glasses of wine.

'Oh gosh, that's plenty!' exclaims Anne. 'I am going to have to nurse this one, I've decided to limit myself to one drink an evening until the marathon.'

'What?' Sasha looks at her with incomprehension.

'On the 10th of September. We're late July and I only have six weeks to get in shape. I tried going for a thirteen-mile run this morning all the way to St George and back along the coast and I had to stop and walk a few times... The heat makes it tougher to run than in London but unfortunately, I am also forty-two now... It's a lot harder to train for a marathon than it used to be.'

'I remember when you ran an ultra at the end of our third year of uni,' reminisces Louise. 'Didn't we go out like almost every evening the week before?' Anne does not answer. 'Yes, I remember,' Louise carries on. 'The race coincided with our last week of university. Exams were over and we wanted to celebrate.'

'Oh yes!' exclaims Thomas. 'I remember that time as well. We went out for nearly seven consecutive nights in a row. I would die if we did that now.'

Anne nods a few times, but she has opted out of the conversation. So have Liliane and Sasha. They did not know Victor, Anne, Thomas and Louise back then and it always feels strange to be reminded that the four of them have been friends for longer than they have.

'Wasn't that the week just before we all moved away from Durham? We went to that graduation formal, didn't we?' adds Victor.

'Oh yes!' exclaims Louise. 'We went to the pub after leaving the ball and Thomas decided to climb on one of the tables and sing at the top of his lungs.'

'And then he made friends with those random Scottish lads, didn't he?' inquires Victor playfully.

Anne's gaze drifts above the terrace's balustrade towards the sunset, patiently waiting for the topic of conversation to change. She takes a small sip of wine.

Ever so sensible, thinks Louise. Who other than Anne – beautiful, badass, hardworking Anne – to decide to train for a marathon during her only three weeks of annual holiday? Louise reflects that as much as she admires her friend, she also envies her. Maybe that is why she wants what is her friends for herself.

'I must have looked like an absolute wanker standing there in my ball robe…' says Thomas.

Victor roars with laughter. 'I remember that evening! You got super drunk because you were trying to keep up with how much the table next to ours was drinking. Anne and I had to carry you home and put you to bed.'

'Not one of my proudest moments, unfortunately,' grins Thomas bashfully. 'It was the sambuca that tipped me over the edge. Sambuca always does it for me.' Thomas smiles and takes a sip of his drink.

Like his friends, he seems to enjoy reminiscing about his partying days. So much so that Louise almost misses the disgusted look that distorts his features for a split second. Just as suddenly, Thomas re-joins the conversation effortlessly and Louise cannot help but wonder if what she saw was not just a fragment of her imagination.

CHAPTER 9
SUMMER 2022

Willow

I am so excited to see Katie, I practically leap out of the car and throw myself into her arms. I know the last time I saw her was only a few days ago, but I have missed her so much. I turn around to grab my suitcase from the boot so I can quickly put my stuff away in my room and spend time with her. I quickly notice that Alex, Thomas and Dad have already started unloading the car, so I figure I better leave them to it. They do not need my help. Before anybody can stop us, we scurry away to find a quiet corner to hang out in the garden. Katie links arms with me and asks me if I saw this video she sent me on social media earlier. I barely have time to reply to her before she drags me across the garden until we reach our secret spot, which is located behind the house. We walk behind some thick bushes and sit down on the stocky tree logs Marco, Diana, Leo, Katie and I carried over to this side of the garden a few summers ago. We call this place the secret spot because the bushes are so tall and thick, they completely conceal you from view. It is a great place to get a bit of privacy from our parents and the five of us used to hang out here all the time when we were younger. Our parents have always respected the secret spot and never ventured behind the bushes. This place makes me very nostalgic. It reminds me of all the games I used to play as a child. I wish the five of us were still as close as when we were in primary school. It is a shame we drifted apart when we moved to secondary. Especially with Diana. She has become a completely different person. But I do not want to think about it. I have Katie. That is all that matters.

Now that Katie and I are alone, I suddenly go shy. I can feel her warm body next to mine on the tree log and I do not know where to look. I stare at the dry grass underneath my feet. What should I do next? What should I say? Thankfully, Katie is more confident than I am. She reaches for my hand and squeezes it. I can feel her scooting closer to me and her hair tickles my nose as she rests her head on my shoulder.

'I can't believe how lucky we are,' she whispers. 'We are going to spend the whole summer together in the same house. We can be together all the time!'

'I know, I can't wait!' I reply. I want to mention something about our parents letting us have sleepovers, something they would never allow if one of us were a boy, but I do not know how to bring that topic up without sounding super forward.

Katie lifts her head from my shoulder and I can feel her staring at me. I turn around to face her and her face is suddenly only inches away from mine. I did not realise we were sitting this close to each other. I stare at her for a few seconds. I am afraid to make the first move. Thankfully, Katie takes the lead and she leans into me slightly. Our lips brush against each other softly. The kiss does not last very long, it is only the second time it has happened and we do not want to move too fast. Part of me is also scared of getting caught, which is why I break away first. I wish I was not so afraid.

Katie smiles at me.

'So, what do you want to do before everybody else arrives?' she asks me. I want to stay hidden behind these bushes and spend the whole evening with her and no one else, but I do not say that. It would sound too cringe.

'I don't mind,' I reply instead. 'I suppose I should shower and change into something different...' I look down at my white t-shirt. My skin is clammy and I can see aureoles of sweat forming under my armpits. I push some hair away from my face which feels shinny and greasy. All of a sudden, I feel self-conscious. I have been travelling for the whole day and as a result, I look atrocious. I do not want Katie to see me like this.

'I need to get changed as well,' Katie replies. She hesitates and a mischievous smile forms on her lips. 'How about we both go back inside and get ready for tonight? I have a little something hidden in my wardrobe that we could have in my room to get this party started without the parents...'

I frown. I have no idea what she is talking about.

'What do you mean?' I ask as she grabs my arm and practically drags me out of the bushes and back into the villa. 'What do you have in your wardrobe?'

'You really haven't guessed?' She giggles, her playful smile widening across her face. I shake my head. She leans into me and whispers, 'Wine!' I look at her, surprised.

'How did you get wine?' I whisper as we walk into the villa and head towards the stairs. I do not want any of our parents to overhear this conversation. It might get us into trouble.

'Well, I went to the wine shop with Alex earlier and I just sneaked one of the bottles he bought out of the carrier bag and into my bag,' she explains, clearly proud of herself.

I giggle nervously. I cannot believe she has done that, I almost admire her courage. I would never be able to pull a stunt like that. I am too much of a stickler for the rules whereas Katie is a little bit more of a free spirit. As we run up the stairs, Katie still pulling me in her wake, we run into my dad.

'What is so funny?' he asks, confused.

'Nothing, Dad,' I reply quickly. 'You wouldn't understand.' We rush past him before he notices my discomfort. I doubt he suspects what we are up to.

CHAPTER 10
SUMMER 2022

Sasha

I drop my suitcase on the floor and slump down heavily on the bed. I lean back and sigh in relief. My lower back is complaining from having sat in the car for so long and it feels wonderful to be able to stretch my limbs. I feel a little bit guilty about my lack of enthusiasm when Thomas took me downstairs to the game room to have a look at the pool table, but I really need a few minutes of alone time before our big social gathering tonight. I kick my shoes off and let my legs dangle from the king-size bed. Anne and Thomas's guest bedroom is just as big as Liliane and mine's own room in London. It is decorated very elegantly in blue and white tones to match the colour of the ocean which I can see from the window. I stare at the framed photograph that is hanging up next to the door to our en-suite bathroom. I recognise the *carrelets de la Crique du Concié*, the fishing huts which are located along the small cove de Concié. I also recognise the signature at the bottom left of the frame. The picture was taken by a famous local photographer in Royan. Laughter filters into the room from the open window. I get up and look down into the garden. My wife Liliane and Anne are standing close together facing the ocean. They seem deep in conversation. Another noise catches my attention. I look to my left and I spot Alex leaving the villa through the back gate, a beach towel underneath his arm. No doubt going for that swim he was talking about earlier. A bead of sweat rolls from my forehead into my left eye. My body is struggling to adapt to the harsh, French summer heat.

Fifteen minutes later, I feel much better. I have had a shower and changed into a pair of clean clothes. I am ready to interact with other human beings again. I walk up to the window to check if Anne and Liliane are still outside. I cannot see them anywhere, but Thomas is unfolding some garden furniture and setting up chairs around a large wooden table. When he is done, he starts bringing out some food and bottles of wine from the kitchen. I head downstairs to give him a hand. As I open the bedroom door, I almost collide into Willow and Katie running up the stairs hand in hand, almost bent over in fits of laughter.

'What's so funny?' I ask, curious.

'Nothing, Dad,' my daughter replies, waving me off dismissively. 'You wouldn't understand,' she adds and the two of them race off into Katie's room, giggling like the two teenage girls they are. I shake my head, a faint smile on my lips. I walk down the stairs and I find Anne and Liliane in the kitchen. They are sitting around the central island plating out some *fromage et crudités* for *l'apéritif* whilst enjoying their first rosé of the summer together.

'Oh perfect, honey!' Liliane exclaims as she sees me. 'Could you help me carry some food and wine glasses outside?'

'No problem at all,' I reply. I grab a handful of glasses, balance a platter of *charcuterie* with my left hand and follow my wife outside. Thomas has decided he deserves a break from setting up and we find him sitting comfortably in one of the garden chairs, a glass of rosé in one hand and a large helping of peanuts in the other.

CHAPTER 11
SUMMER 2022

Thomas

'*Ahhhhh!*' With relief, I sink into a garden chair facing the ocean. I cross my right ankle on top of my left and extend my legs in front of me. Alex and Katie came back from the shops an hour ago and I have poured myself a glass of rosé, which has had time to chill in the fridge. Content, I raise my glass, cheers myself to a well-deserved break, and take a large sip of wine. I exhale the stress slowly out of my body. The transition from London to France has successfully allowed me to forget about my work problems. Often, it seems that geographical distance from the office is the only efficient way to distance my thoughts from the stock market, from rising and falling shares, from making and losing money. There is a bowl of peanuts on the garden table and I grab a handful.

My thoughts trail aimlessly from one thing to the other. I am hoping to get back on the bike over the next three weeks. I twisted my left ankle back in May after going to one of these cross-fit classes with Victor and I have only just recovered. Damn box jumps! Having an injured ankle has been quite a pain for the past two and half months. I have had to take the tube to work and it has not been a pleasant experience. When we get back from France, I will finally be able to ride my bike into the office again and I will not have to put up with impatient crowds and sweaty, sticky bodies compressed against each other on public transport any more. I will no longer have to twist my limbs into awkward positions around strangers' bodies to get a hold of the handrail before the train jerks into motion when departing from the station. And most importantly, Anne will no longer have reasons to complain about me getting back home late (signal failure), clammy (small, overcrowded carriage without ventilation) and grumpy (the results of all of the above on top of a tiring day at work).

'If it's that bad, just take the car to work!' she huffed impatiently one evening after a particularly long rant over dinner.

'Are you mad? Driving from West London into central during peak rush hour? It would take me hours.'

'Surely if you hate taking the tube so much, you'd have a better time driving instead.'

'I'm not even sure where I would park. Oh, and I'd probably end up paying a fortune in congestion charges. Honestly, Anne, driving is the worst idea possible.'

'Well, I'm trying to suggest solutions to improve your daily commute.'

'It's a rubbish solution. Honestly, cycling to work is life-changing. You exercise and it's faster. I reckon it saves about twenty minutes cycling to work instead of driving. And traffic jams are never an issue. The roads could be gridlocked with cars and buses sitting behind each other at a standstill and it wouldn't affect me. I would just fly past all the traffic.'

Her eyes narrowed and scalded me over a forkful of rice and chicken, 'Right. You love to cycle to work. We get it. The problem is your ankle is injured and since the doctor said it would take another six weeks for you to be able to exercise again, it is fair to say that you are not cycling anywhere anytime soon. So, you are either driving to work or taking the tube to work and it feels like you have decided that the tube is the lesser of two evils. So, the reality is that in the foreseeable future, whether you like it or not, you are taking the tube and there is nothing you can, or really want to, do about it, since you refuse to drive. So, since it seems inevitable that you are going to have to deal with the District line and its flock of sweaty, smelly, grumpy Londoners, which, by the way, you have become a member of, will you just stop whinging about it already, get on with it and eat your stir fry!'

The memory makes me smile feebly. It was a superficial bicker, an argument fuelled largely by exasperation and bluntness from both parties. When we were still at university and had only been together for three years, we used to argue about superficial things like this all the time, but these arguments would often blow out of proportion. That is because at the time, these superficial problems tugged at deeper-rooted issues. Our relationship was rocky, we were even broken up for a short period of time. Even twenty-five years later, I hate thinking about that time. But everything changed when we found out that Anne was unexpectedly pregnant. Now we bicker, but we hardly argue.

I bring my thoughts back to cycling and start planning my route for tomorrow morning. I will probably cycle south along the *sentier des douaniers*, the old coast guard path that runs along the entirety of French Atlantic coast. I am hoping to take the route past St George to see the

when he was studying at St Andrews. But I suppose it's hard for Anne to accept that even though he now lives in London, we still see as little of him as when he lived in Scotland. I think she thought we didn't see much of him because of the distance, but now it's a bit more obvious that the reason we don't see him too often is because he probably has other priorities.'

'That can't be easy to accept.' Sasha nods sympathetically.

'It's just how it is, isn't it,' I reply, resigned. 'He's an adult now. He needs to get on with his life without us.'

CHAPTER 12
SUMMER 2022

Diana

'Marco, get the hell out of my room!' I yell at the top of my voice.

Marco laughs, I can tell he is enjoying winding me up. I cannot help it, I know my anger is giving him all the satisfaction in the world, but I am growing increasingly frustrated and losing self-control.

He is leaning nonchalantly against the door frame of my bedroom, grinning.

'Relax, Lady Di! Stop being such a diva—'

'Do. Not. Call. Me. That!' I shriek. I feel like I could throw something at him. Ideally something heavy and sharp.

'What on earth are you screaming for?' bellows Mum from the bottom of the stairs. I can hear angry footsteps making their way to the first floor. Marco turns around, he clearly finds the whole situation very amusing.

'She's just all flustered about seeing Alex tonight.'

'Shut up, Marco!'

'She's taking absolutely ages getting ready. I swear this is the third outfit I've seen her try on since she got out of the shower. And I've never seen anyone concentrate this hard whilst applying eyeliner!'

Mum's face twists in annoyance. 'Marco, leave your sister alone and come downstairs. You can help your dad, he's getting the groceries out of the car.'

'OKaaayyyyyyy!'

Marco struts off, wiggling his hips as if he were on a catwalk. He turns around once he reaches the top of the stairs, pretends to flick his hair and blows me a kiss. I flip him off.

'Diana!' exclaims Mum with shock.

'Oh, come on, he completely deserved that!'

'Just because your brother is being immature doesn't mean you should stoop down to his level. I've told you this before, behaving just as poorly as he does takes away your moral high ground to feel outraged.' I can tell Mum is starting to get worked up.

'What are you taking his side for?'

'I am not taking sides, I'm calling it as I see it. Now stop worrying so much about what you look like and get ready. We are leaving in fifteen minutes.' Mum turns around abruptly and disappears down the stairs.

I turn around and stare into my hand mirror. My face is distorted into an unpleasant expression, the corners of my mouth raised into an aggressive snarl. I have been feeling apprehensive about seeing Alex all afternoon, and this argument has left me feeling even more on edge. I cannot stand my younger brother right now. The little pot stirrer. Marco is convinced I have a crush on Alex and loves tormenting me about it. But if I am completely honest, Marco's teasing is nothing compared to the shock on Mum's face when she found out there was some truth behind Marco's assumptions. I can tell she was disappointed in me. What bothers me the most, however, is the fact that Marco sees right through me. I find it infuriating. I am taking a lot longer than usual getting ready. Clearly, I still care about what Alex thinks about me and a small part of me hopes he starts to see me more as a grown up and less as the girl I used to be when I was 14. I take a deep breath and pick up my eyeliner once again. I try to compose myself, but there is no use. I put the eyeliner back down. I do not want to look like I am trying. I wish I could skip this *apéritif* tonight and go straight to Cédric's with Tala and Nora instead. 'Let's go, Diana,' Dad calls from downstairs.

'Coming,' I shout back. I get up abruptly and painstakingly make my way down the stairs.

CHAPTER 13
SUMMER 2022

Alex

I walk through the open-planned kitchen, cross the living room and reach the bottom of the staircase. I climb up the stairs two at a time and I wave at Leo as I pass the guest bedroom. My own room is at the end of the corridor, up another flight of stairs, to the left. I close the door behind me and partially draw the shutters together to obstruct myself from outside view. I make sure to leave a narrow gap between the two shutters to let a stream of natural daylight into the bedroom. The sunlight is gorgeous this evening, tinting the ocean, beach and houses surrounding the promenade golden, and I do not want to miss a minute of it.

Quickly, I strip out of my swimming trunks and step into the shower of my en-suite bathroom. I turn the tap to its coldest setting. The icy water comes as a welcome relief from the outside heat. I scrub and my thoughts drift to the evening ahead.

I am apprehensive about seeing Louise. The last time the two of us were in a room together last summer… events took a nasty turn. Louise did not hold back and shouted abuse at me for what I did to Diana. No one knows about that, about what happened. Certainly not Mum and Dad, and I am sure Diana and Louise both want it to stay that way. I know I certainly do. So, I am just going to have to put on my biggest smile, act like everything is normal, nurse a steady supply of alcohol throughout the night to medicate the awkwardness and self-loathing, and hopefully make an early exit to one of the neighbouring bars.

I turn the shower off and grab a towel. I stare at myself in the mirror as I pat my body dry. I am twenty-two, but I think I look much younger. My face is wide and angular, you could almost trace two straight lines from my temples to the bottom of my cheeks, and then a right angle where my mouth meets my jawline. My lips are narrow, my jaw square and set. I have brown eyes and short brown hair. I have a natural, permanent tan. Personally, I feel like I have got an overly serious look about myself. It is my jaw; its shape makes it seem like my face is always clenched in irritation. I used to be skinny, but I have put on some muscle since I turned 16. Therefore, I have gotten used to people calling me attractive. I quickly spray on some deodorant and dispassionately start selecting clothes for tonight. A breezy flannel shirt and some shorts will do. I sit on my bed and stare at the new high-end watch I just bought myself with my bonus money. Seven five p.m. Any minute now. I strain my ears in an attempt to work out what might be happening in the front garden, but I cannot hear a thing. That must mean the Munroes have not arrived yet.

My watch has just reminded me of work. I have been employed for roughly a year now, and I am slowly getting used to the new routine of working life. I have to admit, starting an office job was a shock to the system after spending four years at university. Undergraduate life did not prepare me for working life. I doubt it prepares anybody for life as a financially independent adult. For four years, you get used to working around your own schedule and having only yourself to take into consideration when organising your time. You get used to spontaneous nights out on a Tuesday evening, or taking a random Friday off because you feel you have worked hard that week and really deserve a three-day weekend. Hell, if you prefer to be in the library on Saturday and Sunday and instead take the Monday and Tuesday off, nobody is going to stop you. You are the sole owner of your time at university. When you start to work, that freedom disappears. The company you work for is entitled to nine hours of your time every day from Monday to Friday. Suddenly, especially when you live in South Brixton, you have to get up at six a.m. five times a week if you want to make it into your central London office before eight a.m. Since you have not gotten up before nine a.m. in over four years, your body needs to go through a long, painful phase of adaptation. You need to teach it how to be productive, alert and efficient from eight a.m. to seven p.m. again (has your body ever been able to concentrate for that long in the first place?), instead of being at its peak working condition around midnight.

The first two months at work were positively exhausting and morale sapping. I was tired and perpetually short-tempered, and dragging myself out of bed felt like an insurmountable battle every morning. A battle that I had to repeat day after day after day. I experienced my whole week as a countdown until Friday night, urging time to go by faster. Then Friday night arrived and a different countdown started, the countdown until Sunday evening, a countdown during which I pleaded time to slow down. And just like that, it was Monday again and the countdown was back on. Furthermore, being part of a competitive graduate scheme meant performing the most boring and unexciting tasks for the first month or so. I did not know enough about the business to be entrusted with any responsibility and the nature of my daily work reflected that. What I found the hardest at the start was my lack of independence at work. Performing the smallest task for the first time required asking a dozen different questions to a dozen different people. Every task felt like a big ordeal because instead of just getting the job done, I also had to figure out how to perform that task in the first place: the files I would need for it, the people I would need to talk to, and finally the steps I would have to follow.

Thankfully, work is easier now. I have worked out a routine, I have become more independent, I have figured out how to organise my time. I have even made a few work friends, and every Thursday evening, like most of London's consultants, we like to meet up at the local pub in Bank for a few pints. Unoriginally, we moan about our bosses, we complain about time-consuming tasks which do not seem to lead to any tangible results, and we kick up a fuss about how we should be getting paid a lot more for the amount of time we spend at work. I remember the last conversation Julian, Charlie, Patrick and I had just before I flew over to France.

'Honestly, does anyone even have a look at this spreadsheet?' wondered Charlie that Thursday over her third margarita, her favourite. 'Took me freaking three hours to input all the data and then Rachel walks into the office and tells me she has just updated the formula to calculate the ARR. Literally, that woman just wasted three hours of my time. Going to have to start all over again tomorrow.'

'Rachel is so disorganised, honestly,' added Julian. He was on his second larger.

'The worst thing is, her disorganisation always becomes other people's problem,' added Rachel, tequila fuelling her irritation. 'She messes up and we have to pick up the broken pieces. Honestly, I am so annoyed at her. And it's not like I can say anything to her, can I? After all, she's the boss. She knows best apparently. Even when she makes freaking incompetent decisions, we have to do as we are told…'

'I know what you mean,' answered Patrick. 'You just have to accept that more senior people will always get their way when you first start out. Our time will come in ten years' time after we've proven ourselves competent. Then we'll be able to speak up our minds when we feel like it.' Patrick had a large glass of red wine in his hand. Patrick always drinks red; according to him, it's the cheapest way to get properly drunk in London. He usually has the worst hangovers out of the four of us.

'Gosh, I'm not sure I still want to be doing this in ten years' time,' I said, sipping my pint.

'You have to stick it out till then,' said Julian. 'That's when you start making real money.'

'That makes me feel a bit depressed… Ten years before this becomes worth it?'

'I don't want to think about that,' interrupted Patrick. 'Let's get tequila shots. My round.'

Obviously, we end up getting pretty drunk that evening (there was no food) and the next morning, after an evening of moaning about our bosses, complaining about time-consuming tasks and getting upset about how little we get paid, Charlie, Julian, Patrick and I whinged about our hangovers and the wickedness of tequila. I felt rougher than usual that particular Friday and unfortunately for me, first thing in the morning, I had to sit through a presentation from HR about how to make the workplace a more positive environment. I could not decide if I thought it was ironic or amusing. One thing I knew for sure was that I desperately needed to throw up. However, I felt like I could not exactly just run out of the conference room in the middle of the meeting. It would not have looked very professional.

Now, sitting on the edge of my bed in Royan, waiting for this dreadful *apéritif* to start, I reflect that this drunken conversation a few days ago encapsulates my current misgivings about work. It is not that I dread going into work every day. On the contrary, I do not mind my job most days. Mostly, I do not mind going to work because realistically, there is not much else for me to do from Monday to Friday. I do enjoy the feeling of having done something productive with myself by the end of the day. But I do not relate to people who say they wake up every day excited to go to work and get things done. I am not excited by what I do. Ultimately, I work to pay the bills and enjoy myself with whatever money I have left. I look forward to every evening at home, every weekend, every Bank Holiday, ever trip abroad. Consequently, I am very excited about the next couple of work-free weeks. I am just worried about the truth coming out. Of friendships being ruined as a consequence of my actions.

Contrary to what Mum and Dad might think, I want to be here, in Royan, with them. Our family holidays are always very relaxing, and I crave some down time. But Louise and her family always spend their summers in France, and there is no way to avoid them when we live on opposite ends of the same promenade. Unfortunately for me, Mum is like a dog on a bone when she has an idea in mind. I remember the phone call she gave me, a little over a month ago. Even though I could not see her, I could imagine her stern face on the other end of the line just by the intonation of her voice. She sounded both bossy and disappointed at the same time.

'The four of us haven't spent more than one evening together in over a year, Alex. You are always working, in the office until ungodly hours and you have been very poor at carving time out of your schedule for us. I understand you have your new work friends and they are more fun than us, but after all, we are your family. Or maybe there is a girl who you'd rather spend all your time with, but then I do not understand why you wouldn't introduce her to us...'

'Mum, there isn't any girl—' I didn't get to finish my sentence. She carried on as if I hadn't spoken. That happens a lot when I have her on the phone. She tends to confuse reciprocal conversations with one-sided monologues. I often wonder if becoming a successful investment banker has not led her to become a bit self-centred. Clearly, she works in an environment where people come to her for advice and her opinion is valued. She often has the final say over business transactions at work. As a result, I think Mum has developed the false belief that her word should be valued over everyone else's in all aspects of life.

'I'm starting to feel like you only come to see us now when you need something from us. That makes me sad. I know it would mean a lot to your dad if you came to France with us. He loves it when the two of you go on these long cycle trips and discover new parts of the coast... It's been hard for him recently not being able to cycle because of his ankle, and I know he is looking forward to finally being allowed back on the bike. If you were there for him when that happened, well, I reckon he'd be absolutely over the moon.'

'I know, Mum, I just don't know if I can afford to take this much time off work at the moment. I feel like I still need to prove that I am a hard worker and that I can be trusted to put the hours in when necessary. That's the only way my manager is going to entrust me with more important work. If I show I am serious and a team player. Going off on holiday for a few weeks doesn't exactly send that message.'

'And I think it would do Katie some real good to have her big brother around as well,' Mum soldiered on, clearly on her own conversational trajectory. 'She has been rather quiet recently. She won't tell me what is bothering her, I guess she is too old now to confide in her mother. However, she might speak to you. I just want to make sure she isn't being bullied at school or anything like that.'

'Mum, just because Katie has become a little bit more introverted doesn't necessarily mean she is being bullied—'

'To be honest, Alex, I think you are being rather selfish. It's not like I am asking much from you, is it? I literally just want you to come on holiday to France with us. How is that a chore? Everything is paid for, the only thing I am asking from you in return is for you to show interest in your sister and father.'

I stare at my watch again. Ten past seven. Still no noise from outside. I shake my head, clearing the conversation with my mum from my mind. Obviously, she eventually got her way and I begrudgingly booked return flights to Bordeaux. That is Mum's secret power. She will badger you relentlessly until you realise the only way to make your life easier is to give in, so you do. She is like a child in that aspect. Now, I am just going to have to be creative in coming up with excuses to avoid the Munroes for the next two weeks, or, when avoiding them is not an option (like tonight), ways of keeping our interactions to the bare minimum.

A delusional part of me hoped the Munroes would holiday somewhere different this year, sparing me this headache. Surely, spending every single holiday in the same tiny, albeit picturesque, village would have become rather monotonous by now. I was hoping the Munroes would be curious to discover new countries in Europe this summer, or at the very least, another part of France. After all, Louise disappeared to Berlin after she found out what happened with Diana.

Consequently, it seemed reasonable for me to believe they would not be in Royan this year. Clearly, she seemed to be willing to go to extraordinary lengths to avoid seeing me. Part of me wonders if she also took the sabbatical in Berlin to get away from her daughter. I hope that is not the case. I cannot imagine what it might feel like, not being able to look your own daughter in the eye.

'Alex!'

I jump. My bedroom door creaks slightly ajar and Leo's face appears. It looks like his head is floating in the air, detached from the rest of his body.

'What are you doing sitting on your bed like this staring at your hands?' he asks. I shrug. 'You're strange sometimes, you know that?'

Again, I just look at him in silence. I do not think his comment warrants any reply. I am strange, and this has been established many years ago.

'Anyways, man, everyone's here so we should probably go down.'

I strain my ears. Indeed, I notice indistinct chatter and laughter coming up from the front garden. I sigh and push myself off the bed. I open the door and I put my hand on Leo's shoulder.

'Let's go,' I say and we make our way downstairs.

CHAPTER 14
LAST SUMMER, 2021

Louise

For the past thirty years, Cédric's has been located in the middle of the Royan's promenade. It is an imposing, white, brick building adorned with expansive large bay windows that offer stunning ocean views and fill the dining area with natural light. The wooden beams that ornate the roof are painted a light sea blue, and so are the rails of the second-level outdoor terrace. A row of tables and chairs is set up outside the restaurant, against its white wall. A second row of tables, chairs and parasols is set up closer to the edge of the beach, creating a narrow passage for *flâneurs* to make their way up and down the promenade. Walkers usually slow down when they get closer to Cédric's. They take their time strolling between tables, looking left and right at what clients are eating, drinking and eavesdropping on strangers' conversations. They enjoy the spectacle just as much as clients enjoy being seen.

This evening, the section of the promenade in front of Cédric's has been cordoned off by two red ropes, creating an exclusive feel. If you are not part of the guest list, you have to make your way down the stairs onto the beach and walk a few meters in the sand to get from one side of the promenade to the other. From the upstairs terrace, Louise is observing a group of tourists who are taking off their shoes before walking through the sand. She is standing slightly apart from her group of friends and leaning against the balustrade, people watching. She enjoys social events, but there are often moments during the night when she does not feel like participating in conversation. When that happens, she removes herself from the group, and enjoys a short moment of solitude. She enjoys the respite of being alone because it comes with the security that whenever she feels like it, she can turn around and throw herself back into light-hearted conversation. She often stares at people and romanticises their lives in her head, disconnecting herself from reality.

'How are you doing, Louise?' Sasha leans against the balustrade and hands her a freshly poured glass of rosé. 'Thought you might want a second

until their stomachs, appetite stretched by alcohol, started growling for food. When they were not having dinner with Louise's parents, they would stay and eat *moules frites*. After a while, Cédric started recognising them. Back in the days where Royan was an almost exclusively French summer destination, a loud group of Brits stuck out like a sore thumb. Cédric was keen to practice his English, and over the years, they developed a friendship. Holding the six Brits responsible for drinking most of his stock of alcohol each summer has become a recurring joke between them.

As per usual, Anne feigns shock upon hearing this accusation. 'Oh, come off it, Cédric, you make us sound like drunkards!'

Cédric holds his hands up high in excuse, one of them clutching a now empty bottle of rosé as if to prove his point. He has just poured the six of them sizeable glasses of wine. Cédric knows how to keep his clientele happy. 'I'm joking, I'm joking.' He laughs. 'But my business is changing, I want to make sure you know about it, spread the word and love it so that you come back and continue spending all of your money here,' he confesses bluntly.

'The place looks great,' approves Liliane loyally. 'I love the ambiance you've created, very relaxed yet lively. I'm sure you'll have a huge success.'

'Agreed, this place is for everyone. People our age can sit down and enjoy the food, but being able to come just for a drink means you will also attract younger customers like our Alex. You've been clever, Cédric,' adds Anne.

'*Merci beaucoup*,' says Cédric. He shouts towards the bar, 'Oh, Antoine! *Sers-nous six shots de notre meilleure vodka s'il-te-plaît.*'

'Oh no, Cédric, you don't have to. I don't think any of us have done a shot in years,' exclaims Louise. 'It's probably not a very good idea.'

'Don't be ridiculous, it's the expensive kind, not that cheap stuff you used to drink all the time twenty-five years ago. It will keep your head clear, unlike that junk that you used to love.'

'We didn't love it,' interjects Victor. 'Unfortunately, it was the only thing we could afford. Tasted horrible but when you are a university student, you buy booze which has the cheapest price tag for the highest percentage of alcohol possible.'

Antoine, the bartender, appears behind Cédric. He is balancing a tray of shots. He places them one by one in front of Cédric, who starts handing them round the table. Victor looks amused, Thomas feels ridiculous, Sasha and Liliane sniff the vodka, recoiling at the scent, and Anne and Louise are both thinking about how awful they are going to feel the next morning.

Cédric lifts his shot, and shouts, '*Santé!* To the success of Cédric's.'

It would have been impolite not to toast with the host, so the six of them raise their glass in unison.

'*Santé!*' they exclaim in chorus.

Liliane knocks her glass back quickly, hoping to swallow the clear liquid before being able to taste it. For the first few seconds, she feels nothing, but then the vodka starts burning its way down her throat. She has to resist the urge to throw up.

'Gosh, I feel like I am a student again,' she moans.

'I don't,' answers Louise. 'I don't remember this being as unpleasant.'

'Really? On the contrary, I was surprised by how easy that felt,' says Sasha. 'I miss those days sometimes, you know? University. It was a lot of fun.'

'I don't get that,' interjects Anne rather bluntly. 'I think it's a bit sad, thinking of university as the best days of our lives... Most of our time at university was spent either drunk or hungover. How can these be the best days ever? I mean, these are such superficial experiences, surely there's more value to life than that. Have we not achieved more in our lives since then? Surely, we feel more fulfilled as adults, with families we love and jobs we care about, than we did when we were confused, twenty-something-year-old students... Personally, uni was fun, I'm glad I had these experiences, but I wouldn't repeat any of it for the world. Too messy.'

'Jesus, Anne, calm down... I was just saying those were fun days, I wouldn't mind a few more fun days once in a while to unwind from work and stress and just to break up the monotonous routine,' replies Sasha, eyebrows frowned. He does not want to escalate the conversation into an argument, but he is not ready to let Anne paint such a shallow portrait of him. 'Of course, I care more about my family than about getting plastered in a dingy club with strangers, but I'm sorry, being a parent is hard work and I don't think it's a crime to admit that once in a while I wouldn't mind a break from it.'

An uncomfortable silence sets around the table. Louise is looking at the empty plate in front of her, Victor is staring at his hands, and Liliane and Thomas's gazes are skimming across the room.

Nobody knows how to break the awkwardness and everyone is avoiding direct contact with either Anne or Sasha. Even Cédric has gone unusually quiet and he is shifting his weight from one foot to the other. He is thinking hard about what he could say to break the tension, but his mind is drawing a blank. Anne regrets snapping at Sasha and she is wondering how to rectify the situation. After all, it is not fair to let her insecurities about what happened at the end of their time at university put a damper on everyone else's evening. She is not usually one for creating drama and awkward situations, and she wants nothing more but to drop the subject and move on.

'I know, I'm sorry, Sasha, this came out a lot harsher than I intended. I didn't mean to sound so judgemental. I just don't want to be one of these middle-aged women who still wishes she were twenty...'

Sasha smiles at her, the kind of smile that indicates that he is ready to move on but would probably be badmouthing her to Liliane in private later. Cédric looks relieved.

'Right, maybe no more vodka for a little while then. Oh, there's some friends from the surf club, I'll see you guys later!' Cédric moves away swiftly, greeting his other guests just as exuberantly as he had greeted them.

'Let's have some food!' exclaims Thomas. He is sitting across the table from Anne and gives her a supportive smile as their friends slowly break into conversation and help themselves to the dishes around the table. Anne smiles back at her husband gratefully; clearly, he wants to diffuse the tension and make sure everybody is having a good time. Anne takes a sip of her rosé and helps herself to some *melon et jambon de parme*. She chews slowly, absentmindedly tuning in and out of the conversation around her. Quickly, she loses track of what her friends are saying, completely lost in her own memories, reliving her last months of university over and over again in her mind.

Thomas sneaks a quick glance at Anne from across the table. She seems lost in thought, Thomas is fairly confident she regrets snapping at Sasha. Anne does not like to relive university, he is fully aware of that. She regrets some of the states she got in during her first year at Durham, which they both now refer to as her rebellious period. Anne's parents were very strict with her when she was a teenager. Even when she turned 18, they would not allow her to go to parties or see friends past nine p.m. As a result, she spent most of her last years of school feeling like she was missing out. At school, her friends would be gossiping about house parties she had not been allowed to go to and about the new, 'cool' people they had met she knew nothing about. After a while, because she was never seen out during the weekend, she started getting a reputation. She as a bore, a goody touchy only interested in school work, and she stopped being invited to parties altogether. Telling Thomas about her school years, Anne recognised those were trivial problems, but they had greatly affected her confidence as a teenager. As a result, she did not know what to do with all her newfound freedom when she moved to Durham. During the first months of her fresher year, she compensated for missed time. Thomas did not know her back then, but he did not like what she sounded like. Apparently, she dabbled with a druggy crowd, and got herself embarrassingly drunk on more than one occasion. Thomas does not know much more than that. Anne likes to believe that if she does not talk about her first year of university, she can pretend it never happened, and if he is completely honest with himself, Thomas is happy to be kept in the dark about this period of his wife's life. In a way, he is glad they only met in their second year of university. He suspects he would have found her very unattractive if he had seen her in one of those states she used to get herself in.

In second year, when they met at Halloween, Anne had started to calm down. Granted, that party lasted until the early hours of the morning, but that was one of the rare times the two of them stayed up that late. A few months after they had started dating, Anne told him about her wild first year experiences. She explained how her strict upbringing at home had resulted in her acting out at university. She confided how she first turned to drugs and alcohol for fun and escapism. Finally, she described how getting high and wasted did not stay fun for very long.

'After a night out, it would take me days to stop feeling gross about myself,' she told him one evening as they were lying cuddling in bed. 'I would spend hours and hours worrying about the things I had done or said to other people. I was convinced everybody was judging me for getting so fucked up and acting like an absolute shell of a human being. Sometimes, I wouldn't be able to get out of bed for a day or two because I was too scared to see anybody. And when I eventually did leave my room, I would then spend another few days regretting the time I had wasted in there watching stupid TV and eating junk. I would be angry at myself for not doing anything productive with my time and for not achieving anything worthwhile. After a while, going out stopped being fun... I started hating how unhealthy I was becoming and eventually, I realised how sad it was that all I seemed to be interested in was going out… So, I decided something had to change. That's why I decided to move in with Louise at the end of first year. I wanted to distance myself from the people I used to go out with and that druggy environment. I hoped that Louise, who has always been a very sensible girl, would positively influence me.'

Thomas also considered himself a good influence on Anne. Seeing him meant she had less time to spend with some of her more questionable friends, and gradually, ties with her first-year crowd fizzled out. Anne had been a very serious student at school, hardworking and rigorous. She had lost sight of her ambitions and love of learning when starting university, but rediscovered her work ethic the more time she spent with him. Thomas had a plan, he was hoping to get a graduate job at one of the UK's top five banks when he graduated and he sold the London lifestyle to Anne. For the whole of their second year at university, they were great as a couple, almost inseparable. They studied hard whilst making the most of university life and the opportunities it offered them. They joined the student union board and helped organise a wide range of university events. They raised money for various charities by completing multiple long distance races. Anne subsequently discovered a passion for running, and whilst Thomas was happy to say he had once run over 21km without stopping, he vowed never to put himself through such an ordeal ever again. They both became part of the Business Society and attended most socials. By the end of second year, Thomas and Victor both spent most of their nights at Louise and Anne's. The four of them rapidly became very good friends and during the spring and summer months, they would often go for walks together along the Wear. They enjoyed watching the rowing club train and mingled on the cricket court with many of Durham's university students. Their lives had become so intertwined, Thomas simply assumed his dream of moving into a corporate job in London had also become Anne's. Therefore, it came as a total shock when she told him she was considering taking a gap year after graduation.

The blow came midway through the second semester of third year. Their time at university was rapidly coming to an end and Thomas was focused on finding a job in London. He had already applied to a few big banks and he was waiting to hear back about interviews. One day, as he and Anne were sitting opposite each other in the library and he was applying for a postgraduate job in to become an investment banker, he asked Anne how she was getting on with finding a job. Her reply took him completely by surprise.

'I haven't applied anywhere yet. To be honest, I'm not too sure what I want to do after uni.'

'What do you mean?' His fingers froze over his keyboard and his head jerked up in alarm.

All of a sudden, he had forgotten all about the personal statement he was working on.

'I quite like the idea of a gap year. Travel, maybe do some teaching or something to make a bit of money while I figure out what kind of long-term job I really want.' Anne fiddled nervously with a strand of her dark, curly, thick hair. Thomas was absolutely gobsmacked.

'A gap year?' he whispered, self-conscious not to make a spectacle of himself in the middle of the silent library.

'It's just an idea. I just don't know what I want...' Anne looked uncomfortable, she was avoiding all eye contact with Thomas and shifting anxiously in her seat. She had been apprehensive about having this conversation for a few weeks, and she was upset it was now happening in the library. She did not feel she could say exactly how she felt in such an open and public space. Furthermore, Anne was a private person and she was worried people around them would eavesdrop into what was becoming an intimate conversation.

'I'm not sure the post grad route is for me. Or maybe it is, but even though it sounds a bit cliché, I would like to see the world and have new experiences before I commit to a career. All these post grad jobs, they will still be here in a year's time. But this is probably one of the only times in my life I could do this. Before I have responsibilities and a job and no holidays.'

'But... I mean, where would you even go? For how long?' Thomas muttered in dismay.

'You always talk about how much you loved traveling to Thailand and south-east Asia the summer you left school before starting university. I don't know, I've always thought I should do something similar. I've never been outside of Europe. Sometimes, I think my life is a bit plain and boring. I think it's time for me to be more adventurous.'

Thomas felt a wave of anguish constrict his chest. Without even knowing it, he was the one who had inadvertently planted this idea of gap year in her mind.

'But, how long do you want to travel for?' he asked again. Anne had ignored the question and therefore, he knew he was not going to like the answer she was going to give him.

'I don't know, six months, one year? Isn't a gap year about being spontaneous? Making plans as you go along?'

'It is… if you only have yourself to take into consideration.' He had said it. He could not take it back. He had voiced the idea of a life without him. Is that what she wanted? Some independence? Or did Anne want to do long distance? Did she want to travel for a year and then move to London with him? Was he willing to wait a whole year? Or was she trying to tell him she didn't necessarily see a future with him? Thomas felt like the world was constricting around him. He did not want to be having this conversation, but now the cat was out of the bag, he needed answers. Immediate answers. How could he have been so blissfully unaware of what his girlfriend had been thinking all this time?

Anne had gone silent. She was staring blankly at the wall to her right. She hoped that concentrating hard enough on a small patch of peeled plaster would keep the tears at bay. Pressure was building behind her eye sockets, she feared she might start crying at any moment. She felt guilty. She loved Thomas and ever since they had started dating, her life had greatly improved. She did not want to break up with him. But she was scared of letting her love for him influence some of the big life choices that lay ahead of her. If they ended up separating, she might be left with nothing but a broken heart and a handful of regrets.

Thomas sensed her distress. It gave him hope. Clearly, she had not made her mind up about this gap year yet. He whispered, 'We should go back to yours. Where we can talk. Properly.'

Anne nodded. They quickly packed up their books, notepads and water bottles into their backpacks. Anne held her head down as they walked past Louise and Victor on their way out of the library. She hoped they had not noticed anything unusual. Victor shot Thomas an inquisitive look which the latter chose to ignore. Thomas put his arm around Anne, who looked like she was about to burst into tears at any second, as they walked silently through the hilly roads of Durham back to Anne's house on the Avenue. He did not understand how he was the one consoling Anne when she was the one who had just pulled the rug from under his feet. Surely, he should be the one who was upset and not the other way around?

77

When they arrived at the house, Anne and Thomas went straight to her bedroom and closed the door. They needed privacy. Anne sat on the edge of her bed and looked up at Thomas.

'I am worried we are too young to be making decisions around each other.'

'Moving to London and getting a grad job isn't just about me. Surely you realise it's the smart thing for you to do regardless of our situation. The sooner you start to work after graduation, the quicker you'll move up the professional ladder. The longer you wait, the longer it is going to take for you to build a proper career. Make some real money.' Thomas's shock was slowly morphing into anger. This idea of a gap year, it was preposterous. Nothing more than a modern, middle-class fairy tale full of false promises of freedom, cultural awakening and life-changing experiences. How could Anne be buying into that pipe dream?

'It's just such a big commitment. A commitment I am not ready to make because I am not sure I want the big career, the big money… I just want a job I love. Even if that means being less successful. And I am not too sure what that job is yet.'

'And how is going to Thailand going to help you figure out what your dream job is exactly?'

'I don't know. That's the thing, Thomas, I don't want to have everything planned out just yet. I'm sure things will fall into place naturally at some point.' Anne choked.

'That's ridiculous. You just want to live the student life for a little bit longer. No responsibilities, partying all night, sleeping around…' Rage was creeping into his voice.

'How can you say that? Just because I want to travel doesn't necessarily mean I want us to break up. We could do long distance.'

'No way.' His voice was uncompromising. 'You can't have your cake and eat it. If you want to go and travel and waste a year of your life, then go ahead. But you cannot expect me to wait around and just pine after you. I know how these stories end, you'll end up cheating on me anyway and shortly after that, you'll break up with me because you are too busy trying to "find yourself" to be tied down by a boyfriend. I don't need to wait around for that to happen.' He was speaking out of anger. He did not know how to deal with the wave of sorrow that was threatening to drown him at any moment. Therefore, he had chosen to transform his despair into ice-cold infuriation, an emotion he felt more comfortable with and better equipped to cope with.

Despite her best efforts, Anne was not able to fight her tears any longer. She did not expect this much venom in Thomas' voice.

That night, they argued for many more hours. They argued through tears, hurtful words and crushed emotions. But ultimately, that was the night Anne and Thomas broke up. Almost twenty-five years later, Thomas takes a large sip of his rosé and looks at his wife. Yes, the pain of their break up still feels as fresh as it did when he woke up all those years ago, alone and miserable in his small, abandoned apartment.

CHAPTER 15
SUMMER 2022

Victor

I am walking along the promenade, Louise to my right, my daughter Diana and my son Marco to my left. I look at my wife furtively. Louise has an elegant profile, a straight nose and a long neck, like a ballerina. Her face is midway between oval and round, the baby fat that used to fill her cheeks until her late twenties has melted away with age, and her cheekbones now stand out more prominently. Her blonde, wavy hair is pinned back in a strict ponytail. She is dressed rather drably tonight, a plain cream t-shirt and a pair of old jeans. I remember those jeans from our pre-wedding days; she must have dug them up from the very depths of her closet. They used to be white, but they are so worn out their colour reminds me of a grey, rainy, mid-autumn sky. I do not recognise my wife. She has never been vain, but she has always been one of the better-dressed people in the room. She has always taken care of herself, and she used to have an eye for clothes that stood out from mainstream fashion trends without looking tacky nor hippy. Now, she dresses for camouflage purposes, as if she wants to blend into her surroundings, disappear from people's view.

What she wears is one of the many things I do not recognise about my wife. For the past year, Louise has gradually become a mystery to me. It is an unsettling feeling, especially after eighteen years of marriage. I always thought I knew Louise better than she knew herself. For example, Louise struggles to connect with her emotions, she often feigns cheerfulness when she is actually feeling insecure or down. I used to be able to see through her act and provide her with the comfort and reassurance she did not always realise she needed. Nowadays, however, her sunny nature has vanished. Instead, she can be taciturn. Never in front of the children or when we are with friends, however. Only in private. And she has become extremely closed off when I try to talk to her about her feelings. I can tell there is something she is not telling me, but she denies anything is wrong. Louise's decision to move to Berlin for work has not only created a geographical distance between us, but also an emotional one.

'Victor, stop being ridiculous, I am just absolutely exhausted. I've had a hard week and just travelled over six hours to spend the weekend with you and the kids. Just let me go to sleep, please,' she would say when she arrived in London after spending a month in Berlin.

She did not seem happy to see me, and her words made me wonder if she even missed me when we were apart. We often spent the first night back together sleeping on opposite ends of the bed, as if Louise was scared to touch me. I would act hurt in the hope of getting her attention. I was rarely successful on the night. The next morning, however, Louise would wake up feeling bad about her frosty demeanour. She would consequently spend the entire weekend overcompensating, making me feel like she was walking on eggshells around me, overly keen to please. Louise came across shifty and that is how I imagine a guilty person would behave.

Eventually, I asked, 'Are you having an affair? Have you met someone? In Berlin?'

'Someone? In Berlin? You cannot be serious.' Louise was incredulous.

'You never come to visit. There always seems to be something more important to do in Berlin than seeing your family.' I should not have said that. From this moment onwards, the whole conversation became about her resentment towards the implication that she did not spend enough time with her family. She wondered why it always had to be her who had to fly to London and why I never travelled to see her. She asked if I thought she should feel apologetic about putting her career first. I could tell she was ready to pounce down my throat   if I took the bait and answered her question.

Louise looks away from the beach and catches me staring. She smiles a thin smile, her lips tightly pressed against each other. I smile back and push my worries to the back of my mind. Maybe we are just going through a bit of a rough patch. Maybe things will revert to normal on their own. Either or, now is not the time to ponder over all these questions. It has been a whole year since our three families have been reunited in Royan. It has also been a long time since my last holiday. Thinking of it, I do not think I have taken any annual leave since Christmas. I intend to enjoy my summer holiday and some down time with friends and for this reason, any problems concerning Louise and me can wait until we get back to London.

We arrive at the front gate of the Villa Grand Large. I can see Thomas and Sasha talking around the garden table, a glass of rosé in their hand. I

'Did you enjoy Berlin? I mean, surely it must have been hard being separated from Victor, Diana and Marco for a year...'

There is a small pause. Louise is taking a sip of her wine and I am worried the silence does not feel comfortable. I feel an urge to fill in the gap in conversation.

'It was very tough,' I say. Liliane prying into our private life annoys me, but I do not want to let it show. I want to squash this topic of conversation as quickly as possible and move on.

'It took some getting used to start with, of course, but we made it work,' answers Louise breezily. 'It was an opportunity I couldn't miss out on. Teaching French to German-speaking students instead of English ones, it's not the same. It's given me lots of ideas for a linguistic paper, which will hopefully support my application for a professorship in the near future.' This is Louise's standard answer when she talks about Berlin, a very untruthful answer. Like me, she is a private person and we are both keen to keep the tension this move has caused for our family between us.

'Well, I'm sure the kids and Victor will be very happy when you are back in London for good,' smiles Liliane.

'Oh definitely,' I grin. 'No more sabbaticals for a few years after this!' I fake laugh.

Liliane opens her mouth but we never get to find out what she was about to say. We are interrupted by a loud, shocked squeal. The sound is coming from the other side of the garden where the children have gradually gravitated towards. All six of us, the adults, turn urgently towards the direction of the scream. Katie is holding a phone, her hand clasped over her mouth, her eyes wide in stupefaction. I look around and catch Anne and Thomas' gaze. They look confused. I turn my head back towards the children. Something inexplicable happens next. I stare in incomprehension as Alex strides towards his sister, nostrils flared in anger, hands stretched out as if ready to snatch the phone ferociously out of Katie's hands. Luckily for her, Anne gets to her first.

CHAPTER 16
SUMMER 2022

Diana

Dad pushes the gate leading to the garden of the Villa Grand Large and all of a sudden, we are surrounded by the Dalton and Brandson families. Everyone is hugging everybody and asking for updates, 'How have you been?', 'When did you get here?', 'Isn't the weather just amazing?', 'So nice to see you guys!'. Thomas is quick to pour us all a drink and we stand there, congregated around the garden table. Alex is not here yet, and I am relieved. My chest, tightened in anticipation when we arrived in front of the villa, relaxes for a fraction of a second. However, I quickly realise that his absence just means he is bound to appear at any moment now. My nerves flare up again, I am on high alert, afraid his presence will catch me by surprise. I brace myself for a forced hello. Hopefully, that will be the extent of our interaction tonight. We have gotten pretty good at avoiding each other during these reunions over the years, so much so that I had started to become less apprehensive when Mum and Dad organised days out with the Daltons. But last summer, Mum found out about everything and now, I feel just as embarrassed as I used to feel when I was fourteen. Potentially even more embarrassed, I can only imagine what Mum must think when she sees the two of us together in a room.

Katie puts her arm around my shoulders and pulls Willow and me slightly aside from the group of parents.

'Gosh, what boring conversation, why do adults only seem to be able to talk about their jobs? To this day, I still have no idea what Mum and Dad do on a day-to-day basis even though they always talk about their work problems over dinner. It's all these corporate words they use, dead confusing. I swear it sounds like their work is basically the same but then according to them their jobs are radically different. I dunno…'

'I guess it's a bit different for my parents, my mum especially,' I reply. 'Being a university lecturer, everybody has an idea of what that entitles.'

'Very true, very true,' answers Katie. I like Katie a lot. She is very cheery and an upbeat person. A bit like Willow, but the latter has a more serious and academic side to her. Part of me feels bad that I lost touch with both of them after primary school, especially given the fact that we all go to Lady Cecilia. We hang out during the summer holidays when our parents take us to Royan. I guess it makes sense, up until recently we were the only Brits in town, we only had each other to keep ourselves entertained. However, we do not spend that much time together at school. We always say hi when we cross paths in the corridors and we have a bit of small talk when we run into each other at the library or in the lunch hall. But we have very different interests and very different friends. That is probably why we do not spend much time together at school. Willow is smart and very much into her studies, we all know she is going to be applying to the UK's top universities when the time comes to think about high education. She spends a lot of time with Katie, who is also hardworking but a bit more of a free spirit. Their friends seem a bit too serious to really get on with mine. They like to discuss latest social media trends and prefer Art and PE over Maths and English. Just like me.

'You know, I think I'm slowly starting to enjoy rosé,' says Willow. She is swirling her wine around her glass and looking at the vortex of liquid intently. 'Last summer, I was not a fan but it's growing on me. It's like coffee, tastes disgusting at first but you can teach yourself to love it by having it over and over again until you get used to it.'

'Have you ever tried amaretto?' I ask. 'It's my favourite, tastes like marzipan.'

'I haven't,' replies Willow.

'Neither,' says Katie. 'Doesn't sound like something the parents would buy though, where did you try that?'

'It was Laura's… She's a friend from school,' I specify just in case although I suspect Katie and Willow know who I am talking about. 'So it was Laura's older sister's twenty-first this year. She had this big party in Soho. Parents paid for it. Anyway, Laura was allowed to invite a few friends to keep her company so that's why I was there. They were serving amaretto then. It's like a little shot, but doesn't taste of alcohol at all.'

'Must have been fun,' says Willow.

'How is Laura?' asks Katie. 'I heard about her dad, how is she holding up?'

'Yeah, they got the cancer diagnosis shortly after that party actually,' I reply. 'They are doing OK, thankfully they caught it early. He's had to cut down on work quite a lot, mostly working from home and less responsibilities. Laura says he's exhausted all the time and he's lost a lot of weight from the chemo. But they are being very strong as a family.'

'Ah that sounds tough,' says Willow.

Katie nods. There is a lull in the conversation and consequently, I overhear Thomas exclaim, 'Ah, there they are!'

I know what to expect and knots of nervousness tighten inside my stomach. Surely enough, as I look away from Katie and Willow, I spot Alex and Leo walking towards us. I watch Alex give my mum a hug, a quick and awkward affair, they bodies are quick to disconnect from each other and Mum cannot look Alex in the eye. Leo gives me a warm hug and suddenly Alex is standing behind him.

'Hi, Diana, good to see you,' he says.

'You too,' I mumble, trying to act normal. I let out a silent sigh of relief when he turns away to say hello to my dad. I watch them have a short conversation before my brother pulls Alex to one side. I try to shift my attention back to Katie and Willow. Neither of them seem to have noticed anything weird. Good. They are too busy trying to discreetly pour themselves another glass of rosé. Dad catches them and tells them off with a laugh. They turn back towards me, all giggles and I catch Willow mid-sentence, '... part-time job in a small café next to home. It's only on Saturdays and some Sunday mornings but it's decent money. I'm trying to save to buy a car when I get my driver's license.'

'It's so good you have a job in the first place. How did you get it? Did you know the café owners?' asks Katie.

'No, there was a sign up on the shop window advertising for a part-time vacancy. So I wrote a CV and gave it to them. Obviously, I'd already done some waitering when helping Mum out during some of her events, which is why I reckon I got the job.'

'How do you manage with homework if you are working all weekend?' Katie wants to know.

'Not going to lie,' admits Willow, 'it's a bit of a struggle. I have to get quite a bit of work done during the week when I get back from school if I want to keep up. Obviously, Mum and Dad wouldn't let me keep this job if it started affecting my school work, so I just need to make sure I keep on top of everything.'

Despite my best efforts, I struggle to get involved in their conversation. I check my phone, I do not have any signal but it has automatically connected to the villa's Wi-Fi. However, we must be pretty far away from the main box because my social media feed is struggling to update. I check the time. 7.45 p.m. Still too early to leave and no news from Tala and Nora. Next, I try to refresh my text messages. Once again, no success. The currently loading sign nags at me. I put my phone away.

'So when are we going to take the boards out?' Katie wants to know. Many of the adults and children of our large, heteroclite group took up surfing numerous summers ago. I cannot remember which summer exactly, but it was sometime when I was still in primary school. Thomas was the one who suggested it. I remember how the idea came about. It was a sunny afternoon and we were at the *Côte Sauvage*, the Wild Coast.

The Wild Coast is a half-hour drive away from Royan and the beaches are very different up there. Royan's beaches are very family friendly. They are small, usually about 500m in length, and they are enclosed in rocky coves, which means the water is very calm despite it being the Atlantic Ocean. Old houses, such as the Villa Grand Large, restaurants and bars circle the beaches of Royan; therefore, they are busy places with lots of animation and activity throughout all hours of the day. On the other hand, the Wild Coast, as its name suggests, is ruled by nature. It is one, long, continuous stretch of sand which extends for kilometres and kilometres on end, all the way to l'Île d'Oléron. Getting to the Wild Coast is an ordeal, and therefore, it does not attract many tourists as it is slightly off the beaten tracks. The journey starts by driving along a narrow country road bordered by tall, lanky pine trees. There is no formal parking near the Coast, so most cars end up tucked off the main road underneath the canopy of trees. Once you have parked, you need to walk along one of the forest's narrow dirt tracks, which gradually transforms into a sandy path covered in pine needles. You can spot surfers and locals walking along these tracks, board or sun umbrella in hand and wearing old trainers or slip-on shoes. An unusual choice of footwear for the beach, but better than walking barefoot on the sharp pine needles scattered along the way. After a five-minute walk, you reach the bottom of sand dunes so tall they cut the ocean away from view. The ascent is a breathless affair, especially, as we discovered when we started surfing, if you are carrying a heavy longboard. When you finally reach the top of the dune, you are greeted by the breath-taking view of a near-empty beach and the noisy, foamy waves of the Atlantic Ocean crashing disorderly on the shore. These are waves that make the Wild Coast popular with surfers.

The summer Thomas suggested we try surfing, we were having a beach picnic on the Wild Coast. I remember playing in the sand, building a sandcastle, and Mum and Dad instructing me not to go too far into the water when I went to clean my beach bucket and spade. The waves were powerful and the tide tugged at my toys as I submerged them underwater. However, these must have made for good surfing conditions because the water was packed with surfers. Thomas was observing them from our towels and I overheard him talking to Katie and Alex as I got back from the water.

'You know, they're pretty impressive. Look at this guy on the far right, he keeps doing these insane skills. Maybe we should try one day. I'm pretty sure there is a surf club on the far-left side of the beach back in Royan.'

'Oh yes, Dad,' they shouted. 'That would be sooooo cool.'

The idea stuck and for a few summers, five days in a row, the surf club would take Katie, Alex, Willow, Marco, Leo, Thomas, Anne, Liliane and I (the other adults found surfing too scary) to the Wild Coast with some other beginners, and teach us how to catch waves. We have stopped taking lessons now, and most of us have given up on surfing. It is hard to make progress when you only practice a few days a year. Personally, I stopped surfing because I got scared after wiping out on some powerful waves. Only Katie, Willow and Thomas have kept up with it, and they bought second-hand boards two or three years ago to go surfing on their own without the club.

Therefore, I am not surprised that Katie is asking about catching some waves.

'I don't know,' answers Willow. 'First of all, we need to check with your dad when he wants to go surfing. We need him to drive us to the Coast.'

'True, might be worth checking the tides to find out what day will have the best waves before we ask him,' answers Katie. 'I left my phone upstairs in my room, can you check on yours, Willow?'

'*Urgh*, I don't think the Wi-Fi reaches this far into the garden,' she moans. 'What about you, Diana? Is your Internet working?'

I check my phone once again. 'No, it was the same earlier, it's not loading, we are too far away from the box.'

'*Urgh*, I'll go inside and get my phone,' says Katie. She walks off, her glass of rosé in hand. She is back almost immediately. 'I just got Alex's phone, it was charging on the kitchen counter, cannot be bothered to walk all the way upstairs. Look, Willow, I got the wave forecast up inside.' The two of them lean over the phone, their heads almost touching, pointing and discussing numbers I do not understand the significance of. My attention drifts off again, I wonder how much longer I am going to have to stay here until I can meet up with Tala and Nora. I vaguely overheard Katie whispering, 'Right, let me put this back before he realises, he really hates it when I use his stuff… Let me just close this… Oh shit, that's not what I wanted to do… What the…'

My head snaps up as she lets out a loud, horrified scream, her hand clasped over her mouth with shock. Two seconds later, Alex is striding towards us, he looks alarmed and his fits are clenched in anger. From the corner of my eyes, I also notice Anne marching purposefully towards us.

CHAPTER 17
SUMMER 2022

Willow

'Sttttooppppp!' I half shout, half giggle as Katie chases me around the room with a makeup brush. The wine has made me slightly giddy and I throw myself on her bed before I lose balance. Katie jumps next to me and waves her makeup brush resolutely in front of my face, which I bury in a pillow to avoid all contact from.

'Trust mmeeee,' she wines, biting her bottom lip and fluttering her eyelids at me. 'This colour would look great with your eyes.' I shake my head vehemently.

'No way, Mum would never let me wear something so dark,' I reply. Katie pouts, unconvinced. 'Believe me,' I continue, 'if I turned up like that, she would make me go back upstairs to wash it off my face. Not happening, that would be so embarrassing!'

'Fine...' Katie sighs in defeat. She jumps off the bed and grabs her empty glass and the almost empty wine bottle. She looks at me interrogatively and rolls her eyes as I shake my head.

She pours the rest of the wine into her glass and hides the empty bottle back into her blue shoulder bag. 'Suit yourself,' she says. 'More for me!'

I cannot help but wonder if Katie finds me a bit boring. She certainly likes to break the rules more than I do. I feel self-conscious. Maybe I should loosen up and have another glass of rosé. But I already feel quite light-headed from my first glass and I know I am probably going to be drinking more later. I do not want to get too drunk, I do not like that feeling of losing control that usually comes with drinking. I only had too much to drink once in my life and it was during Mum's 43rd birthday party a few months ago. I felt so disgusting and embarrassed the next day, I promised myself this would never happen again. I hope that does not make me too boring for Katie.

'How do I look?' she asks, twirling in front of the mirror. Her figure snatches me out of my reverie. She looks gorgeous in her tight black dress and open-toed sandals. I wish I could look as effortlessly glamorous as she does.

'You look fabulous,' I reply shyly. Katie stares at me and I blush. I wonder if she realises how much I like her. Some days, I am worried I like her more than she likes me. I try not to be too obvious about the way I feel, I know people can get put off if they think you are too keen.

'So do you,' she replies, 'that top looks amazing on you.' She says this very seriously, no longer exuberant nor intoxicated. I think she really means it, and her sincerity surprises me. Snippets of conversation filter through the open window and I recognise Victor, Louise and Diana's voices.

'We should probably go downstairs,' I say to Katie. 'I think the Munroes have arrived.'

Katie pauses and tilts her head towards the window. Suddenly, her dad's voice bellows across the room as if he were standing right next to us: 'HONEY, CAN YOU GET VICTOR A BEER FROM THE FRIDGE?' We both jump up in surprise and burst out laughing.

'Yep,' Katie replies, 'I think the Munroes are definitely there. Let's go!'

I slide off the bed and slip on my Birkenstocks. Katie and I leave the room hand in hand, but we let go of each other as soon as we reach the bottom of the stairs. Our relationship is a secret and we do not want anybody to find out. Katie and I have briefly discussed coming out to our parents and she is less nervous about the prospect than I am. I do not know why I am so scared to tell my parents I like girls, they are very open-minded people and I know that their perception of me would not change because of that. It is more about me. I do not think I am ready to admit and accept that I am different. The only thing you want to do when you are seventeen years old is blend in. What scares me the most is people at school finding out. My friends and classmates are generally pretty inclusive, but teenagers gossip and as a shy person, the last thing I want is to do is become a topic of conversation.

We step into the garden and we are instantly greeted by a whirlwind of faces and loud voices. I diligently make my way around the whole group, hugging and smiling at everyone. The buzz of the rosé I had earlier is slowly wearing off so I feel safe having another small glass. I grab one of the many bottles stashed into the wine cooler and start pouring glasses for Katie, Diana and myself. I quickly realise that I did not check with the adults if they were OK with us drinking. I scan the crowd for Mum, but she is engrossed in conversation and I only manage to catch Louise and Anne's eye. I look at them questionably and they give me a nod. Relieved, I pour two more glasses and hand them over to Katie and Diana. The three of us move away from the group of adults so we can talk more privately. I have not seen Diana in a while and I am looking forward to catching up with her. I look at Katie to check how she is doing. I know she feels a little bit uncomfortable around Diana since they lost touch. I think Katie is a little bit resentful about the fact that Diana dropped her for 'cooler' and 'better' friends when we got to secondary school. Katie looks fine, if not a little bit glassy-eyed. Maybe I should not have poured her that last glass of wine.

We engage in small talk for a while and talk about everything and anything, avoiding serious topics of conversation. We get briefly interrupted by Leo and Alex's arrival and Katie tries to pour us another glass of rosé, but Victor catches us red-handed and tells us to slow down. I jump when he calls us out, slightly embarrassed at being told off but secretly relieved. I am feeling the buzz and I have only had two glasses, so I am slightly worried about how much Katie has had to drink. I tell Diana about my new job as a waitress at my local café, but I get the impression she does not care about what I have to say. She is constantly checking her phone and her answers are short and distracted. There is another lull in conversation and Katie jumps in to fill the silence.

'So, when are we going to take the boards out?' she asks.

'I don't know,' I answer with enthusiasm. 'First of all, we need to check with your dad when he wants to go surfing. We need him to drive us to the Coast.' I love surfing, it is one of my favourite activities to do in Royan.

'True, might be worth checking the tides,' she replies.

We try to get the tide times up on my phone, then on Diana's, but both of us are struggling to get any reception out in the garden. Katie runs off to get her phone and for a moment I stand awkwardly next to Diana, wondering what to say to her. Thankfully, Katie is back within seconds, holding a phone which is Alex's, she informs us. We both look at the screen, trying to figure out the best time to catch some good waves in the upcoming days. Diana does not get involved in the conversation, but then again, I remember she does not enjoy surfing any more.

'Look,' I say to Katie, pointing at the screen. 'Tuesday morning looks good, tidal coefficient of 90. That should give us some decent waves without them getting too big.'

'Agreed,' she says. 'I'll ask Dad tomorrow morning if he can take us to the Wild Coast. Shouldn't be a problem, I reckon. Right,' she continues, pointing at Alex's phone, 'let me put this back before he realises, he really hates it when I use his stuff…' She moves away from me and as she closes the Safari browser, her thumb accidentally brushes again the text message icon. I know she did not mean to do that because she immediately says, 'Oh shit, that's not what I wanted to do…' Then, her scream pierces through the air so loudly, I jump back in surprise.

immediately, their moves ripple on the surrounding crowd, and suddenly, the restaurant has transformed into a dance floor. Liliane rolls her eyes.

'That's it, I'm going downstairs. I need a cigarette and some silence.'

'How very French of you,' mocks Louise.

'I thought you had given up smoking,' accuses Anne.

'Oh goodness, what is this, the health police? I'm on blimming holiday in a country where it's literally more unusual not to smoke than to smoke. Too much temptation. I'll be good once we are back in London. Come on, girls, come with me; hopefully, we'll find someone to pour us a glass of water on the way.'

'You guys go,' replies Louise. 'I'll meet you down there, I need to go to the loo first.'

'Should we let the husbands know?' wonders Anne.

'*Pfff*, I don't think they will even notice if we leave,' huffs Liliane, amused. 'Look at them, entranced in conversation, I wonder what they are taking about.'

The three women stand up and divide into two groups at the top of the staircase. Louise finds an empty restroom and locks the door behind her. Immediately, the thick wooden frame muffles the noise of the nascent party outside. Louise looks at herself in the mirror and smiles. Miraculously, the alcohol has dissipated the guilt and fear she has been battling against all night. For the first time that evening, with no remorse, she lets her thoughts trail towards him. He looks so handsome tonight in his light blue shirt and white trousers. The light colour of his clothes accentuates his tan. Her heart skipped a few beats when she saw him come out of the Villa Grand Large earlier. They locked eyes for a second, a fleeting second, forever tiptoeing around each other to make sure nobody suspects a thing, constantly worried about seeming too fond or too indifferent towards each other.

Louise closes her eyes and wills herself to picture every single one of his features in detail. She sees his face with all its laughing lines and sharp edges. His face is what she finds most attractive about him, how it naturally sets into a serious frown, his jaw squared as if he were forever ruminating about an important issue or debating an intellectual topic. She pictures him running his hand through his hair in slow motion. Her body tingles when he does that, she loves how his biceps flex as he raises his arms up in the air. Louise closes her eyes and visualises his thumb running along his lower jawline, a habit of his when he is laughing. Her cheeks flush, she finds it so attractive when he uses his hands, when she can see the tendons of his fingers tense under his skin. His powerful hands make her think of how easily he can lift her off the floor and prop her onto the kitchen counter, of the way her back arches when they slowly trail their way underneath her skirt...

Louise snaps her eyes open and shakes her head to dissipate her thoughts. She really should not be thinking about him like that. Part of her still does not understand how she can possibly see him in that way. Never in her wildest dreams would she have thought that she would one day fancy him. She has known him for so long, she has seen him go through so many awkward and uncomfortable phases in life, surely all these old memories should have made him impossible to fancy? Louise sighs. She is tired. Every day for the past three weeks, she has been battling two conflicting urges. The urge to be with him and the urge to end this madness now before it is too late. She almost managed to break it off that one time. She was on a solitary, post-dinner digestive walk along the *Sentier des Douaniers*, the coastguard path, when she ran into him along the *Plage*, the beach, *de Nauzan*. He was running shirtless, beads of sweat trickling down his skinny yet muscly body. They did not get many opportunities to meet alone, especially by coincidence, so they walked across the beach onto the rocks that surround the cove and found a quiet space secluded from eyesight. His tongue was warm in her mouth, his hands cupping her breasts, when they heard the voices of people approaching. They broke apart in fright, but it was only a group of teenagers looking for a private spot to drink some beers. They quickly moved on. Louise, however, was struggling to shake off the momentary panic that had caused her stomach to drop.

'All this heavy petting outside... Having to find somewhere quiet to mess around... I feel like I am a teenager again,' she whispered.

'Welcome to the dark side.' He laughed, trying to pull her back towards him. Angrily, she pushed him away.

'No, you don't understand, I don't like this... This feeling. This feeling that I have to constantly be on high alert, that I need to worry if someone is going to catch us. I don't want to have to feel this way anymore. It's embarrassing. I'm a grown woman acting like an absolute idiot.'

He leaned away from her, annoyed. 'I mean, what did you expect really? What we are doing is kind of sick in a way... Of course, you are going to worry about people finding out. It's too late now, anyway. It's done. There is always going to be something to find out now. I'm not sure stopping is necessarily going to make it less likely for Victor, Anne and everyone else to find out the truth.'

'If you think it's sick, then why not just stop?' she wanted to shove him off the rocks into the ocean. She resented him for forcing her to face the music.

'Because I don't want to. Because it's hard. Resisting lust is very, very difficult. This is why this started in the first place, isn't it?'

Louise was not happy about this conversation. She left their hiding place alone, almost breaking into a jog, hoping the exertion would dissipate the outrage that was bubbling inside her. She realised she was projecting her self-loathing onto him because she was not ready to accept the type of person she had become. A liar. A sick, twisted liar.

That day, after this argument, Louise had truly believed that whatever had been going on between them was over. There were no complicated, intricate feelings to pull her back into the relationship; as he had said, it was just lust. But that was precisely the root of the problem. Lust. It tugged at her senses when their three families met up on the promenade a few days after the events on the Plage de Nauzan. Everyone was excited about the 14th of July firework display, but all Louise could think about was how the fabric of his t-shirt stretched over his shoulders and upper arms. She tried her best to look anywhere but in his general direction, but eventually, in the middle of the show, unable to help herself any longer, she stared long and hard at his profile. He must have felt the intensity of her gaze upon him because he turned his head halfway towards her and they locked eyes. The explosion of the final firework bouquet jolted both of them out of their trance. They turned away from each other, resuming the role of family friends. But exactly as he had described to her on the beach, the temptation had once more become too powerful to resist. They met up the night of the fireworks and they have been stealing as many moments together as possible ever since.

Tonight again, in the small restroom of Cédric's restaurant, Louise feels her desire for him obliterating her morals. She hopes they will be able to catch a few moments together later. Maybe the Villa Grand Large might be empty, or they could go to hers. After all, Marco and Diana are out with friends. Louise suddenly realises she has been standing in front of the mirror for much longer than reasonable, she wonders if she has not just heard a female voice on the other side of the door complaining about needing to use the loo. Alcohol and deep introspection must have skewed her appreciation of time. She rearranges her hair swiftly in front of the mirror and steps out of the restroom. She was right, two girls are waiting outside the door, an impatient look on their faces. They look about twenty, Louise wonders if they are part of the group Alex greeted when they first arrived. She makes her way across the lower floor of the restaurant and spots Liliane and Anne on the promenade.

'*Ah*, there you are!' exclaims Liliane, a cigarette in hand. 'We were wondering if you had gone back upstairs.'

'You've missed quite a bit of a *remu-ménage*,' adds Anne.

'*Pardon*? A what?' inquires Liliane. 'A threesome? What are you talking about?'

'Oh, my goodness, no!' Anne explodes in laughter. 'Not a *ménage à trois* ! *Un remu-ménage*! Drama,' explains Anne.

'Ohhhhh...' realises Liliane. 'Easy mistake to make.'

'Oh gosh, what happened?' Louise's curiosity is tickled.

'Cédric,' declares Anne. 'Cédric happened.'

'Oh dear, did he start screaming at some poor waitress again?' inquires Louise.

'What else?' answers Liliane.

Louise shakes her head. 'He really needs to learn how to control himself, especially if he wants his establishment to become the "classy" place to be of Royan.'

'Definitely not "classy" to cause a scene in front of clients. It's so uncomfortable. It can definitely put a damper on your evening,' adds Louise.

'To be fair, some people seemed to really enjoy the drama,' says Anne.

'What happened exactly?' Louise wants to know.

'So,' starts Liliane, 'we were about to step onto the terrace when we heard raised voices. They seemed to be coming from the back of the restaurant, that's where the kitchens are.'

'Cédric's completely redone them too. It's one of these open kitchens where you can basically hear and see everything that's going on inside,' explains Anne.

'Exactly, so not the best place to be having an argument,' adds Liliane. 'Surely Cédric realises everyone must have heard him screaming at that poor girl.'

'I don't think he would really care, to be honest,' says Anne. 'I mean how often have we witnessed something like that over the years? At least this time he didn't do it in the middle of the actual restaurant surrounded by tables of customers having dinner.'

'Gosh, that was awkward,' says Louise, remembering the incident Anne is referring to. 'He's a bit fake, isn't he? Such an entertainer and charmer with us but a dick with his staff.'

'I think it speaks volume about someone's personality,' adds Anne, 'when you are unkind to the people who work for you and only nice to those you work for…'

'I see what you mean. So, what was he screaming at that girl about?' inquires Louise.

'Well, from what we understood,' explains Liliane, 'the waitress completely messed up a huge order for a table of 10 customers. Got the most of the dishes wrong. And it sounded like the customers had been waiting for their food for a while so they were not happy when it came out wrong. They complained to Cédric about it.'

'Oh, the poor girl. Was Cédric absolutely furious?' Louise wants to know.

'It sounded like it,' replies Anne. 'He was also pretty angry about the amount of food wasted on that first, incorrect order. And the money that represents.'

'Poor girl, honestly, she was in tears. I mean, as a customer, can you imagine being served by a waitress who is basically weeping in your food?' asks Liliane.

'If I were a first-time client and witnessed the restaurant owner yelling at his staff during service, I don't think I would want to come back,' concludes Louise.

'I agree with you,' mutters Liliane, a new cigarette pinched between her lips. She leans forward to shelter the flame of her lighter from the light breeze, inhales deeply and exhales away from Anne and Louise. The three women stare into the darkness ahead of them, a darkness where the evening sky and the still ocean meet on the horizon and blend into one dark shade of black. If they strain their ears, they can just about make out, over the animated conversations around them, the faint sound of waves crashing on the sand. Louise notices that her thoughts are starting to lose their previously fogy quality, the noises around her are becoming sharper and she feels more in tune and responsive to her surroundings. She has not had a drink in the past forty-five minutes and she is happily sobering up.

'I wonder what time it is,' she says, fumbling into her clutch for her phone.

Before she has the chance to locate it, Liliane answers, 'Nearly midnight.'

'Gosh, already?' exclaims Anne. 'I wonder what the men are up to. I'm going to go upstairs and check on Thomas... Might be time to call it a night soon.'

'You guys go ahead,' says Liliane, 'I'll finish my cigarette and come find you.'

Anne and Louise make their way back into the restaurant and up the stairs leading to the second-level terrace. Anne is craning her neck left and right, clearly looking for something.

'Have you seen Alex?' she asks Louise.

'No, I haven't seen him since we got here and he left us to hang out with his friends.'

'*Umm*, I wonder where he has gone.'

'He's probably still around here somewhere, I doubt he would have gone home before us.'

'Maybe his friends and him are off to the Bodega?'

'It's a bit early for that, don't you think? Remember when we used to go? Clubs in France, they usually don't fill up before two a.m.'

'You know what I used to love the most about our nights out?' reminisces Anne. 'Grabbing a fresh *croissant* or *pain au chocolat* from the *boulangerie* on the way home.'

'Best hangover cure!' approves Louise. 'I still cannot believe we used to stay out until seven a.m. in the morning.'

The two women reach the landing of the second floor and walk towards their table.

'Where have they gone?' exclaims Anne. The table is empty, the only trace of their earlier presence being empty plates, bottles flipped upside down in wine coolers, jumbled up cutlery and creased napkins. Louise scans the room, looking for their husbands.

'Oh, there they are!' she exclaims, pointing at the bar on the outdoor terrace. 'I think they have made some friends.'

Anne and Louise walk in their direction.

'We've been looking for you,' smiles Anne, slipping her arm around Thomas's waist.

'Thought we'd mingle with the younger crowd,' laughs Sasha, nodding at Alex and three of his friends next to them. 'Where is Liliane, by the way?'

'Downstairs still, she's finishing her cigarette.'

'We were starting to feel old, just the three of us sat in a dark room at the back of the restaurant while everyone else was outside having fun and dancing,' adds Victor.

'Louise, can I get you anything?' asks Thomas. 'And you, Anne?'

'A margarita would be nice, thank you,' replies Louise with an appreciative smile.

'I think I'll stick to rosé,' answers Anne. 'Mixing alcohols is not a good idea for me anymore.'

Thomas busies himself trying to grab the attention of the bartender, a difficult task given the number of people standing around the bar. Next to his father, Alex, slightly glassy-eyed, is chatting animatedly to his friends, two girls and another boy. Sasha and Victor seem to be dipping in and out of the young group's conversation, their interventions always accompanied by the loud laughter of their impressionable crowd.

'Darling,' intervenes Anne, edging closer to her son and leaving her husband behind to fight for her drink, 'introduce us to your friends, maybe?'

Alex smiles indulgently. 'Of course. Elsa, Jade, Eddy, this is my mum Anne, and her old friend Louise. They have known each other since university.'

'Oh my goodness!' exclaims the blonde girl named Elsa. 'You are Alex's mum? You look so young to have a twenty-something-year-old son!'

'Elsa!' cries out Jade, the petit brunette.

Elsa clasps her hands over her mouth and laughs nervously. 'Gosh, sorry, that was a bit rude of me, I didn't mean it in that way!'

Anne throws her head back and laughs, waving her hand dismissively. 'Don't worry, sweety. I'll take that as a compliment! Thomas and I did have him when we were still quite young. I was actually pregnant with him on graduation day. Unplanned but the best surprise we could have possibly wished for.'

'*Aw*, how adorable,' chirps Elsa.

'Very cute,' comments Jade. 'You and Thomas are like uni sweethearts in a way.'

'I guess we are,' confirms Anne before swiftly moving the topic of conversation along. She is used to such comments about her age when people realise Alex is her son. Therefore, over the years, she has perfected the narrative around his conception, bending the truth and keeping the tone light-hearted to make people feel endeared by her story instead of sorry for her. Jade and Elsa would definitely not think of her and Thomas as 'adorable' if they knew what really happened.

'There you go, ladies!' Thomas appears, a drink in both hands. 'Rosé for you and a margarita *pour vous*,' he says, handing Anne and Louise their respective drinks.

'Thank you, Thomas,' smiles Louise.

'*Merci, mon chéri*,' flirts Anne. She spots Alex rolling his eyes.

'So what were you all talking about?' inquires Thomas.

'Oh,' Elsa jumps in, 'your wife was telling us about when you had Alex and how you have been together since uni. Very sweet.'

'Yes, very sweet indeed,' laughs Thomas, putting a hand around his wife's waist and pulling her close. He knows how to act in order to live up to the image of a happily married couple. *If only you knew,* he thinks to himself.

Thomas

Post-break-up, Thomas was a wreck for days. The first morning he woke up alone in his bed, he felt so depressed he took his duvet and pillow and set camp in the living room. He had grown used to waking up next to Anne and rolling over to spoon her in the morning and he was not ready to face his new reality. He curled up in a foetal position on the couch and spent three, whole, consecutive days mindlessly watching TV. He switched between channels, fruitlessly attempting to keep his mind off his ex-girlfriend. He only got up to make himself some toast when he was hungry or to go to the bathroom. He refused to go back to his room and fell asleep, late at night and sometimes in the middle of the day, in front of the TV. After day one, Thomas came to the conclusion that daytime television did not have many interesting programmes to offer. He was heartbroken and bored. After day two, he started feeling gross about himself. He was, he thought, a slobbish, unclean, lazy, television-hooked zombie. Not only was he heartbroken and bored, he was also pitiful. Thomas knew he would feel better if he got up, had a shower and saw some friends. But he did not have the willpower nor the energy to do any of these things. So, he curled up tighter around himself and let another day go by.

Victor, who was usually always over at Louise and Anne's house, got so worried about Thomas's behaviour that he started coming back to their flat more often to check up on him. Whenever Victor was keeping him company, Thomas would ask him how Anne was doing, hoping he would feel better about himself if he knew she was taking the breakup just as bad as he was. Victor would always give him half-hearted answers; he did not think keeping tabs on Anne was going to help him move on. To Thomas, even though Victor would never outright say so, it sounded like Louise and him were spending a lot of time with Anne to keep her distracted. Thomas was jealous of Victor being around Anne so much. He was also resentful towards Anne for developing such a strong relationship with his friend. He feared he and Victor might grow apart as a result. After all, Victor was caught up in a very uncomfortable position; his girlfriend's best friend on one side, his flatmate on the other. Thomas was not sure how much longer Victor would be able to stay friendly with both parties. Eventually, midway through another, television-filled day, Thomas snapped himself out of his misery. He had wallowed long enough, he said to himself, and he was too proud to let Anne 'win' the breakup. He finally got up from the couch.

The next stage of his grief was not much healthier. He started going out a lot, drinking in bars and clubs until closing time. Most nights, he was not ready to go home when he left the club, so he would seek out friends or loose acquaintances until he found a place for afters. He was committed to drowning his sadness in alcohol and superficial fun and often stayed up until sunrise, trying to convince himself he was living his best single life. Deep down, he was aware he was deceiving himself, but he tried to keep that feeling buried at the very bottom of his sub-conscience for as long as possible thanks to a steady supply of alcohol. As long as he kept going, he could suppress the hurt, anger and incomprehension Anne was causing him. Eventually, there would be no one left to party with and Thomas would go home alone and dejected, the feelings he was struggling with assailing him from all directions, magnified by all the alcohol he had consumed that night.

At first, Victor would always go out with him for moral support. But after a week, he told Thomas he did not think the constant partying was the best way to deal with the breakup.

'Maybe you should tone it down a little, you know. Do something a bit healthier, start cycling again, look for jobs. You haven't filled in a job application in weeks.'

Thomas was not ready to hear all of this. Therefore, when Victor could not, or would not, go out with him, Thomas started rallying some boys from the netball or hockey teams. These lads were always keen for a bender and for a while, he preferred their company to that of his best friend. They enabled his drinking and most of them were single like him; it was nice to spend time with people who were not a walking reminder of what he had lost. They convinced him the best way to get over Anne was to 'get under someone else' and Thomas fell down the rabbit hole of one-night stands. This self-destructive cycle carried on for a few weeks until the day Thomas got a text from Anne. It was the first time they had spoken to each other since the breakup.

Anne: *Hi, Thomas, I hope you are doing well. I have some of your stuff. I was thinking you might want it back? Just let me know when you have time to pick everything up, and maybe you could bring those speakers I left at yours? I think I also left some clothes, that red top I wear all the time and my favourite grey jumper x*

His heart skipped at beat when he first saw Anne's name pop up on his phone screen. Quickly, however, as his eyes darted from one line to the next, his initial excitement was replaced by bitter disappointment. She wanted her stuff back. She wanted to get rid of any memories of him. All of a sudden, this breakup felt very final, the small chance of getting back together he had been secretly nursing for weeks obliterated by a single text message. He stared at his phone for a long time. He wondered if the kiss at the end of her message had not been added out of pity. He could picture Anne carefully composing this message, deliberating how to sound friendly and considerate while signalling she was ready to move on. He did not have the strength to pretend he was on the same page as her. His reply was curt, hopefully the less he said, the less apparent his pain would be.

Thomas: *No problem. I can come by tonight, around six p.m.?*
Anne: *Perfect, I'll see you then.*

No more x, pondered Thomas. Did she feel self-conscious about putting one in her first message and then not getting one in return? Or did she think that if he was not going to put any effort into pretending they were friendly, then she would not bother either? He spent a long time attempting to decipher the potential hidden meanings of their short conversation. Eventually, he gave up, frustrated at himself for reading so much into an insignificant conversation and overthinking every single word he had read or typed.

If the messages had caused Thomas some degree of stress, it was nothing compared to how he felt when the time finally came to meet Anne. He wanted to look his best, handsome, upbeat and happy. Hopefully, she would realise she had made a massive mistake breaking up with him. He showered and spent too much time putting gel through his hair. He considered wearing some after shave but decided against it. After all, he did not want to look like he was trying too hard. He shoved Anne's speakers into a shopping bag but had absolutely no idea where her clothes had gone. His room was a tip, he had not done any laundry in a while and he was rapidly running out of fresh socks and underwear. Finally, he found the red top she had mentioned on his desk chair, under an unsteady tower of clothes that had been thrown on top of each other over the past week. However, he could not find her jumper anywhere in his room. He turned the living room and kitchen upside down but no luck there either. Eventually, he realised it was in his laundry basket, he had checked it multiple times already but clearly, he was distracted and not paying close attention to anything around him. After this strange game of hide and seek, Thomas realised he was running late. *Good*, he thought to himself. *That will make her think I'm busy, maybe she'll wonder who I am with and get jealous.*

Their first interaction in two weeks was an awkward affair. Thomas was surprised when he saw her; she looked fragile, tired and somewhat vulnerable.

'Hi, Thomas, how are you?' she asked as she opened the front door.

'I'm OK. And you?'

'Fine, just trying to keep myself busy, you know, nothing too exciting. And you? What have you been up to?'

'Oh, not much. Same, just trying to fill in all this free time now that dissertations have been handed in.'

Their conversation felt unnatural and forced. They had become two strangers who had nothing to say to each other beyond mundane small talk.

Thomas looked up at the digital clock on Anne's bedside table. 'Ten a.m. Are you hungry? We could get breakfast at the Riverside Roasts? Or do you have some toast and eggs? I could make us something to eat?'

Anne looked uncomfortable. '*Umm*, I'm not really hungry.'

'Oh… OK… Do you want a coffee?'

'No, thank you, coffee usually makes my hangovers worse…'

'Oh right…'

'I think I might just get up and shower. Go to the library.'

'On a Saturday? What for? Exams and dissertation are over.'

'I have to sort out some admin stuff, …Figure out what I want to do after uni… You know…'

'If you want me to leave, you can just tell me!' Thomas was starting to get worked up.

'No, of course not, you can stay.'

'Well, that sounds very unconvincing. So, what was last night about? Just a one-night stand?'

'No, I wasn't thinking about the consequences of sleeping together last night. I just missed you and wanted you there.'

'But you don't want to get back together?' Thomas was fighting hard to keep his voice under control.

'I don't know, Thomas, I'm so confused!' Anne sounded close to tears. 'I miss you so much and I never wanted us to break up in the first place. But we don't want the same things right now and I don't want you to give up on your London dream. But at the same time, I am not ready to compromise my plans and future for you. It's just all so confusing.'

Thomas did not know what to say. Only a few moments ago, he had been happy and content waking up next to Anne. Now, he felt completely deflated. Clearly, Anne was not ready to be single again but at the same time, she did not want to be in this relationship any more. She was torn between two opposite feelings and she was using him to try to come to terms with her emotions. This was not healthy, and she would keep using him if he let her. One of them needed to bring this relationship to a clear cut end and Thomas doubted she would be able to. He had to be the one to do it.

'I'm going to go, Anne,' declared Thomas firmly. 'I don't think we should have slept together last night. I thought it meant you wanted us to get back together, but clearly that is not what you had in mind. We need to move on and the only way we are going to be able to do that is if we stop texting and seeing each other.'

Thomas got out of bed and put his clothes on as quickly as possible. He had just said his piece, and he did not want to spend any second longer than necessary in Anne's room in case she would try and change his mind. However, Anne seemed to accept his decision. She sat up in bed, duvet wrapped around her shoulders and looked at him blankly as he laced up his trainers. She smiled at him apologetically and their eyes met fleetingly as he walked out the bedroom door.

Thomas did not hear from Anne for a while. It felt like they had broken up all over again, but to his own surprise, he did not take it as hard this time around. He was upset and mourned the life he used to share with Anne, Victor and Louise, but he did not descend into a pit of self-destruction and self-loathing like he did last time. On the contrary, he spent his last month at university keeping himself as busy as possible to distract himself. He spent most days in the library submitting job applications and got two interviews. He commuted to London for both and he was ecstatic when he found out he had gone through the second round of interviews. Thomas was determined to move on and after rearranging another meeting with Anne to get the belongings he had left at hers back, he asked Victor to handle the transaction for him. He knew he needed some distance from Anne in order to get over her.

As the days went by, Thomas began to get used to the idea that he might never see Anne again. He still thought about her constantly, but he was growing to accept the fact that maybe, their relationship was not meant to be. Consequently, it came as a shock when she slowly started creeping her way back into his life. It all happened very gradually, they ran into each other on campus a few times, she started messaging him again and because they had a lot of friends in common, they eventually started bumping into each other on nights out. They slept together once, twice, three times, which led to breakfast in the morning, which led to dinner, which led to suddenly spending most of their time together again. All of this happened without them realising and without them ever discussing the state of their relationship. They were just going with the flow and not thinking about the future and Thomas had to admit it was nice for things to be back to normal. Louise, Victor, Anne and him were inseparable again and they spent their last week of university going out constantly. Thomas had a blast, but everything took a turn for the worst again the night of the graduation formal.

Standing on the terrace of Cédric's surrounded by his wife and his son's friends, Thomas shakes the unpleasant thoughts out of his mind. To this day, he refuses to think about that night. He wants to pretend it never happened. He fast forwards his memories to a few weeks later, when he found out Anne was pregnant. It all started with a text message she had sent him one afternoon.

Anne: *Hi, Thomas, I really need to speak to you. Could I come over to yours sometime tomorrow? It's important.*

Thomas was intrigued by Anne's cryptic message. He had no idea what Anne might want to talk about and his curiosity had been piqued.

Thomas: *Hey, what's going on?*
Anne: *I think it's best if I tell you in person. Do you have any free time today?*
Thomas: *Are you all right? You can come over whenever, I'm not doing much today and mostly staying at home.*
Anne: *Ok perfect, I'll be over within an hour or so.*

Thomas was taken aback by the urgency of her last message. Both of them had left Durham by that point and they were both living at home before he moved to London and she figured out what she wanted to do next. They had not seen each other for a while, much to Thomas's relief. He had been avoiding her ever since the night of the ball. Therefore, he was surprised she was suddenly willing to make the journey from Surrey to Teddington. What could she possibly have to say to him that could not wait, he worried. In his head, he started going through every possible scenario, each one more dramatic and improbable than the previous. Ultimately, he gave up trying to guess what Anne needed to talk to him about. Whatever it was, and surely it could not be good news, he would soon find out. He was biting his thumb nail when the doorbell rang.

'Hi, Anne, come in,' he greeted her.

'Thank you, Thomas.'

'Should we sit down in the living room?'

'Good idea.'

'Tea, coffee?'

'No, I'm OK, thank you.' Anne sat down on the sofa and looked around the room restlessly.

She was fidgeting with her hands.

'So, what did you want to tell me about?' asked Thomas. He did not have the patience to beat around the bush.

Anne paused, words struggling to come out of her mouth. The pause stretched into an ominous silence. Finally, before she could change her mind, she blurted out, 'I'm pregnant.'

There are no words strong enough to express the shock and horror he felt at that moment. Twenty-four years later, standing on the rooftop terrace of a French restaurant with his old friends and two complete strangers, Thomas can almost taste the deep, paralysing panic that had threatened to drown him all that time ago. As people say, life is full of surprises, but out of all the unexpected events that Thomas could have envisioned befalling upon him, an unplanned pregnancy with his ex-girlfriend, girlfriend, friend with benefits (he still did not know what they were to each other) at the age of twenty-one was the last thing he wanted. The irony was, he had always wanted children, and when they were together, Thomas thought he and Anne would eventually start a family someday. But not straight out of university. Not whilst separated.

Thankfully, Anne dealt with the news a lot better than he did. Thomas remembers her resolute acceptance of the unexpected turn of events, he recalls her stating convincingly that the situation was far from ideal but maybe, they should interpret the pregnancy as a sign meant to bring them back together. Thomas can still picture her admitting that she had been debating for weeks if she had made the right decision breaking up with him. She told him she missed him horribly and that she was relieved that to some degree, the decision of getting back together with him or not had been taken out of her hands. Thomas remembers her saying she was now ready to move down to London if that was still what he wanted. She would get a job, they would have the baby (she already had a name in mind, Alex) and maybe, some at point down the line, they might have the big family they had always talked about.

Looking back on those times, Thomas recognises he handed the reins of his life over to Anne for a short while. He had been torn between two conflicting emotions. On the one hand, everything he wanted – Anne moving to London, them getting back together – was finally happening. On the other hand, he could not forget the grief Anne had put him through for the past few months, his trust in their relationship was broken and consequently, he found it very hard to make any decisions involving the pair of them. In a way, it was a relief that Anne was ready to do most of the decision making for him.

Ultimately, the shaky foundations of their unexpected reunion strengthened over the years. Events had initially taken control over Thomas's life but a year after Alex was born, he genuinely believed things could not have turned out any better. Thomas proposed shortly before they had Katie and both bride and groom were radiant with happiness on their wedding day. Their love story did not have a fairy tale beginning, but as the years went by, Thomas believed they were gradually living up to the image of the picture-perfect couple they liked to project around them. If only appearances could be true.

CHAPTER 20
LAST SUMMER, 2021

Louise

'Ah, there you are!' exclaims Liliane, who has just rejoined their group from her cigarette break. She turns to Louise. 'By the way, I have just spotted Diana and some of her friends walking back from the Bistro de Cordouan along the promenade. She looked kind of upset.'

'Really?' replies Louise. 'Did you see where she was heading?'

'I'm not sure, could have been home, but it's hard to say really.'

'I might shoot her a message. If she's back home, she'll have signal and should be able to reply.'

Louise steps away from her friends and finds a quiet space at the back of the restaurant. She relishes the sudden silence around her. Louise sits down on a velvet armchair, a piece of furniture she would have expected to find in a boudoir rather than in a restaurant, and gets her phone out. She fumbles with the lock button, worrying about her daughter. Hopefully, she has not had too much to drink. Hopefully, she is not upset because of some sleazy French boy who was bothering her. Or worse, a middle-aged man. Louise deplores the fact that her daughter lives in a world where sexual harassment is the first risk that jumps to mind when it comes to women on a night out. Slowly, she types on the tiny keyboard in front of her, her manicured nails tapping rhythmically against the glass screen.

Louise: *Hi honey, hope you are having a good night? Liliane said she saw you walking past Cédric's, are you home?*

Louise stares at her phone with satisfaction before pressing send. Diana often accuses her of worrying unnecessarily; therefore, Louise has chosen her words carefully to avoid coming across like the concerned and overbearing parent her daughter believes her to be. She drops her phone into her clutch and leans back against the velvety headrest. She closes her eyes and tilts her head up towards the ceiling. She needs a minute of calm before rejoining the party waiting for her outside. She needs to recharge her batteries before engaging in more small talk. Louise wonders, as she has many times before, if everyone finds socialising as hard work as she does. She does not consider herself a loner; on the contrary, she likes to be surrounded by people and seeks out company, but often, she feels most comfortable when she can be around others in silence. She has never been bothered by a lull in conversation and is always happy to keep the silence going if she has nothing interesting to add. However, Louise knows that most people find it uncomfortable to be around others without talking. That is why she always forces herself to keep the conversation going when she goes out. Nevertheless, however much she tries to convince herself that she enjoys socialising, she has to admit to herself that her favourite part of the night is always when she gets to finally leave the party and go home by herself. There is nothing better than the silence and calm of your own house after a whole evening eating and drinking with friends. Naturally, the exercise is a lot less painful with people she has known for a very long time rather than with loose acquaintances or even worse, work colleagues. But even now, surrounded by her closest of friends whom she has known for decades, she needs a short moment to herself and her thoughts. Which, incidentally, are trailing away into forbidden territory.

Louise opens her eyes and glances towards her husband, friends and the group of young people that has formed around them. For a split second, she gets Victor confused with Alex and she cannot work out which of Jade or Elsa is standing next to her husband. Everybody looks the same in the dim lighting and it is hard to see anything properly from where she is sitting.; She squints to work out who is laughing with one of Alex's blonde friends. Thomas. Actually, it looks like most of the men are enjoying the attention of Alex's female friends. A twinge of jealousy pinches at Louise's heart. She glares at her husband and 'lover' (she abhors that word, it highlights her deceitfulness) ruminating that all men are the same. Dangle a new and shiny toy in front of them and you have lost all of their attention. Talking of the devil, she notices that her 'lover' (she needs a new name for him, one that does not make her whole being swell with guilt every time she pronounces it. Partner in crime? No, that belittles her treachery towards Anne and Victor) is scanning the room around him, probably trying to spot her for a discreet, one to one chat. He has chosen a clever time; everyone else is occupied drinking and chatting near the bar. It even looks like Anne and Liliane are trying to lead the group onto the spontaneous dance floor that has started to form in the middle of the wooden-planked terrace. Finally, he spots her. Their eyes lock and he moves towards the staircase, as if he were making his way down to the promenade. She is surprised when he suddenly appears on her left. She did not see him coming.

'I've been hoping to speak to you all evening,' he asserts in a low voice. He stays standing on the left of her velvet chair, probably to avoid being seen from the terrace. After all, if he was able to spot her from there, there is a risk that one of their friends or family members might glance in their direction and see them together. They probably would not think anything of it, just that they are having a friendly conversation, as they always do, but cheating can make you paranoid.

Louise replies, staring resolutely ahead of her, resisting the temptation to look at his handsome features – she reflects that she must look like she is talking to herself – 'It's difficult to get a moment alone with so many people we know around us. I see you've made some friends though, kept yourself entertained.' Despite her best efforts, she cannot keep a note of cattiness out of her voice.

'Am I mistaken, or are you jealous?' He laughs. Louise is immediately annoyed at herself.

He must think she is very keen.

'No, just calling it as I see it. You like female attention.'

'Maybe that's because you don't give me enough,' he declares bluntly.

From the corner of her eyes, Louise notices that his smile has dropped and his jaw has squared in displeasure. She does not know what to say.

'I want to see you tonight. At the villa. Look at everyone, they are plastered, we could both make a discreet exit, no one would be any the wiser. You could pretend you want to check up on Diana and Marco, I could say I'm tired and going home. We could have a short hour to ourselves at the villa. No one would suspect anything.'

The temptation is hard to resist. He is right; it looks like everyone is having a really good time, she doubts anybody would be going home anytime soon. As if to help make up her mind, Cédric appears next to Anne and her friends and starts handing them some shots. She looks at her best friend and husband knocking back the small glasses of clear liquid and grimacing as the vodka makes its way down their throats.

'You are probably right. You should leave first and I'll wait fifteen minutes before I head out as well.'

His voice drops an octave lower as tension and lust sizzles through his body. 'I'll see you there. Come through the back door, I'll leave it open for you.'

They look at each other briefly before he disappears again. He crosses the room purposefully and walks down the staircase out of the restaurant. Clearly, he does not feel the need to justify his movements and sudden departure to anybody. It is this confidence, this independence, that attracted her to him in the first place. Not many other men in his situation would have had the courage to come on to her so determinately. The first time he looked at her inappropriately, the first time he stepped so close to her their bodies were practically touching, he ignited an impulse in her she did not know existed. Up until that moment, Louise had always considered herself a very measured and controlled person. She is the kind of woman who always thinks about the consequences of her actions before she acts upon them. She has always been like that, even at university. Anne was definitely the wild one out of the two of them. That is why she surprised herself when she gave into the temptation that had materialised in front of her. After a lifetime of repressing impulses, maybe it was not surprising that she gave into the biggest of them all.

Snapping out of her thoughts, Louise gets up. After all, she has fifteen minutes to kill, she might as well have another drink.

'Louise, did you know Royan's famous classical beach music concert is back this year?' Anne asks as she rejoins the group.

'Really? That is so exciting!' she replies enthusiastically. 'How did you find out?'

'Cédric just told us,' replies Liliane.

'That must mean the *mairie* has got some money again!' cries Louise.

'We should definitely go,' interjects Sasha who is swaying his hips lazily to the beat of the music. 'Buy some tickets.'

'We don't need tickets,' objects his wife, Liliane. 'The best way to listen to the concert is on a towel on the beach. With a picnic and an ice-cream from Mirabelle.'

'Is it being held at the *Plage de la Grande Conche* like it used to?' wonders Louise.

'I didn't ask Cédric,' answers Liliane. 'I would assume so. It's the biggest beach around and you need quite a lot of space to build that stage.'

Every summer, a classical music concert used to be held on Royan's main beach, *la Plage de la Grande Conche*, until the *mairie*, the *local council*, ran out of money two years ago. The cost of building a huge stage and bleachers on the beach for a few weeks over the summer holidays massively outstripped any money the city of Royan made from selling tickets, so the concert, very popular amongst the Royannese population and regular tourists, was discontinued, to the general discontent. Louise was particularly heartbroken when she found out about it. The classical concert reminded her of the summers she used to spend with her parents as a child. Every year, they would get their picnic towels and arrive at the beach hours before the concert was meant to start to find a prime spot with view of the stage. The three of them would set up camp for the evening, adding extra layers of clothing as the hours ticked by, the sky growing darker and the temperatures colder. Finally, it was a family tradition to get a *glace* or a *gauffre* from Mirabelle, the famous local beach front confectionary that already existed when her mother was a small girl, before the concert started. Louise loved to lie back on her beach towel and feel the cold sand between her toes whilst listening to the soft melody of the orchestra and watching the stars in the sky. In her opinion, this feeling of communion with music and nature was the epitome of being on holiday. Consequently, Louise is over the moon at the news that the concert is coming back this summer.

'This is the best news ever!' she cries in excitement. 'I need to find Cédric and find out about dates.'

'He's over there,' says her husband helpfully, pointing at the restaurant owner who is standing near the music booth and shouting something in the DJ's ear. He is too far away for Louise to overhear what he is saying, but his facial expression indicates that he is not happy.

'*Umm...* I'll probably wait until later,' decides Louise.

'Good call,' approves Sasha. 'This doesn't look like the best time.'

'That man needs to learn to keep his temper in check,' says Liliane, 'especially when there are customers around. It's uncomfortable to witness him abusing his staff all the time. Brings the whole cachet of the restaurant down.'

'There's this stereotypes that people in the hospitality industry can be ruthless. Cédric lives up to that stereotype,' says Anne. 'It's sad. I feel sorry for his staff.'

'I reckon he must get a fair amount of grief from his customers... And because he can't say anything, he lets out his frustration on his staff instead,' suggests Victor.

'You are probably right, but still, it's a job like any other. There are rules about what you can and cannot say in an office. Why should it be any different in a restaurant?' argues Louise.

'I completely agree with what you are saying,' replies Anne. 'It's just not acceptable and they shouldn't get away with it just because there's some sort of weird, unspoken understanding that this is how things work in the hospitality industry and no one is going to change it. Goodness, I remember what it was like working as a waitress at the Blue Boat during our second year at Durham. Really put me off, the chefs especially were some of the rudest people I have ever met in my life. And misogynistic as well. They used to make me feel so uncomfortable every time I walked in and out of the kitchens. I could hear them exchanging lascivious comments about my figure, they didn't even try and be discreet about it. So inappropriate. Honestly, I would rather Katie do any other job than waitressing. Work in a clothes shop, babysit, supermarket, I don't care, just hopefully not in a restaurant.'

'*Um*, I agree with you there,' says Liliane supportively. 'Unfortunately, you can only get tips in the service industry. And that's what young people want. As much money in as little time as possible. That's why Willow sometimes likes to help me out during events. So far, she's not complained about anybody being inappropriate with her; hopefully, that stays that way.'

'I mean, we can't protect them from their own femininity forever, can we?' interjects Louise. 'That's the sad truth of the world we live in, isn't it?' Her statement is met with a resigned silence from Anne and Liliane. Sasha and Victor have the common sense not to say anything. It is not their place.

'Where has Thomas gone, by the way?' wonders Anne.

'I think I saw him walk downstairs a few minutes ago,' replies Victor.

'I wonder what he is doing,' says Anne.

'Probably just needs the toilet,' replies Sasha. 'Or a breath of fresh air.'

'Alex and his young group of friends have also disappeared,' realised Sasha.

'They probably had enough talking to old farts like use,' jokes Liliane.

'*Hem, excusez-moi*,' objects her husband vehemently, a twinkle of laughter in his eyes. 'Call yourself an old fart maybe, but I still feel like I'm 20.'

'Oh, honey, unfortunately, you don't look it,' teases Anne.

Sasha rolls his eyes and clenches his hands over his chest, pretending he has just been stabbed in the heart. 'How can you say that?' he cries out in false indignation.

Alex's name to come up.

'OK, and what happened?' Louise encourages her on.

'He wouldn't look at me, barely met my eye... Just made me feel so pathetic.'

Incomprehension floods Louise's mind. *Where is this going?*

'Why would you feel pathetic about that?' she asks her daughter.

'Because of what happened a few years ago...' sobs Diana.

'What happened, honey?' Louise urges her on. 'What does that have to do with Alex?'

Bravely, Diana attempts to collect herself. She believes it might be easier to tell the truth in one go rather than constantly stopping and starting between sentences. So far, every pause has challenged her resolution to come clean. Finally, Diana stops crying and she feels ready to tell her mum everything.

'It was few years ago, when I was in Year 9. That was also Alex's last year at Chelsea's School for Boys. You know, Lady Cecilia, we are kind of like their sister school, we are the all-girls version and they are the all-boys version. Anyways, most days after lessons are over, the two schools mix on the green. Obviously, I recognised Alex, but we never really talked that much because he was so much older. We'd say hello to each other, that's about it. Anyways, you know Nathalia, well, she kind of had this crush on one of Alex's friends—'

'Which one?' inquires Louise.

'What?' asks Diana, not expecting the interruption. 'Oh, *uh*, Bill. Why? Do you know who that is?'

'I'm not sure, was he at Alex's 18th?'

'I dunno, I wasn't there, was I?' Diana looks at her mum with incredulous eyes.

'Oh right, you weren't, that's right.'

'Anyways,' continues Diana, slightly resentful about the interruption, 'it doesn't matter, Bill is not important.'

'Sorry, honey,' apologises Louise, 'carry on.'

'So, Nathalia had a crush on Bill. Anyways, they kind of started messaging on social media—'

'What do you mean he was messaging her?' exclaims Louise in outrage. 'Wasn't he about four or five years older than her?'

'Please, Mum, let me finish. If you are going to be that judgemental, maybe I shouldn't tell you anything,' snaps Diana.

Louise bits her tongue. She should not have said anything, but the words escaped her before she could stop them. 'Sorry, honey, please carry on.' Diana glares at her in silence. 'I won't interrupt you again,' promises Louise.

'OK... Thank you. So, Nathalia and Bill were messaging for a bit. Eventually, he told her about this Year thirteen party that was being held on the weekend in Chelsea. He said she should come and bring a friend or two if she wanted. So, Nathalia asked me to go with her. I wasn't sure at the start, I thought it would be bit daunting to turn up as two year nine to a year thirteen party. Like people would definitely wonder why we were there, maybe make fun of us. But Nathalia was super keen. She wanted to see Bill, but I think she was also excited at the idea of going to like an "actual grown-up party", as she called it. You know with alcohol and stuff...'

Diana had drawn air quotes with her fingers when she said 'actual grown up party', but as she mentioned alcohol, she looked away from her mother bashfully. Her mum might be fine with her having a casual drink when on holiday now, but she doubts she would have let her touch alcohol at the age of fourteen. Diana pauses for a second to catch her breath and soldiers on.

'I dunno, I guess ultimately I caved to the peer-pressure. Nathalia kept saying that no one our age ever got invited to a six-form party, and the fact that we did meant that some of them must think we were cool... But they might change their minds if we didn't come, and never bother inviting us ever again. She said I would be a lousy friend if I couldn't do that for her, and that really she wasn't asking for much, just for me to go out and have some fun. So, I went with her that night.' Diana looks up at her mother and pre-emptively answers the question she knows must be burning on the tip of her tongue.

'I just told you I was having a sleep over at Nathalia's. You and Dad didn't question it. And Nathalia parents were away for the weekend so she told them she was staying with us while they were gone... Anyways,' Diana moves on quickly, 'so we got there and it was super awkward. Like I could feel everyone staring at us and wondering what on earth we were doing there. Nathalia basically ditched me straightaway as well. She hung out with Bill most of night. I felt a bit sorry for her, I could hear people whispering about her and Bill, how he was playing her, how young she looked… That someone should tell her she should be careful. That he would try something on her. But, yeah, I was by myself for a while until I saw Alex.

'He was super kind to me, got me a drink, introduced me to a bunch of his friends. It was a laugh to start with, we played beer pong and they were all very nice to me, saying that I was very mature for a Year eleven. That's when I realised Nathalia had lied about her age to Bill. He had no idea just how young she really was. I thought Alex would realise that his friends had gotten my age wrong, but I guess he didn't know exactly how old I was either, just that I was a few years below him. Anyways, the thing is, I quite enjoyed the way they perceived me. I liked being this mature Year eleven. So, I kind of went along with it. One of Alex's friends started flirting with me after a bit and gave me a bunch of drinks. That's when I got quite drunk. I think the guy tried to kiss me, but Alex stepped in. Said I had a bit too much to drink and that he should leave me alone. I thought that was really sweet of him. He could tell I didn't feel great so he took me outside for some fresh air. We went for a little walk around Chelsea.'

'So, yeah, we just walked for a bit. I was definitely quite drunk, I was very giddy and silly and just making a little bit of a fool of myself, I suppose. But I think Alex thought I was quite funny. He said it had been a while since he had seen anyone get drunk so quickly and be such a happy drunk. He said that there was usually a lot of drama at these parties because people didn't know how to hold their liquor and got angry or sad. I enjoyed feeling like he would rather hang out with me than his Year thirteen friends. And then I'm not too sure how it happened – I was quite drunk, after all – if I'm the one who instigated it or if he is the one that leaned into me, but as some point we started kissing. In the middle of the King's Road. It got quite intense pretty quickly. He suggested we go back to the flat and find a quiet place to have some alone time. Mum, I just didn't really think it through, I wasn't thinking at all actually, I was out of it.' Diana sounds almost pleading now.

'But I think he didn't realise just how out of it I was. Because I wasn't throwing up or anything and I was quite coherent. So, we snuck back in, I don't think anyone noticed us, they were all pretty gone at that point. We went into the parents' room and for a while it was fine, we were just making out. Then it started to be a bit more. Alex stopped and asked me if I had done this before, he said he assumed I had, because I was sixteen and very pretty, surely lots of boys were interested in me. And I just lied to him. I was really drunk and I thought this was a good idea. I thought I was ready to… To…' Diana chokes on her words. She is scared of saying it out loud. Once she has said it, there is no taking it back. Once she has said it, it will make what happened that night so much more real.

'…To have sex.'

Louise does not know what to say. How to react. What to do. She just sits there and looks at her daughter with incomprehension. The enormity of what she has just learned, her little daughter being intimate with a boy at the age of fourteen, with Alex of all people, is too much for her to take in. She does not want to hear it. She does not want to believe it. She fells slightly nauseous just thinking about it. However, now that she has started, Diana is desperate to get to the end of her story. She wants to share the weight she has been carrying around on her own for the past three years with someone else. With a trusted adult. With someone who is better equipped to make sense of and deal with the events that fell upon her.

'He was nice about it. Like very sweet, offered to walk me home after. But after it happened… it's like it sobered me up. I felt awful. I didn't feel right in my own skin. I just wanted to get as far away from him as possible. But I had to act normal; after all, I had told him I had experience. I had told him I was someone else. So, I tried to act cool, I said I was just going to get Nathalia and leave with her. It took me a while to find her, but eventually I located her in a dark corner, making out with Bill. His hands were all over her. To be honest, I think she was relieved about the interruption. I wish I had a friend who had interrupted Alex and I. I told her I wanted to go home. She was super giddy on the way back to hers, super excited about her evening with Bill and that they had kissed. I think she was already picturing them as boyfriend and girlfriend. Clearly, she didn't think lying about her age might be a problem at some point. I don't think she noticed I wasn't being myself.' Diana pauses. She has reached a turning point in her story.

'Obviously, Bill eventually found out about Nathalia's real age. I don't know what she was thinking, lying to him about that in the first place. In small schools like Lady Cecilia and Chelsea's School for Boys, someone is bound to know someone who actually knows which year you are in. Of course, the moment he found out Nathalia was fourteen, he called it off. Her must have told Alex about it and Alex must have worked out that I wasn't sixteen either. He used to like, say hi or something when we ran into each other on the green or when we were hanging out together with Bill and

Nathalia, but when the truth came out, he wouldn't even look at me. Or speak to me. Well, apart from that one time he cornered me at the end of the school day. That must have been the day he had just found out. He was livid, I remember him grabbing my arm really tightly and whispering angrily in my ear. He asked me if I had told anybody about what happened and I said no. He said I better keep it that way. He made me promise not to tell a soul. Which I haven't. You are the first one to know about this, Mum. Marco thinks I have a crush on Alex because ever since that night, whenever we meet up with the Daltons and he speaks to me, my cheeks go bright red and I get very embarrassed. That's why he is always teasing me about Alex. Because he thinks I like him, when really, it's because I am super ashamed of the things he said to me that day after school. Alex said it was disgusting, it was basically like he had slept with a child. That I was actually just a small, immature little girl and a liar. He said that if he had known how old I really was, he would have never touched me, not even with a ten-foot pole. He said that if I ever tried to start a rumour about sleeping together, he would deny everything and find a way to turn it against me. That I should be smart about it all and just keep my mouth shut if I wanted to avoid ruining my life… He made me feel so ashamed of myself. Or at least, even more ashamed of myself than I already was. I still am ashamed. Since that night, I feel like my own body doesn't really belong to me anymore. I don't think I'll ever be able to like… Do it again…' Finally, Diana has gotten to the end of her story. She sits still and waits for her mother's reaction, which worries her.

Louise remains motionless for a few seconds. She is shell-shocked and trying to process her emotions. She is mainly disgusted at Alex. How could he have slept with Diana? Her own daughter out of any girl? Her sense of betrayal is immense. Slowly, that disgust transforms into anger. How dare he disrespect them both so deeply? Diana, a powerless, shy, vulnerable fourteen-year-old girl? Her, his mother's best friend, who has known and trusted him for decades. Who has always believed, up until now, that he was a decent and honest man. Louise glances up at her daughter and suddenly, she snaps out of the whirlwind of emotions that are raging in her head. Diana has confided in her for a reason. She needs to be reassured. This is about Diana's feelings, not her own.

'Oh honey!' cries Louise. 'You have no reason to feel ashamed. You were drunk, yes, but you were also a vulnerable, young child. Alex was the adult in this situation. He should have known better. He should never have propositioned you in the first place.' Louise reaches over to her daughter and wraps her in a motherly and protective embrace. She can feel Diana's body relax into her arms. Diana buries her head in the crux of her neck and starts sobbing tears of relief. Louise can feel the salty water running down her skin. She strokes her daughter's long, shiny dark hair until it is flat and smooth.

'I want you to know,' she continues, 'that nothing you have said changes anything about the way I think about you. I still think you are a smart, strong-willed, fierce little person. You can't let that night define your sense of self-worth.'

In between two hiccupy sobs, Diana's muffled voice replies, 'Thank you, Mum… I love you so much.'

'I love you too, honey,' says Louise, her voice heavy with emotion.

In her head, she is already planning the heated argument she is determined to have with Alex the next time they cross paths.

CHAPTER 21
SUMMER 2022

Anne

I am standing in my garden, a rosé in hand, surveying my guests. Everyone looks content. Victor has got his beer; the children are hanging out and everyone seems to be having a good time. Recently, longer periods of time than usual have gone by without seeing each other and I am proud I managed to get all of us back together this evening. Royan has always been a special place for us, it is where we all first went on holiday together as a group of friends, and it is great we are now able to bring our children here. Hopefully, when they are older and have kids of their own, they will be close friends as well and pass down the tradition. I know that is an idealistic wish, but sometimes it is nice to romanticise the future. My husband, Thomas, snaps me out of my careful survey of our reunion. I want to make sure everybody is having a good time.

'Do we have any plans for dinner, honey?' he enquires. 'At some point, we are going to have to get food into everybody's bellies or people are going to get absolutely trolleeeyyed.' He says trolleyed with his silly voice, clearly pleased to have found an occasion to use this new piece of vocabulary.

'Well,' I reply, 'we could always go to Cédric's. We haven't booked a table though, and it's high season. I'm worried there won't be any space for us this late notice. Especially for such a large group of us.'

'I agree. Do we have food in the house?' wonders Thomas.

'I mean, we do,' I reply, 'but cooking for twelve with nothing prepped is a bit of a feat. Worse comes to worse,' I add decisively, forever the problem solver, 'we'll just get some of the kids to go pick up some pizzas from Mario's in the centre of town.'

'Oh yes, very good idea. You always have everything under control, don't you?' giggles Thomas before planting a playful kiss on my cheek.

I guess I do. I like being that person. At the start of my twenties, I was overly organised and put together to compensate for my wild first year at university. I wanted people to change their opinion of me. But now, it has become a central part of my personality. A character trait that calms and centres me.

Thomas and I both rejoin the conversation around us. It feels good to be reunited with close friends. Apart from my husband Thomas, Victor, Louise, Liliane and Sasha are the people I feel more relaxed and comfortable around. That is because we are life-long friends, and there is nobody else I can have such easy-going conversations with, not even my colleagues in London whom I have known for years now. I get on with my co-workers very well, we occasionally go for a drink on a Friday evening or plan a dinner over the weekend to celebrate a birthday, but my relationship with them is not as relaxed as with those four. I catch a snippet of conversation, Liliane is quizzing Louise about her sudden move to Berlin. I tune in, I would like to know more about the reasons behind that decision as well. It has never made any sense to me, Louise deciding to move to Berlin. It was a rash decision, almost as if she were trying to run away from something. Every time Louise came back to visit during her sabbatical year, she tried her best to sound excited about living in Germany, but her smile never reached her eyes and her praises of the German culture never sounded one hundred per cent genuine.

However, I never get to ask the questions that are burning on the tip of my tongue. A sudden shriek completely distracts me from Louise and Liliane's conversation. My head snaps around in alert, trying to identify where the sound came from. It sounded a lot like Katie's voice. Sure enough, a curious spectacle unfolds in front of my eyes. My daughter's gaze is glued to the phone she is holding in her hands, she will not look up. Whatever she has seen or read must have shocked her because she is holding her free hand in front of her month as if to stifle another scream. Her eyes are wide with confusion. I can see them darting frantically from one side of the screen to the other. I put my glass of rosé down on the garden table and quickly walk towards Katie to find out what is causing such a commotion. Probably just some silly teenage drama. I will calm Katie down, move our little gathering along, and in a few hours and rosés' time, we will all be laughing about my daughter's dramatic tendencies. It is only when I am almost in front of Katie that I notice Alex is walking in her direction as well. But his walk is almost a sprint and the look on his face takes me by surprise. He looks angry. No, furious. But curiously, also terrified. Now I am starting to get a little bit confused. Katie and Alex do not spend much time together, so why would Katie's distress be in any way, shape or form related to Alex? This does not make sense. Curiosity piqued, I close the last few meters separating me from my daughter with a decisive stride and hold my hand out.

Firmly, I say, 'Now, Katie, what's all his drama about? Show me your phone.'

To my surprise, Katie doesn't argue with me and hands the device over. That's odd. Katie is usually very private about her phone. It's her private space and she never wants me snooping in. That's when I realise I am not holding Katie's phone. The blue protective phone case, that's Alex's. I look up at my son, who has frozen in his steps.

'Why do you have Alex's phone?' I ask my daughter.

'It was on the kitchen counter, I just borrowed it to check the tides to see if we could go surfing tomorrow. I didn't mean to open his messages...' she whispers.

His messages? For the first time, I look down at the rectangular screen. I can see message after message, of what seems like a heated discussion.

'Mum,' whispers Katie in a fearful voice. 'Mum. You should probably read these messages. Look who they are from...'

At this point, Alex tries to intervene. He almost lunges towards me, trying to snatch his phone out of my hands. I evade him in the nick of time. I can tell he is trying to avoid a scene and that is the only reason he does not attempt to wrestle his phone out of my grip.

He looks me straight in the eyes and snarls through his teeth, 'Mum, give me my phone. You have no right to read any of my messages. Neither do you, Katie. What were you thinking borrowing my phone without asking me for permission? You would absolutely flip out if I did anything like that to you.'

I do not move. Alex insists, 'Mum, give me the phone now. I am not your child anymore and you should respect my privacy. If you start snooping around my business as if I were a teenager, there will be no trust between us anymore.'

I hesitate. On the one hand, I know it is inappropriate for me to be reading my grown son's messages. I am going to look like an overbearing and controlling mother if I do. But on the other hand, Katie's reaction worries me. I feel like there is something sinister going on here. I am worried Alex is in trouble, and it is still my duty as his mum to make sure he is safe. Even if he does not want me to get involved. I look down at the screen, determined to read the messages I caught a glance of previously. I can hear Katie breathing in sharply, probably waiting for my reaction.

Alex's face twists in fury, or maybe fear, and I truly believe that if I were not his mother and if we were not standing in front of all our friends, he would not hesitate to wrestle his phone out of my hands. I read the first message, sent this afternoon at five thirty p.m. It's from Alex and, to my surprise, rather lengthy.

Alex: *Hi, how are you? I know you told me not to get in touch with you again, but I thought it would be a good idea to clear the air. After all, we are going to be spending the next few weeks together, so it would be good if we were on speaking terms. We wouldn't want anybody to start suspecting anything because we are being awkward around each other. I just wanted to tell you one more time that I am truly sorry about last summer. And I am sorry about what happened with Diana. I know it's not an excuse, but I've tried so hard not to think about that evening that in a way, I managed to convince myself that it never happened in the first place. I know we'll never get back to how we were, but it would be nice if we could be friendly at least? I'll see you this evening.*

My eyes dart to the top of the screen and my heart skips a beat. Alex sent this cryptic message to Louise. I stare at the screen, completely confused. Why would Alex message Louise? I am surprised they even have each other's numbers. It does seem a bit odd. Almost inappropriate. Furthermore, none of this message makes sense. For some reason, Diana seems to be involved in this conversation, but I do not understand how. 'Get back to how we were?' What does that mean? Eyebrows frowned, I search for Louise amongst the crowd of silent guests around me. She looks as white as a sheet. I keep on reading. It looks like Louise replied about half an hour later.

Louise: *Listen Alex, don't worry about it. I'll be friendly and normal around you; after all, that's what we did all summer long last year and no one ever suspected a thing. But I want to make one thing perfectly clear. What you did was repulsive.*

My mind is positively racing at this point. What did Alex do? I thought I was stepping in to help Alex out of a tricky situation, but now it sounds like he might be the source of the wrongdoing. My hands are clammy, my mouth is dry. Part of me wants to hand Alex his phone back and never find out what Louise wrote next. I want to continue living in ignorance. Unfortunately, ignorance is not an option for me right now. I carry on reading. Bile rises in my throat with every passing word. I am worried I might throw up.

Louise: *You slept with my fourteen-year-old daughter, treated her like a piece of garbage and then you seduced me?* I would have never *slept with you if I had known about Diana. This is so disgusting. It's twisted, almost psychotic. I have felt dirty in my own skin ever since Diana told me the truth. Honestly, if it wouldn't destroy my family and your poor mother, I would have told everyone the truth about you. You're not the perfect golden boy you pretend to be. You are a sociopath. So yes, rest assured, I'll be friendly and act like everything is OK. But you better stay away from Diana. And be around me as little as possible.*

events. But there is no reasonable way for me to justify her absence. Therefore, on a regular basis, my small, fragile daughter, needs to stand in the same room as the man who defiled her. Who robbed her of her innocence. Over my dead body will I ever let that same man also be the reason why her parents are not together any more. He will not cause her any more harm and pain than he already has. Because of Diana, and my motherly impulses to protect my baby daughter from all the harms I possibly can, I am fiercely determined that no one will ever find out about this twisted, almost incestuous love triangle.

The four of us walk through the large garden that surrounds Anne and Thomas's imposing mansion. The grass is orange and patchy, burnt from the strong and unforgiving sun that is currently making its way down across the horizon. It has been a hotter summer than usual, the French department of Charente-Maritime issued a drought warning early June and as a result, restrictions have been put in place surrounding domestic water consumption. Inhabitants of Royan have not been allowed to water their gardens for weeks and the neighbourhood's lawns are looking rather sad.

I am snatched away from my thoughts by an enthusiastic greeting. Thomas and Sasha are standing next to the garden table and look thrilled to see us. They are both holding a drink, which might contribute to their upbeat spirits. Victor smiles. He has been looking forward to our annual group reunion in Royan a lot more than I have. I suspect it is because for a few weeks, this holiday gives him the opportunity to revert back to how things used to be. I wish I could also forget about the tension that has grown between us in the past years. But I cannot. Unlike Victor, who is unknowingly blessed with the gift of ignorance, I know too much.

My husband waves and shouts, '*Bonjours les amis! Comment ça va?*'

I smile. It is a relief to realise that I still find it endearing when Victor attempts to speak French. I wish my friends had learned to speak better French by now. After all, we have been coming to Royan for over two decades. But to be fair to them, apart from when we go out for dinner or to the market in the morning to buy local products, we do not mix with French people that much. We have the six of us, twelve with the children, and we tend to stay amongst ourselves. Consequently, they have never had many opportunities to practice. In the past, waiters and shop owners did not speak any English, so once in a while, when they were hungry mostly, my friends had to at least try and speak French. If they really struggled to communicate with the waiters, I would step in and order for the group. I did not mind. I enjoyed it actually, it was one of the rare occasions I got to speak French in France. Nowadays, however, everybody seems to speak English, and most French people speak English better than any of my friends speak French. In restaurants, waiters overhear us and automatically switch to English. They usually love it, they say they do not get to practice it that often. Although I am sure that is slowly changing as well. Royan is attracting an increasingly international crowd, it is no longer the French tourist destination it used to be. Soon, people in the service industry will also be speaking more English than French. If teaching French was not my job, I would be worried about forgetting how to speak it due to lack of practice. I used to speak French with my family all the time, but that is not possible any more either. I miss my parents. It feels strange being in their house without them. I always knew the beach house would be mine one day, I just did not expect it to be this early.

Thomas and Sasha walk towards us and we embrace in the middle of the garden. Immediately, Thomas is in host mode.

'Let's get you something to drink,' he says. 'Victor, beer?'

'That would be amazing, thank you.'

Whilst Victor and Thomas yell across the garden for Anne to get some beers out the fridge, I walk towards the garden table and pour myself a glass of rosé. I turn to my two children, 'You know the rules, just the one drink.'

'Yes, Mum, you know you can trust us. We are very sensible teenagers,' smiles Marco playfully.

I always wonder if Victor and I are too relaxed about Marco and Diana drinking alcohol in front of us. Some parents would definitely criticise our decision and argue we are enabling our children. I believe that teenagers are going to drink no matter what, so I would rather it be in an environment that is controlled and safe. Furthermore, I am hoping that the more casual we are about alcohol, the less likely they are going to turn to it to rebel.

I look up. Anne and Liliane are walking down the garden steps, a six pack of beer in hand. Victor is stereotypically British in his drink choices. I suppose I am stereotypically French, the only alcohol I like apart from wine is cognac. Anne greets us with effusion. She fusses about how tanned we all look and how fast Marco and Diana are growing. My two children smile benevolently, they must get tired of adults constantly reminding them about the changes their bodies are going through. A few minutes later, we are joined by Katie and Willow. The children gravitate towards each other and away from the parents. As if by obligation, we cheers to being back together in Royan. Alex is nowhere to be seen so far. I relax ever so slightly, then quickly pull myself back together. If he is not here yet, that means he is bound to appear at any moment. I need to keep my poker face on.

Eventually, Leo steps out the kitchen and slaloms down the winding garden path. He is followed closely by Alex. My heart twists. It feels like a hand of steel has reached through my chest and is squeezing it as hard as possible. He looks much more mature than he did last summer. He has cut his hair short and he holds himself with confidence. His jaw is set and his lips meet in a thin line. He seems so sure of himself. I wonder if his new job in London and the responsibilities that come with being a young adult are the reasons behind his new-found assurance. Alex has always been confident, but in a more noisy, obvious fashion. He would dominate conversations and express his opinions unapologetically. Now, his confidence is silent, it oozes from the way he walks and his body posture. It feels more authentic. Abruptly, I jump off this train of thought. I am angry at myself; if I could, I would give myself a hard slap across the face. I should not feel attracted to him anymore. I cannot believe I am still able to voice sexual thoughts about Alex. That is unacceptable. I do not like that man. No, that is not strong enough. I despise that man. Not a man, a child. A man would never do what he did. A man would be able to control himself. A man would know right from wrong. I not only despise Alex, I think he is vile. He disgusts me. It is interesting how one person can be the source of such extreme, polar opposite feelings. Alex is making his way around the group, saying hello to all of us. I brace myself for impact. Before I know it, he is standing right in front of me and we quickly hug. I try my best to keep my facial expression neutral, to not let my revulsion show. My skin crawls where we touch. We exchange some platitudes, I try and smile. As he walks away, I sneak a quick glance around me, nobody suspects anything. Just when I start to think I can relax, Liliane corners me and ropes me into conversation about Berlin. I cannot face any more lies today, but I do not have a choice. I put on a smiley mask.

'Did you enjoy Berlin?' she enquires. I bet she has been dying to ask me that question for months. 'I mean, surely it must have been hard being separated from Victor, Diana and Marco for a year...'

I pause for a second. Thankfully, Victor steps in and replies on my behalf. We did find it tough living apart for so long, he says, and Liliane nods sympathetically. I take a sip of wine and I get ready to deliver the answer I have rehearsed so many times.

'It took some getting used to start with, of course, but we made it work,' I say breezily. I waffle some more about Berlin, about the fact that it was an amazing opportunity for my career and my hopes of being able to publish a linguistic paper, which would support my application for a professorship. I keep hoping that the more I say all of this, the more I will start to believe it. So far, that has yet to happen. I would never have accepted that sabbatical year if I had not found out that the man I was cheating on my husband with had also slept with my daughter. Teaching in Berlin has allowed me to gain some different teaching experience, but I had to give up the new postgrad class I was supposed to start lecturing in London. I am still bitter about this sacrifice. It was a self-inflicted punishment, as if it would redress the wrongs I had inflicted upon my daughter and husband. It was a pointless sacrifice in the end, it did not make me feel any better about myself and it is not as if Victor or Diana reaped any benefits from me moving away. On the contrary, I suspect Diana has interpreted my move as an abandonment. I am worried she thinks I decided to move to Berlin because I could not cope with what she revealed to me the night of Cédric's big party, when really, I moved away because I could not cope with the person that revelation had transformed me into. All in all, I took the coward's approach to my problems and ran away. I solved nothing and my self-esteem took another hit.

Liliane is still talking about Berlin. I will her to shut up. Surely, she must realise she is prying. I look at Victor, poor man, he has never been a good actor. He is trying so hard to sound brazen about the whole 'sabbatical year' situation, but he is doing a rubbish job at it. His smile is too forced, the corners of his mouth riding too far up his cheeks.

'Well, I'm sure the kids and Victor will be very happy when you are back in London for good.' Liliane smiles at me.

'So will I, can't wait,' I reply.

Victor says something else. I do not listen to him, I am consumed by my own thoughts. *Goodness*, I think, *that did not sound genuine.* Maybe I cannot lie very well either. What am I talking about? I have been deceiving everyone for the past year. Some days, I worry how easily lying came to me when I used to sneak off to meet up with Alex. Maybe I missed my calling as a spy. When I get stressed or when I feel guilty, I like to deflect my emotions with humour.

Liliane opens her mouth to say something else. *Please let it go,* I think. I prepare myself to deflect yet another question about Berlin and change the topic of conversation. Unfortunately, Victor and I never get to find out what she was about to say. In hindsight, any further prodding into our marital life would have been much better than dealing with what was about to happen.

Katie screams. A long, agonising screech. At first, I am confused. It seems the cause of Katie's distress is linked to something she has read or seen on her phone. Her hand is clasped dramatically over her mouth. I welcome the distraction at first, until I spot Alex. I was not searching for him, my gaze just happened to land where he is standing. He looks pale. He looks angry. He strides towards her, he almost breaks into a run. Next to me, Anne is walking in the same direction. For a second, I wonder who is going to get to Katie first. Ultimately, Anne has a few seconds head start. Katie is holding her phone close to her chest but Anne holds her hand out decisively and Katie does not hesitate twice. She hands over her phone to Anne. Anne is the kind of mother children do not argue with. Unlike me. Diana seems to think every instruction or rule we have at home is up for debate.

Alex lunges towards Anne then seems to think better of it. At this point, I would not be surprised if he attempted to wrestle Katie's phone out of his own mother's hands. *That is strange,* I think. *What does Alex want with his sister's phone?* The whole garden has gone silent, we are watching the scene that is unfolding in front of our eye with confusion. I hear Alex snarling, 'Mum, give me my phone. You have no right to read any of my messages.' He turns angrily towards his sister, eyes blazing. 'Neither do you, Katie.' His voice is thick with venom.

Suddenly, the pieces of the puzzle fall into place. This is not Katie's phone. This is Alex's phone. My stomach lurches and drops as fast as a heavy stone in water. I cast my mind back to the conversation between Alex and I earlier today. How explicit were those messages? How much of our relationship did I reveal? These text messages were out of character. I have always been careful not to leave a written trail between the two of us. We never communicated over phone last summer. We would agree on meetings discreetly, whenever we found an opportunity to talk outside of earshot. I remember how last year, whenever our big group came together, I would keep an eye out on Alex's movements, always trying to work out when an opportunity might arise for us to talk without anybody noticing. I made sure the two of us found a way to inconspicuously run into each other in a corner of the kitchen when clearing plates or topping up wine glasses. Or along a deserted corridor coming in and out of the bathroom.

I rack my brains, desperate to remember verbatim what I wrote only a few hours ago. Unfortunately, I was so worked up, I barely registered what my fingers were typing. I fear I was so angry with Alex, with myself, with the whole situation I created, that I threw all caution to the wind. These messages might be very incriminating. I try to reassure myself. Maybe Katie is upset about something else she has seen on Alex's phone. I know I am deceiving myself. I have got that sinking feeling in the pit of my stomach that indicates my worst nightmares are about to come true. I stand frozen, staring hard at Anne's face. I look as it slowly morphs with realisation. For a few excruciating seconds, nothing happens. I barely register Victor shaking my shoulder. He mutters a few indistinct words. Then all hell breaks loose.

Anne looks up from Alex's phone. She scans the garden until she spots me. I cannot read her expression. She looks almost ill. This time, I hear Victor asking me, 'Why is Anne staring at you?' I do not bother acknowledging his question. I do not know what to do. I want all the onlookers – Liliane, Sasha, all the people who have nothing to do with this and who are standing limply around the garden – to disappear. I am not ready to deal with their judgement.

I watch as Anne's eyes dart rapidly between Diana, Alex and I. And back. And forth. And back and forth. Anne is stuck in a loop. Shock has struck her dumb. Eventually, everyone else is also staring at one of the three of us. Nobody might know what is going on (yet), but they have certainly worked out who is involved in the drama that is slowly starting to unfold in front of their eyes.

All of a sudden, Anne darts across the garden and runs up to the house. She disappears through the sliding doors. She is still holding Alex's phone, but her other hand is clenched firmly over her mouth, as if she is about to be sick. For a moment, we all stand motionless and watch her disappear into the villa. Finally, I order the children to stay outside and run after her. I find her doubled down over the kitchen sink, breathing heavily, hands trembling. Her head snaps up as she hears me cross the landing.

'Louise,' she says with a trembling voice. 'What on earth?'

'Listen…' I start, but I do not know what to say. It would be distasteful to try and justify my actions. It would probably just make matters worse. I stand still, waiting for Anne to unleash her wrath on me.

'That's my son. You knew him as a child. Not just a child, a baby. What is wrong with you?' Slowly, anger creeps into her voice.

'I know. I don't know what came over me. I never should have done what I have done. It was wrong.'

'Wrong?' Anne is properly shouting now. 'Wrong?' she repeats, her cheeks flushed with outrage. 'Wrong doesn't cut it. Wrong is hardly strong enough of a word to describe what you have done. It's disgusting. You disgust me!'

'What is going on here?'

I spin around. Victor has just entered the room, followed closely by Thomas, Liliane and Sasha. Anne laughs. She sounds close to hysteria.

'Of course, Victor doesn't know. I wonder what he is going to think of you when he finds out.' Anne looks around the room theatrically. She holds her arms up, gesturing to the small crowd around us. 'What are any of them going to think of you when they find out about what you have done!'

'Alex is not exactly innocent in this. He was the only one who held all the pieces of the puzzle and he still went ahead with it.'

'Don't even try and deflect the blame onto Alex!' Anne shouts.

'He slept with Diana when she was only fourteen!' I bellow, enraged. I am ready to take the blame that is bound to come my way for cheating on my husband with my best friend's son, but I am not ready to belittle what he did to Diana when she was only a vulnerable child. All the pent-up anger I have been harbouring since Diana disclosed the truth bubbles up to the surface. I am almost relieved to finally be able to talk about it.

'Excuse me, what?' cries Victor.

'Maybe we should go,' suggests Liliane awkwardly. She is talking to Sasha. 'This clearly doesn't concern us.'

'Oh no, you are not going anywhere,' shrieks Anne. 'You are going to stay here and witness Louise's humiliation. You think that's bad? That this is shocking? Oh, you wait.' Once again, Anne laughs hysterically. 'Oh just wait until you find out what she did.'

Victor is not listening to Anne any more. Maybe if he were, her words would have stopped him dead in his tracks. He rams into Thomas, who unfortunately for him is standing next to the bay windows, shoves him out of the way and strides across the garden. He looks murderous. I hear him shout, 'You, you son of a bitch!' and there is a kerfuffle as the remaining five of us try to get out of the kitchen at the same time. Victor is heading straight for Alex, who is standing next to Marco and Leo near the garden table. Katie and Diana are facing each other, talking intensely. Willow is on her own, halfway between the group of boys and girls, unsure what to do with herself. Initially, Katie and Diana do not notice Victor sprinting and shouting his way across the garden, the five of us close on his tail. It is only as Thomas shouts, 'Victor, mate, where are you going?' that they turn around, alarmed. Before any of us can react, Victor is standing in front of Alex. Out of nowhere, his right arm swings out and with a muffled crack, his closed fist makes contact with Alex's jaw.

'What are you doing?' Anne screams. She and Thomas break into a run.

'Get your hands off my son!' yells Thomas in outrage. He shoves my husband away from Alex, who has stumbled a few paces back from the shock of the impact.

'How dare I? That boy took advantage of my daughter! I'm going to knock his teeth out!' shouts Victor.

'Back off or I'll be the one knocking teeth out,' Thomas spits. Thomas and Victor, who have been friends for over twenty years, are now squaring off at each other. In unison, Diana and I both step in between the two men, trying to push them away from each other before the situation escalates any further. Unfortunately, Victor does not seem interested in diffusing the situation.

'Diana, you stay out of this,' he shouts at our daughter.

'Victor, please, you need to calm down,' I plead. 'The children are here,' I try to reason with him.

Victor makes another lunge towards Alex, nearly knocking Diana and I over onto the grass. I have never seen him act this violently before. Thomas blocks his attack and suddenly, the two of them – grown, respectable men, both parents – are rolling on the ground, trying to land punches on each other. Everybody starts screaming and Sasha steps into the fight. Unsuccessfully, he tries to lift Thomas, who is lying on top of Victor, off the ground.

'Dad, get off him,' shouts Alex. He attempts to separate Victor and Thomas, but Anne steps in front of him to prevent him from getting involved. Diana starts crying and Katie is screaming at everybody to stop from the top of her voice. Finally, Sasha, who is by far the most muscular of the three men, breaks Thomas and Victor apart. They stand panting, facing each other murderously.

Anne steps in, intent to add fuel to the fire.

153

'Victor, you are so pathetic. You are taking your anger out on Alex when really it's your wife you should be mad at.'

Victor reels around to look at me. 'How long have you known about this?' he demands.

I don't know what to answer.

'This isn't even about Alex and Diana,' screams Anne. 'It's about her and Alex.'

'What are you talking about?' asks Diana, teary and confused.

'Mum, stop,' interjects Alex.

'Do not tell me what to do,' snaps Anne. She spins around and glares at her son. 'I'm so disappointed in you. I did not raise you to get yourself involved in such a messy situation.'

'What is going on?' demands Thomas.

'This doesn't concern you,' tries to stall Alex.

'This concerns all of us' screams Anne.

'Will someone just please explain what on earth you are talking about?' yells Victor, infuriated.

'Anne, please,' I moan. 'Don't do this here. Not like this.'

'Victor needs to know the truth about you and Alex,' barks Anne.

'What do you mean?' cries Diana. 'What about Mum and Alex?'

'And clearly so does your daughter!'

'Mum, why are you making such a scene? Stop it. It's pathetic,' says Alex.

'I will tell them, Anne, if that's what you really want,' I concede. 'Just not like this, not in front of everyone.'

'So now you are concerned about appearances? Well, you bloody should have thought about this before you decided to have an affair with my twenty-two-year-old son, shouldn't you? Who incidentally also happened to have slept with your own daughter. Isn't that twisted? Fancying the same boy your daughter has been with? '

All of sudden, the whole garden goes quiet. Adults and children stand frozen to the spot, shocked by this gruesome revelation. I feel everybody's gaze burning upon me, judgement and disgust painted all over my friends' faces. Victor looks like he might be physically ill. Diana's face is green, she is clawing at her t-shirt, disgusted by the fact that her skin and my skin have touched the same body in the same way. Alex buries his face into his hands.

I whisper meekly, as if it might absolve me from my sins, 'I didn't know Alex and Diana had ever been involved. I only found out... after Alex and I had already... I broke it off I soon as I found out.'

'You slept with my mum after you slept with my sister?' whispers Marco. He stares at Alex in disbelief. Marco has always looked up to Alex as a brother, a role model. I think that Marco has always wanted to be like Alex, almost a bit envious of his relationship with Victor and their shared interest for the F1. All of that adoration has disappeared from Marco's eyes. He looks at Alex like a fallen hero.

'You cheated on me... with Alex... with Anne's son?' Victor's voice is trembling. He looks up at Anne. 'With your son...'

Something strange passes over Anne's face. Like a second wave of realisation. I cannot explain it. The twelve of us do not move for a few seconds. It is so quiet, I can hear strings of indistinct conversation coming from people strolling past the Villa Grand Large along the promenade. None of us know how to break the silence. Where to go from here? How to process this bombshell which has just destroyed our friendship group? Finally, someone moves. Victor jerks into life, and, very slowly at first, then faster and faster, desperate to escape, walks down the garden steps, flings the door open, and sprints off, away from the villa, away from his lifelong friends, away from his cheating wife and his messed-up family.

CHAPTER 24
SUMMER 2022

Diana

I do not understand what is happening around me. I barely have time to process Katie's shrill scream before Alex and Anne are suddenly standing right in front of us. Anne demands to see Alex's phone, which Katie hands over fearfully. She shoots me a concerned look before she does so, which I do not know how to interpret. Anne reads whatever Katie is showing her on Alex's phone and her face gradually loses all composure as the seconds tick by. She looks up from the screen and scans the garden. Her gaze pauses on Mum who looks frozen in fear. Once again, I do not know what to make of the strange look that passes between them. Suddenly, Anne rushes past me, hands clutched over her mouth as if she were about to throw up. Almost immediately, Mum runs after her.

'Children, stay outside,' she shouts in her wake before sprinting into the villa.

All the other adults follow her and Marco, Leo, Alex, Katie, Willow and I are left alone in the garden. Alex looks worried and Willow, Marco and I stare at each other in confusion. Before I have time to say anything, Katie grabs me by the arm and pulls me away from Willow. She whispers in my ear, 'Is it true?'

'Is what true?' I reply, confused.

Katie pauses, clearly unsure about what to do next. However, her question has piqued my curiosity.

'Tell me,' I urge, 'is what true?'

'I just saw a series of text messages between your mum and Alex.'

My heart skips a beat. I have a feeling I know where this is going. 'And?' I press her on.

Katie looks around her nervously and whispers so quietly I have to in lean closer to catch what she is saying, 'Is it true that you and Alex slept with each other when you were only fourteen?'

'I...' My first instinct is to deny everything, but based on the increasingly loud voices streaming from the kitchen, I have a feeling there

'I think it might be a good idea if I just go out for a bit. Give everybody some space. I'll get food.'

'Sure, sure, you do that,' he replies absentmindedly. I wonder if he has registered what I said.

After Victor, Louise, Diana, Marco, the Brandson family and Mum, it is my turn to head down the garden steps and make my way along the promenade. I look around me; as per usual, Cédric's is heaving with customers. There is not a single chair left empty and I can see a long line of customers waiting to be seated. No point trying my luck here, I will never get a table. All of a sudden, I realise I am craving a strong drink. No, more than just a strong drink. I am craving to get drunk. Maybe even blackout drunk. At this point in time, I want nothing more than to forget who I am, what I did and the inevitable repercussion of my actions. I want to be a normal twenty-two-year-old lad on holiday, out for a good time, flirting with girls his own age, girls who are way too young to be married and old enough to have sex with.

Decisively, I walk past Cédric's towards Royan's small city centre. I hope to find a table at the Bistro de Cordouan. I walk through the small square that marks the centre of Royan. The cafés and restaurants around it are just as packed as the promenade. Some terraces have spilled over in front of other shops and tables and chairs are scattered in front of the *boucherie* and the *boulangerie*, both closed at this late hour. Behind the square, I can see the roof of the covered market, designed to look like the shell of a giant oyster.

Royan's market is famous throughout the region, it is the only market of this size open outside the summer months for miles around. Nevertheless, like most businesses in Royan, it makes most of its profit during the months of July and August. That is because those are the only two months during which the local council transforms the parking surrounding the indoor market into an outdoor market and rents out spots to artisans and small-scale producers from all over Poitou-Charente, the region of France where Royan is located. During the summer, every day from seven a.m. to one p.m., Royan's market becomes the hub of an eclectic mix of products, produce and people from all other the country. As a result, Royan's market is a food lover's dream where you can find almost any French product there exists. Wine, seafood, oysters, *foie gras*, fresh fruits and vegetables, homemade *brioches,* jams, readymade *blanquette de veau, brandade...* The choices are endless and the smells seeping from the different food stalls very appetising. However, Royan's market is not just a food market. You can buy all sorts of random things there such as cheap dresses, watches and shoes for under 10€, and even, if your heart desires, some fluorescent underwear decorated with inspirational or just plain wacky quotes. More than once, I have been tempted to buy some as a joke for my friends back at uni, but there was no point, they would not understand the punch line. They do not speak French.

Finally, I arrive at the Bistro de Cordouan. I am scanning the terrace in search for an empty table when I hear my name. 'Alex! Alex!' I look left and right before I can identify where the voice is coming from. To my surprise, Eddy and Jade are waving at me from the far-right corner of the bar.

'I didn't realise you were in Royan,' says Jade as I pull out a chair and sit down.

'I literally just arrived earlier this afternoon,' I explain.

I met Eddy and Jade a few summers ago. I was out clubbing with some of my uni friends who I had invited out to France for the week. Eddy, Jade and their friend Elsa heard us speaking English in the queue for the Bodega and we have been hanging out every summer ever since. Eddy and Jade are twins and grew up in Paris before moving to the UK for university. Their dad is originally from Royan, they also have a holiday house along the promenade where they spend most of their summers. Last time I saw them, Jade was finishing her civil engineering degree in Bristol, and Eddy his math degree in Edinburgh. Elsa is their friend from primary school, she visits them very often but she is not from Royan, so I do not see her as regularly.

'Fair enough, we got here a few days ago. It's soooo busy, I swear every year this place gets more and more crowded,' says Jade. 'It took Mum thirty minutes to find a parking space at the *marché* this morning.'

'I thought she was going to throw her toys out the pram,' jokes Eddy. 'She kept complaining that 75 matriculation plates were taking over Royan.'

Cars matriculated 75 come from Paris. Locals do not like Parisians. Parisians are the scapegoats of Royan, they get blamed for every single problem, from the lack of parking spaces to the pollution on the beaches and the urbanisation of the littoral.

A waiter walks past out table. I order a beer and recline back in my seat. For the first time this evening, I feel normal, relaxed by Eddy and Jade's easy-going attitude and our mundane topics of conversation.

'So, what have you guys been up to?' I enquire. 'Last time I saw you, you were job hunting.'

My beer arrives. I pay and we cheers to our reunion.

'*Santé*,' we say in unison.

'I got a job in recruitment,' replies Jade. 'So yeah, putting my engineering degree to real good use,' she adds ironically.

'I mean, that's quite common, isn't it,' says Eddy. 'How many of us are actually in a job that is related to what we studied at university?'

'Are you still in Bristol?' I ask Jade.

'No, I've moved down to London. Thought now was the time or never to try it out.'

'Oh really? I live in London too. Brixton.' I reflect that the fact that we have both been living in the same city for a year without knowing about it says a lot about our friendship.

'I had no idea! I'm Clapham, near the Northcote Road.'

'Gosh, everybody moves to London, don't they?'

'Well, that's where most of the jobs are,' I answer. 'Clapham is nice, full of yopros.'

'Yopros?' asks Jade.

'Young professionals,' Eddy answers.

'Well, we'll definitely have to grab a drink when we are back in London!' exclaims Jade.

I nod out of politeness, but I know that it is unlikely to happen. Jade and Eddy are my holiday friends, we hang out because we do not know many other Brits in Royan. Realistically, if we had other options, neither of us would choose to spend our evenings together. I take a swig of my beer and I am surprised to find that I have already drunk it all.

'Another round?' I offer.

'Can't say no to that,' replies Eddy. We flag down the waiter again and place our order. I scan the terrace. True to British stereotypes, we are the one table that seems to be drinking the most, and the fastest.

'So, what about you, Eddy? Have you moved to London too?' I wonder.

'Me? Oh, no. I'm still in Edinburgh. I was working in real estate for a while, but I wasn't really enjoying it. I want to get into urban planning, but you need a master's to apply for those types of positions. So, I'm going back to uni in September to get the right qualifications.'

'Wow, really? Back at uni? Good for you!' I say. I could not imagine anything worse, having to sit through lectures again, attending seminars, being asked to write papers on abstract topics... But some people absolutely love uni. Think of it as the best years of their lives. I wonder if Eddy is one of these people. If he is secretly looking forward to jumping back into student life.

'Yeah, I mean, it's a master's degree, so I am going to be studying with mature students. You know people who have had a similar experience as me, worked for a few years and then worked out they need an extra qualification if they want to progress in their careers. Nothing like an undergrad, hopefully. Couldn't do that again.'

This surprises me. Eddy does not sound like the kind of guy who is craving to relive his wild student years. Maybe I got him wrong. The waiter arrives with our drinks. We split the bill and clink our drinks together. I take a large gulp, a second, a third. When I put my pint down, it is half empty. Jade whistles.

'Jeez, Alex, are you on a mission or something?' she says.

'Just on holiday,' I shrug. Slowly, the alcohol is starting to have its desired effect. I can feel the uncomfortable thoughts in my mind receding into the background of my consciousness. Once in a while, one of them will try and make its way to the forefront of my mind, but I am finding it easier and easier to dismiss these ideas, to push them to the back of my brain. The world takes on a woolly texture, my senses feel strangely numb at times, and then suddenly hyper sensitive at others. I start focusing on small details that would usually elude my attention such as the condensation beads forming around the rim of my glass and slowly snaking their way down onto the table. Paradoxically, it is getting harder and harder to keep up with what Jade and Eddy are saying and what is happening around me.

The rest of the night slowly fades into a blur. I remember buying a few more drinks and eventually, a packet of cigarettes from the waiter at the Bistro de Cordouan. I only smoke when I am really drunk. Every drag seems to amplify the effects of the alcohol. Eventually, the three of us make our way to the Bodega. It's a thirty-minute walk from The Bistro de Cordouan through the market and Royan's public park. A few groups are going in the same direction as us. It is an ordinary night out and the hours slip away from me. All of a sudden, it is two, three, four a.m. and a few seconds later, the club is closing. I am almost surprised I managed to stay out until seven a.m. For a few glorious hours, I completely forgot about the events that transpired at the villa last night. I only remember Mum and Louise shouting at me as I make my way back into Royan and stop at the *boulangerie* for its first batch of *pain au chocolat*. As per usual, there is a small queue of very drunk but also already slightly hungover people forming outside the shop. I grab a *croissant* and a *pain au chocolat* and *bise* Jade and Eddy goodbye.

I have eaten both pastries by the time I arrive in front of the villa. The shutters are open, Mum must already be up for a run. I pray she is still out, I do not want to talk to anybody. I am also aware that coming home at his time, in this state, is probably not going to do me any favours. Thankfully, I make it to my room without bumping into anybody. I kick off my shoes, take off my jeans and t-shirt and fall face-first onto my bed, blacking out almost instantly.

CHAPTER 26
SUMMER 2022

Anne

The night of the disastrous *apéritif*, I toss and turn in my bed for hours, unable to find sleep. I am thinking about Alex, Diana and Louise and disturbing images are keeping me awake. I look at the alarm clock on my bedside table. It is 4:45 a.m. For what feels like the millionth time, my mind replays the end of the evening after Victor ran away from the villa.

Once the Munroes were gone, Liliane and Sasha left hurriedly with their children, mumbling excuses about giving our family some privacy to work out our differences. We did not work anything out. I could not bear to look at my son so I walked straight out the garden after the Brandsons. I stormed off in the opposite direction until my high heels became too painful to walk in. Feet crying for mercy, I finally sat down in a dingy restaurant, one of these places that is built up in a week to make maximum profit during the summer season and then promptly taken down late August as soon as the tourists have left Royan. The outdoor terrace was furnished with plastic chairs and tables and covered by a white tarpaulin. I had not sat down in a place like this in years, since I was myself a tourist in Royan and did not know the places to go and those to avoid. Service was awful. That is what happens when restaurant managers hire seasonal staff instead of professional waiters. Sometimes, these places go through three, four different crews in one season, which makes matters even worse. Furthermore, the food is usually tasteless. Clearly, building a returning clientele is not a number one priority when you run a restaurant in a sea-side resort. It took me twenty minutes to catch the waiter's attention to order a Monaco and a plate of soggy fries. I ate and drank mindlessly while staring at passers-by until I started shivering from the evening cold. But I did not want to go home. In the end, the manager had to kick me out of the restaurant, letting me know in an impatient voice that it was time for his waiters to bring the terrace furniture back inside for the night.

By the time I got back to the villa, Katie and Thomas were in bed. I checked Alex's room, it was empty but I was too drained to worry about his whereabouts. If last night had taught me anything, it was that Alex was officially too old for me to still think of him as mine to protect. On the contrary, it seems that my son is actually the one others should be protected from. Thinking of my son as a threat pierced through my heart like a dagger. I did not have the energy to get changed, so I just threw my shoes across the bedroom and flung myself onto the bed, desperate for oblivion to sweep the events of last night away for a few hours. Thomas did not stir, I do not think he was asleep, but he probably was not ready to discuss last night either. I rolled as far away from him as our king-size bed would possibly allow and waited for exhaustion to sweep me away.

Sleep never comes. I check my alarm clock again. Four fifty a.m. Time is going by painfully slow. Finally, at five a.m., I get out of bed as quietly as possible. I get changed into my running gear and on an afterthought, grab a thin jumper to wear on top of my workout top. I do not usually go out for a run this early, it must be colder than what I am used to. I walk down the garden path past the garden table littered with half drunken glasses of rosé and spilt beer bottles, the remnants of last night's shambolic events. The garden chairs are scattered across the lane (on a normal day, I would never have gone to bed leaving such a mess behind), three of them, the ones next to the dehydrated palm tree, still positioned in a semi-circle where Katie, Willow and Diana had sat huddled up over Alex's phone last night. One chair next to the garden table is toppled over on the grass, probably thrown to the ground by a shocked guest as they found out about the terrible secrets Alex and Louise had been harbouring for the past year.

I emerge onto the promenade and activate my fitness watch. It takes a few minutes for the GPS to work out my location, that always happens on my first run in a new country. I stand still in the fresh morning air. Finally, my watch buzzes, it is ready to record my run. I turn right on the promenade, away from the general direction of Louise's house. Gradually, my walk breaks into a slow jog.

For a few kilometres, I do not think about anything. I am engrossed in the way my body feels. As with every run, it takes me around ten minutes to find my rhythm. I concentrate on my breathing, a barely audible inhale and exhale that breaks the morning silence. I focus on the motion of my legs, heavy and sluggish at first, lighter and stealthier as my body warms up. I direct my attention towards my cadence, making sure my strides are long and efficient instead of quick and short. Finally, I zero onto my arms. They swing loosely by my sides, matching the cadence of my legs. I shake my hands and relax my fingers, I have a bad habit of clenching my fists when I run. Gradually, as movement becomes more and more natural, my attention shifts towards the rolling scenery.

I leave the promenade and the next part of my run takes me along narrow and cobbled residential roads. Some of these houses are truly majestic; four, five storey high mansions that look more like nineteenth-century castles than holiday homes. They might not have the unobstructed view of the sea that the villa offers, but it is certainly much more private and quiet around here compared to living right off the promenade. The second part of my run takes me on the *sentier des douaniers,* the coast guard path. I access it by clambering down a steep staircase squished and dissimulated in between two houses. You would not notice the stairs if you did not know they were there, that is why most tourists access the coastal path the long way around, by walking through the beach and up along the rocks. I slow down as I make my way along the *sentier des douaniers*. The path is narrow and rocky. I usually avoid it during the summer months because it is packed with tourists and I have to stop every 100 meters as it is too narrow for two people to walk side by side. Thankfully, due to the unusually early hour I set off at, I do not have that problem today. In between checking where my feet are landing, I gaze to my left directly at the blue water of the sea. Only a slim patch of greenery separates me from the cliff's edge. Finally, I arrive at *la Plage du Platin*, where the infamous *Pont du Diable*, the Devil's Bridge, is located. The Devil's Bridge is made up of two large chunks of rock, one on the beach, the other in the water, joined together by a thin stone arch. The gap under the bridge is wide, the result of centuries of erosion, and you can see all the way to the next creek if you peer through it. For a long time, I did not understand why it was called the Devil's Bridge. I remember voicing my ignorance to Louise's dad, Jean-Pierre, a local. Unsurprisingly, he had all the answers to satisfy my curiosity. I can still picture him sitting in his comfy chair on the terrace, smoking one of his thick brown cigarettes, a glass of red in the other hand, telling me all about Royan's local legends.

'The name Devil's Bridge comes from a medieval tale,' Jean-Pierre had explained, blowing a cloud of smoke in the air.

'Medieval, really? That far back?' I replied, surprised.

'*Ummm.*' He nodded gruffly. On the surface, Jean-Pierre was a stern and abrupt character. But once you got to know him, he was one of the most caring and selfless person I had ever met.

I was heartbroken when he passed away shortly after we graduated from university. He died from a heart attack, it all happened very suddenly and unexpectedly. I spent a lot of time consoling Louise in the months following his death. She took it very hard, her relationship with her mother had fizzled out years ago when she had divorced her dad and moved to the other side of the world, so Louise felt like she had no family left. I helped Louise through some of the darkest times of her life. And now, look at what we have become... I cast my mind back to Jean-Pierre. I do not want to think about Louise's betrayal.

'According to the legend,' he said, replying to my question, 'one day back in the medieval ages, a fisherman was lost at sea during a violent storm. The waves were rough and the wind unforgiving. Eventually, his boat crashed on the reefs of the Arvet Peninsula. The fisherman sold his soul to the devil in exchange for his life, and the devil built a bridge for him to come back safely to land.'

'The Arvet Peninsula?' I asked, confused.

'Yes, that's what we call this part of the French Coast, all the way from l'île de Ré to La Rochelle down to the Gironde estuary. The Arvet Peninsula, more commonly known as la *Côte de Beauté*.'

'The *Côte de Beauté*?' I asked. At the time, my French was rudimentary.

'The Beautiful Coast. A very fitting name in my opinion.'

To this day still, I agree with Jean-Pierre. He was born and bred in Royan, and like most locals, very proud of his heritage and protective of his hometown. But even as an outsider, it is hard to deny Royan's beauty. The coast is peppered with small conches, beautiful beaches located between two cliffs, fishing carrelets and Belle-Epoque villas, gorgeous nineteenth-century mansions that have survived the bombings and German occupation of World War Two. In contrast to the small conches, the Wild Coast runs for kilometres on end, an interminable stretch of sand bordered on one side by the blue green shades of the Atlantic Ocean, and on the other by an expansive forest of maritime pine trees and wild dunes. The *Phare de la Coubre*, the Coubre lighthouse, itself sixty-four metres high, is perched on top of one of these sandy dunes and towers over the ocean with its red and white stripes. The landscape of the *Côte de Beauté* changes again as you leave the wild coast and arrive at Meschers-sur-Gironde and Talmont-sur-Gironde. This variety is part of the charm of peninsula.

Talmont is a former citadel village and famous for its Roman church called *Eglise Sainte Radegonde*, which was built during the twelfth century on the village's promontory. The fortified village, now completely pedestrianised, is very popular with tourists. In the summer, the narrow alleyways are packed with artisan shops, cafés, restaurants and people stopping to take pictures in front of the *roses trémières*, tall pink flowers also known as hollyhocks which ornate the facades of the villages' small, traditional, white houses tilled with blue roofs. Meschers is located on limestone cliffs, and famous for the *Grottes de Régulus et Matata*. The Regulus and Matata caves are natural cavities dug into the white rock by erosion. They are located thirty meters above sea level and if you were to step out of them, you would fall directly in the sea. These caves were first developed in the eighth century by the Saracens when they invaded France. They used the caves as silos to store grain and added some man-made features and tunnels to the natural structure of the caves. The caves fulfilled different usages through the years, and gradually became larger and more built up. In the fifteenth century, they were used by smugglers to hide salt in order to escape the salt tax. In the seventeenth century, during the Wars of Religion in France opposing Catholics and Protestants, Protestant families used the caves as hiding spots and some of them were transformed into real homes. Nowadays, the caves form a network of several floors, connected to each other by an intricate series of corridors and staircases that run inside the cliffs as well as along the rock in the open air.

Thinking about the hidden gems of Royan has distracted me from my run. All of a sudden, without me even noticing, I have reached the end of the *Plage du Platin*. I duck under the low branches of a maritime pine tree, run across a narrow bridge and find myself along the rocks of the coast again.

Ahead of me, there is a succession of white and blue carrelets. I stop to catch my breath. Reminiscing about the time I used to spend with Jean-Pierre has redirected my thoughts towards Louise. Great. The one person I am trying so hard to forget about.

I pause my run on my watch and turn around to face the direction I have just come from. I observe the irregular outline of the coast. Far in the distance, I can make out the foggy silhouette of Soulac, another sea side village located on the other side of the estuary. Jean-Pierre's favourite restaurant used to be located in Soulac. What was its name? *I will have to ask Louise,* I think automatically. I curse at myself, displeased and annoyed. Clearly, my brain has not processed the fact that Louise and I are no longer friends.

'Get it through your thick skull,' I reprimand myself out loud. 'Louise is out of your life. You will never speak to her ever again.'

I watch as the sun rises above the sea. The water reflects its gold and orange light. A tall and mysterious figure cuts across the horizon. The Phare de Cordouan, another one of Royan's unique cultural heritage sites. Built in the sixteenth century, the lighthouse stands by itself in the middle of the mouth of the Gironde estuary, seven kilometres away from the closest stretch of land. It can only be accessed during low tide, when the retreating water uncovers the stone footpath that leads to it. The window of time to get in and out of the lighthouse is short, a few hours a day, and the waters surrounding the stone structure are traitorous. Indeed, the lighthouse is surrounded by shallow sandbanks, almost invisible during high tides and consequently easy for the inexperienced sailor to get beached on. For a few minutes, I stand still, staring in the distance at the lonely silhouette of the lighthouse. Its solitude echoes my own. In one night, I have lost a best friend and the son I thought I had raised. I have probably also lost my friendship group. Things will never be the same between the six of us and our children after last night. Especially if the other truth comes out. That one piece of information that makes Alex sleeping with Louise and Diana so much worse. Almost unbearable to think about.

Despite myself, my mind takes me back to that other dreadful night over twenty years ago. A night that I have worked very hard to forget about. A night that I have never talked about with anybody. I cannot believe the time has come to wake up the ghosts of the past. I set off on my run again, picking up the pace, hoping the pain of exertion will distract me from the inevitable decision I have come to, and hoped I might be able to evade forever. I need to speak to Victor.

CHAPTER 28
SUMMER 2022

Diana

It is pitch black outside, but I cannot fall asleep. I have been lying in bed for hours now, tossing and turning, rearranging my pillows, pulling my duvet up and down, counting up to a hundred, to a thousand to ten thousand… Nothing works. Horrible thoughts of my mum and the boy I have secretly fancied for years, even after he rejected me, keep barging into my subconscious. I am disgusted. I am furious. Part of me had always hoped that once I left school, once I was older and the age difference between us became irrelevant, Alex might be interested in me again. I am not delusional, I have always known that it would be unlikely, but it was nice to believe it was not completely impossible. After all, at one point in time, he had fancied me enough to sleep with me. But no. It is my mum he is into. My almost-forty-three-year-old mum with her wrinkles and her dyed hair. Does Alex know that her roots are already turning white? Does he know about all the anti-ageing creams she smears across her face before going to bed? I feel worthless. Who is ever going to want to be with me, if my own, old mother is able to outshine me?

I can hear tossing and turning through the wall. Marco must be struggling to find sleep as well. What a night it must have been for him. To find out that Alex, his role model, is about to become responsible for his parents' divorce. Because I do not see any way Mum and Dad are going to be able to recover from this. I can still picture Dad's face when Anne revealed the affair to our whole friendship group. Utter disgust. Shame. I shiver. I wonder what Dad was most disgusted by. Alex sleeping with Mum, or with me? I do not care if he is repulsed by Mum's actions. She deserves it. But I hope he is not ashamed of me.

I wish I could speak to him. But Dad still has not returned home. Once again, probably for the thousandth time since Marco and I left the Villa Grand Large (we refused to walk with Mum, she made her own way back home), I wonder where Dad has gone and what he has been up to. I reach for my phone on my bedside table and press the home button to check the time. 4:32 a.m.

My stomach rumbles. For the first time, I realise I am hungry. After all, because of all the dramatic events that unfolded last night, we never made it to dinner. I do not think I have had any food since the quiche and salad Mum and Dad prepared for lunch. When we were still a happy family, eating and joking together around the kitchen table. None of us knew it at the time, but that was probably our last meal all together in the same room. The thought makes me sad. Tears well up inside me, but I fight them back. I am too angry at Mum to want her to be a part of my life any more. Suddenly, I shove my duvet away and get out of bed. I need to distract myself and I am hungry. It is time to eat my sorrows away. I slide my feet into my slippers and grab a thick jumper before making my way down to the kitchen.

For a while, I stare blankly at the contents of our fridge. The entire top shelf is stacked with bottles of white wine and rosé, nothing else. The other compartments are full to the brim with different types of cheeses, *charcuterie*, summer fruits, vegetables, ready-made meals from the butcher's and uncooked sea food. I cannot make my mind up. I want something cheesy and carby and filling, but I cannot be bothered to cook. I stand there indecisively for so long; goose bumps appear on my forearms from the chilly air of the fridge.

'Can't sleep either?'

I jump around and scream. The door of the fridge slams shut behind me. I was so deep in thought about what I wanted to eat, I did not notice Marco walking into the kitchen.

'Jesuuuussss!' I sigh. 'You gave me such a fright.'

'Hungry?' asks Marco, nodding at the fridge.

'Yeah, just realised we never got to have dinner last night…' I reply uncomfortably, not meeting Marco's eyes. This is the first time one of us has explicitly acknowledged the events that unfolded the previous evening. I feel like I have just broken a taboo. I cannot help but deflect. 'I'm starving.'

'So am I,' my brother replies. Proactively, he strides towards the bread bin and grabs some leftover baguette from lunch. He gives it a squeeze, checking if it is still fresh. Clearly satisfied, he grabs a board and knife and starts preparing us a midnight snack.

A few minutes later, we are both sat opposite each other around the breakfast bar, a platter of cuts of meat, *terrine*, cheese, butter and toasted bread between us. It is only as I bit into my first slice of bread, butter and *comté* (eating cheese with butter – an unhealthy habit I have inherited from my mum) that I realise how hungry I actually am. Ravenously, still chewing, I start stacking a variety of meats and cheeses on my plate. Marco is just as hungry as I am, he is already on his third slice of bread, *jambon de Bayonne* and brie. For a few minutes, we sit in silence. Finally, I am full. I contemplate the crumbs of bread scattered around my otherwise empty plate. I need to talk about what happened, but I am scared of Marco's reaction. I am worried he blames me for some of last night's wreckage. Thankfully, Marco is the first one to break the silence.

'Dad hasn't come back home yet, has he?'

'No… It's late now.' I stare at the red numbers on the oven door. It is past five a.m. 'I wonder what he could be up to at this time?'

'I don't think there is anywhere open in Royan at this time of the night apart from the Bodega,' replies Marco.

I shudder. 'I mean, I hope that's not where he is. That would be depressing, a forty-three-year-old man getting drunk in a club to forget about the fact that his wife had…' I hesitate.

'An affair.' Marco looks at me boldly. It must be easier for him to talk about it. After all, it does not concern him directly. He pauses, then asks, 'Did you ever suspect anything?'

'You mean that Mum was seeing someone else?'

'Alex. Not just someone else. Alex.'

'Fine. Alex.' I pause to think. 'No. They said it happened last summer, didn't they? I guess that explains why Mum took that sabbatical year in Berlin.'

'I hadn't thought about that,' replies Marco. 'You're probably right… That would explain why she made that decision out of nowhere.' He looks at me sheepishly. 'Why didn't you tell me?'

'About what?'

'About you and Alex? I mean, I knew you liked him'

'Yes and you spent most of your time taking the piss out of me because of that,' I cut him off. 'That didn't exactly make me want to confide in you…'

'Fair enough…' acknowledges Marco. He drops his gaze, embarrassed.

I pause. I don't know what to say next. 'I mean… We aren't exactly that close. You've never told me about any girlfriends…' I pause. This conversation is about to get awkward. 'I mean, I don't even know whether you've lost your virginity or not…'

Marco winces uncomfortably and drops his gaze. 'I get what you mean. I guess I wouldn't tell you about that sort of stuff either. I'm just surprised I never heard about it, to be honest. I feel like that kind of gossip usually spreads like wildfire around school.'

'Believe me, he was hellbent on nobody ever finding out about it. He made that perfectly clear. Plus, Alex was a couple of years above you. It doesn't surprise me that you wouldn't know about it.'

'No, trust me, we used to play rugby together. There's a lot of locker room chat.'

'That's gross,' I reply, disgusted. 'Wait, are you saying that Alex is the kind of guy who boasts about his conquests to all the rugby lads? I held him in higher esteem than that.'

'It's not quite like that—' starts Marco.

'Oh really? So, he doesn't objectify women?' I reply angrily. 'All right, tell me how it is then!'

'Jeez, just let me speak. He would never instigate those types of conversations. He was actually quite private about girls. But it's almost like a group effect. After training or a game, it's like an overflow of testosterone. The team starts making crass jokes and everyone is egging each other on and it's like… the environment makes you feel like have to say something. Play up to everybody else. If you don't… I don't know. It just comes across judgemental… So, I always knew what was going on with the rugby lads. And with most of the school, to be honest. I mean, clearly, I didn't know everything.'

I take a minute to digest this information. Eventually, I say, 'I'm not surprised he never said anything. As I said, he was pretty intent on keeping it a secret, and to be honest, so was I. He didn't realise how old I was when… it happened. He only found out afterwards, through his friends. Well, his friend found out that the girl he was seeing, my friend Nathalia, had lied about being sixteen. So obviously, Alex put two and two together and worked out that if Nathalia wasn't sixteen, I probably wasn't either.'

'Our families spend so much time together, you'd think he'd know how old you are,' says Marco.

'Do you know how old Willow is? Or Leo? Or Katie?'

179

'…Good point.'

Once again, we sit in silence, but comfortably this time. It seems that our conversation has dissipated the awkwardness between us.

'What do you think is going to happen now?' Marco's question cuts through the silence like a knife.

'I don't know… I'm not sure I can be in the same room as Mum right now…'

'I'm not sure I can be either. Like, it's bad enough having an affair. But with your best friend's son?'

'Who is also your son's friend…'

'Don't even. What a great friend he turned out to be.'

'So…' I hesitate. Saying the words will make the possibility more real. 'Do you think Mum and Dad… That they are going to get a divorce?'

'Gosh, we're going to be two of them, aren't we?' Marco buries his head in his hands. 'These kids from a broken family. Weekdays spent at Mum's, every other weekend at Dad's. Eventually, one of them is going to get a new, younger partner, like you know, young enough to be our third sibling. That's probably going to be Mum, I suppose. Clearly, she likes younger guys. And then we'll be so confused and angry about the whole situation we'll start rebelling and acting out, getting ourselves in all sorts of trouble.' Marco lifts his head up and his eyes look demented. His voice speeds up as he rants on, 'We'll grow an attitude and develop commitment issues because of the crappy role models our parents turned out to be and we'll carry that trauma into all our future relationships and we'll never be happy until we're like, forty-five, and have undergone thousands of hours of therapy to get over what happened last night…'

At first, I am unsure how to react. I never suspected Marco had such a wild imagination. Then finally, either because of the absurdity of the situation, or maybe because I am slightly unsettled by his long tirade, I start laughing. Marco joins in, and soon we are half crying, half laughing, bent over on the breakfast counter. It is a relief to finally let the tears stream down my face without having to acknowledge what I am really crying about.

'Wow!' exclaims Marco. 'That was dramatic of me.'

'A little bit cliché as well,' I add.

I wipe the tears from my cheeks. Suddenly, I hear the front open and slam shut. Marco and I look at each other. Dad's footsteps echo in the corridor. He sees us as he is about to walk past the kitchen and stops in his tracks. He looks exhausted, there are huge purple circles underneath his eyes. Maybe he has been crying too. I thought he might have been out getting wasted but he looks pretty sober, he is not stumbling nor muttering and when he comes over to encircle us in an embrace, I cannot smell any alcohol on his breath.

CHAPTER 29
SUMMER 2022

Victor

I walk for a very long time. Until the fabric of my canvas shoes start chaffing against the sides of my feet. It is the rawness of my stinging skin that finally forces me to stop. I am almost surprised to find myself standing on the pier of Meschers's harbour. I must have walked for about three hours, there are roughly eleven kilometres separating Royan from Meschers as far as I remember. I have cycled this way numerous times with Thomas before, but I have never walked this far. My thoughts have completely separated me from my body. I look at my watch. It is past eleven p.m. now and the restaurants and bars along the harbour are in full swing. Most terraces have spilt over onto the pier, and in some places, there are barely a few meters separating tables of tourists from the small yachts and sailing boats docked along the jetty. Meschers's harbour is far from impressive. It is nothing like Saint Tropez or La Rochelle, no million-dollar yachts, no three or four masts vessels anchored next to each other. On the contrary, here, oyster farming boats cohabit with leisure catamarans, small sailing boats and tour boats. In order to attract tourists, local tourism companies advertise the various excursion these powerboats offer from small huts scattered along the pier. The ensemble is rather eclectic. I cannot remember the last time I have been on the harbour at this time of the day. We usually avoid this part of town during summer, it is full of tourists and the restaurants here usually serve frozen food at an expensive price point. They are tourist traps in other words.

All of a sudden, I am exhausted and I crave a drink. The effects of the beers I had at the Villa Grand Large wore off kilometres ago. I need something stronger to process the information I have just received. My wife cheated on me. She cheated on me with a boy. A boy who slept with my daughter when she was fourteen, years below the legal age of consent. A boy who I have always thought of as my third child. Once again, the revelations of the past few hours wind me. I spot an empty table next to a rowdy group of middle-aged couples and I sit down heavily, the burden of long-kept secrets and the realisation that my life is quickly unravelling weighing down on me.

It takes a while for the waiter to finally spot me and come over to take my order. Ordinarily, I would be irritated by the inefficient service. But tonight, I do not care. On the contrary, the more time I spend here, the later I will get back home. Home to my cheating wife.

Finally, a young French waiter walks up to me. He is precariously balancing a tray full of empty glasses with his left hand and tapping my order expertly on his tablet with the other. I am impressed by his ability to multitask without dropping anything on the floor.

'*Bonsoir monsieur, vous désirez ?*' he asks. I am in urgent need of a strong drink, beer is not going to cut it for tonight. The time has come for a strong spirit. I order cognac, a speciality of the south-west of France similar to whiskey.

'*Un cognac, s'il-vous-plaît.*'

'*Tout de suite.*'

Despite the waiter's promise that I should be getting my cognac straight away, I doubt it will arrive '*tout de suite*'. After all, it took almost fifteen minutes for him to just realise I was here. Whilst I am waiting, my thoughts inevitably turn back to Louise.

For a while now, things have been rocky between us. It started about two years ago, way before last summer. Work, children, day to day life and worries slowly started to erode our love for each other. We were getting increasingly used to having each other around, our relationship was not exciting any more, we took each other for granted. We were not making a lot of effort with each other. The motivation to try was disappearing. I knew things were far from ideal. But I did not realise they were bad enough for Louise to start looking for thrill and excitement somewhere else. The only time the idea of Louise cheating on me crossed my mind was when she suddenly decided to move to Berlin. The move did not make sense, she had been excited about teaching that new postgrad class for months, I did not understand why she was suddenly abandoning that project to move to Germany. I might have understood it if she had been given the opportunity to do her sabbatical in Italy. Louise has been obsessed with Italy ever since we went there on a romantic holiday when we were students. She has always said it would be her dream country to live in. That is why we spent our honeymoon in Sicily. But Germany? She never spoke about Germany.

Louise loves Italy because of the art, the hot climate, the sea, the outdoor terraces on the little piazzas, hours spent outside drinking coffee or reading and the easy and outgoing nature of Italian people. An environment that I would not expect to easily find in Germany. Therefore, it is not surprising that the idea crossed my mind that she might be cheating on me when she told me about the move. I assumed it was with one of her colleagues who had just moved to Germany himself, or with a visiting lecturer who was based in Berlin. I thought she might have decided to take a sabbatical year to follow somebody abroad. It never crossed my mind that she might be moving away because she was actually trying to leave the person she had cheated on me with behind in London. I remember asking her about it. If she was cheating on me. Her outrage was very convincing. Fake, I know now, but very convincing at the time. I genuinely thought she was telling the truth. I rack my brains. Were there any signs that she was lying? I do not think so, I close my eyes to try and picture the scene, but the details are slippery; after all, that argument took place months ago. Was her attitude a bit shifty? Did she struggle to meet my gaze? Or am I just distorting the past in light of what I know now?

'*Voici, un cognac.*' The waiter suddenly interrupts my train of thoughts. He places a generous glass of amber liquid in front of me and another glass filled with ice. '*Ce sera 3,50€ s'il-vous-plaît.*'

'There you go, oh, I mean, pardon, *merci, voilà, gardez la monnaie.*' I am so distracted I forgot where I was for a second. Naturally, the waiter replies to me in confident English.

'No worries, thank you very much. Have a good night.' He smiles at me. He sounds almost fluent, which makes me feel even worse about my amateurish grasp of the French language. I should be more confident speaking it by now. I was never good at languages as a child, and evidently some things do not change when you grow up.

'*Vous aussi.*' I persevere. The waiter suppresses a smile.

I swirl the cognac around my glass and take a large gulp. The liquid burns its way down my throat. For the first time this evening, I consider what is going to happen next. I have been putting off thinking about what the future holds for my family. But it is time to confront reality. The sting of alcohol has slapped me back to life. I will have to get a divorce. There is just no other way. My ego will never be able to recover from the fact that my wife cheated on me with a twenty-something-year-old boy. I think about Diana and Marco. How will our separation affect them? I suppose Diana might be relieved about spending less time with her mum now she knows the boy she fancies is actually into older women. I will have to make sure Diana understands that I am not upset at her. That the separation has nothing to do with her and Alex. Only with Louise and Alex.

I think of our friendship group. Unfortunately, I do not think we will ever be able to hang out all three families together ever again. I do not think I can bear to be in the same room as Alex ever again. Part of me wants to fight him, shove him to the ground and punch his face, stomach, nose, all of him until his physical pain matches my current, emotional one. I am pathetic. He would probably wrestle me off without too much trouble. He might be smaller than me, but he is dense and muscular. And most importantly, twenty years younger. My loathing for Alex makes me wince. It is not normal for me to feel that way about him. I do not want to detest Alex. I have always considered him as my second son. I oscillate between my natural love for Alex and the newborn resentment I harbour towards him. No, our friendship group will never be the same after last night. I need to cut ties, before the final piece of information, a piece of information that only Anne and I hold, a piece of information that would make last night's scandalous revelations a thousand times more sordid, comes to light. Suddenly, I realise that I need to talk to Anne. Make sure that we are on the same page. Make sure that our secret, a secret we have protected for over twenty years, remains hidden for many more decades to come.

I down my drink and get up. It is almost two a.m. Now, the restaurant is closing. The waiters are starting to usher drunk customers out of the premises, prompting them to continue their night at the Bodega.

I realise I need to walk all the way back to Royan; eleven kilometres back the way I came. It's not like I can flag down a taxi in Royan, it's a small of town. Resigned, I start walking past the boats docked along the harbour and then up along the coast. I cannot see much, the sky and water blending into one homogenous shade of black in the horizon. I can only hear the sound of the waves crashing onto the rocks to my left. I am exhausted, I want to sleep, but I am not impatient to get home.

CHAPTER 30
SUMMER 2022

Anne

I make it back to the villa around six-thirty a.m. Everybody is still asleep. I push open the sliding door leading to the kitchen and take off my running shoes. Large beads of sweat are dripping down my temples and into my eyes. Despite the early hour, it is already hot and humid outside. I look at my running watch. 12.2km, 5:45 minutes per kilometre average pace. I am pretty happy with that result, especially considering the lack of sleep and all the wine from last night. I pour myself a big glass of ice-cold water from the fridge and drink it in avid gulps standing in front of the terrace. I gaze at the promenade and the beach in front of me. Despite having spent the past twenty years holidaying in Royan, I never tire of that scenery. Gradually, my heart rate calms down, my body temperature regulates itself, and I stop sweating as profusely. I tear the top piece of a baguette lying on the breakfast counter and lather the soft bread with butter and raspberry jam. I eat on my way up to the bathroom, I am starving, but I also desperately need a shower. I walk past Alex's room. The door is still slightly ajar, exactly how it looked like over an hour ago when I left for my run. I peek in through the crack to confirm what I already know: Alex has not come home yet. For a moment, I pause and try to work out how I feel about his decision to cope with last night's drama by going out and probably getting mortally drunk. I realise I am too tired to care. I also realise I am so angry at my own son I cannot summon the natural, motherly impulse to be worried about him being out so late. I sneak into my bedroom. Thomas is still fast asleep; unlike me, he went out like a log last night. Thomas and I have always coped with stress differently. Whereas stress keeps me awake and sends me into overthinking mode, it seems to deplete Thomas of all his energy, like a battery being suddenly entirely drained. I rapidly strip and leave my sweaty running clothes in a pile at the bottom of the bed. I should put them in the laundry basket, it is right there but bending down and picking them up feels like too much of an effort right now. I smirk. That is very unlike me. I am a neat freak as Thomas likes to say. Leaving clothes

how big or unforgivable some of our mistakes might seem to be, at some point we need to find it in ourselves to forgive.'

Katie nods slowly, eyes fixed blankly on the wall opposite her bed. I stand up and give her a final hug.

'I am going to make us breakfast and then I will probably go to the market to get some fresh fruit and vegetables. You should come with me. It might take your mind off things. Distract you.'

Katie smiles weakly. 'Thanks, Mum. I'll think about it.'

I cannot blame her. When I was seventeen, I never liked to accompany my mum when she went food shopping either.

Thomas has already made me a cup of coffee by the time I get to the kitchen. We sit silently opposite each other around the kitchen island. I toast some bread and once again spread some butter and raspberry jam on it. I eat a nectarine, my favourite summer fruit. Once in a while, I glance up at the garden and the furniture and cutlery scattered across our usually immaculate lawn. I need to tidy up, erase the memories of last night, but I do not have the energy.

'I think I am going to take the bike out,' Thomas interrupts me deep in thought. 'Ride in the direction of Meschers.'

'That sounds like a good idea, honey,' I reply encouragingly. 'You have been saying you want to get back into it.'

'Yeah… Hopefully it will distract me.'

'Hopefully,' I repeat. 'I'm going to go the market while you're gone. Maybe I'll be able to catch Magalie, let her know we have arrived. Maybe she'll have time to go and grab a coffee with me.'

Magalie runs a fruit and vegetable stall in Royan's market. Her stall is one of the only ones open all year round, therefore, I got to know her a few years ago, when Thomas, the children and I travelled to France during most school holidays. We had just bought the house and felt like we needed to make the most of this pricy investment. Now, we only tend to come to France over the summer holidays, preferring to discover new countries during the shorter school breaks. Royan is really dull outside of July and August. I am surprised it is financially viable for Magalie to stay open outside of the summer season, I cannot imagine she sees many clients between September and June. I like her a lot, she is very chatty and outgoing and she is a gold mine of information when it comes to Royan's small town politics, gossips and scandals. I also feel like I know a surprising amount about her personal life. She has disclosed some very private details with me over her fruit and vegetable counter, sometimes in the middle of rush hour with a small line of customers building up behind me. 'If you do, don't forget to send my regards,' says Thomas before standing up and putting his plate and coffee mug into the dish washer. 'I'm going to check if the tyres are pumped up and I'll get changed.'

'Sounds good, honey,' I reply distractedly. I am already thinking about how Thomas has just offered me a great opportunity to speak to Victor without him knowing about it. When Thomas goes cycling, he is always out hours longer than he originally expects. He always cycles further than he can manage and usually needs a long coffee break with a *croissant* on the way back. I have got a good six hours ahead of me.

By the time I leave the Villa Grand Large, it is close to eleven a.m. Katie has decided to stay home and the Brandsons left in the early hours of the morning for Soulac. It is clear that they are trying to spend as little time as possible in the villa and I cannot say that I am surprised. I stroll along the promenade and walk through the terrace of Cédric's. A few couples and groups of young people are already sitting under the parasols, drinking coffee, smoking cigarettes and staring at the sea. I crane my neck to check out what is going on inside the restaurant as I pass the open doors. I cannot see Cédric. I might come back after the market and ask some of the waiters if he is around. I will probably stop for a coffee in front of the beach as well. Louise and I used to do it every single time we went to the market together. *Not any more*, I think bitterly.

The market is crowded. Cars are driving around the surrounding streets, desperate the find a parking space. It is not an easy feat in such a small town like Royan. The streets are narrow, the space is limited, and consequently, especially when people are in a hurry to get out their stuffy cars and onto the beach to enjoy a well-deserved holiday, arguments between drivers often disturb the peace and quiet of this otherwise monotonous little town. Once again, I tell myself that I am lucky to live within walking distance from the beach and the market.

I slalom between the fruit and vegetable stalls and the displays of freshly (and smelly) caught fish and sea food. For a second, I am tempted by the smell of freshly baked *brioche* as I walk past one of the market's many *boulangeries*. The sweet and sticky aroma that tickles my nostrils is simply divine. In a way, I am glad we do not have *boulangeries* on every other corner of the road in London. I simply could not resist the temptation to buy a fresh *croissant* every time I walked past one if there was. Although the price might quickly bring me back to my senses. While it is perfectly affordable to buy a *croissant* in France (in most places, there are just under 2 euros) I remember paying almost £4 for one at one of those fancy bakeries in central London. Delicious, but extortionate. Finally, I arrive in front of Magalie's stall. There is a small line of customers in front of me, so she does not see me straight away. Eventually, as I shuffle slowly towards the counter behind a thin lady ahead of me (her skin is so tanned, it has acquired an off-putting wrinkly texture) Magalie recognises me.

'Anne! *Mais quelle surprise !*' she exclaims. She goes around the counter and kisses me three times, once on the left cheek, twice on the right. Three *bises*, '*à la Bordelaise,*' as Louise once explained to me. I wish I could get her out of my head!

'*Alors*, what can I get you?' she asks energetically. 'Some cherries? Strawberries? They were picked this morning.'

'Sounds good, can I have a kilo of each please?' I instruct as she shoves handfuls of fruit into paper bags.

'*Avec ceci?*' she asks.

'I'll have some apricots A little bit more... A bit more... That's perfect. So how are things in Royan?' I ask as Magalie leads me to the till. The market is buzzing around me, lots of clients are waiting to be served, but Magalie is never one to say no to some gossipy chit chat.

'*Oulala,* you know, there's not a lot of excitement around here,' she answers untruthfully. I have noticed that the smaller the city you live in, the more people seem connected to each other and consequently, the juicier the scandals.

'What's happened to Pierre?' I ask, nodding to the new cheesemonger stall to the left of Magalie's. It used to be a butcher's. Pierre's.

'Oh, he's moved to the market of Saint-George,' she replies.

I cannot hide my surprise. 'Saint-George? But why?' It makes absolutely no sense to me. Saint George has a tiny market, barely a quarter of the size of Royan's and far less popular. Furthermore, it closes outside of the summer months, it makes no financial sense for a business to give up a prime spot in the market of Royan to move to Saint-George.

'*Oulala,* that was quite the drama,' Magalie whispers.

I refrain from pointing out that she has just told me that life in Royan is quite uneventful. I want to find out what happened more than I want to highlight Magalie's contradictory nature.

'Really?' I say instead. 'What happened?'

'Well, Pierre's wife, Madelaine, left him. Turns out she was having an affair with the... How do you say in English? *Le poisonnier*. Charles.' I follow her gaze to the other side of the market.

'Oh, you mean the fishmonger!' I reply. Surely enough, I spot the fishmonger, Charles (I know his name now), with a middle-aged lady I used to see helping out behind the butcher's counter.

'Oh blimey...' I gasp.

'*Oui, pas bon, pas bon du tout,*' agrees Magalie. 'So obviously, Pierre didn't want to have to see them together every day he went to work. So, he gave up his stall and moved shop to Saint George... What a shame.'

'I can't believe it,' I reply, shocked. What is happening right now? Why are so many people having affairs? Why can people not just leave their partners if they are unhappy instead of betraying them like this? 'They should be the ones moving to another market. They are the ones in the wrong. That's the least they could do...'

Magalie looks at me and raises an eyebrow. 'Unsurprisingly, people who cheat do not seem to have the straightest of moral compasses.'

She has a point. I am about to ask if she wants to grab a coffee later when I spot a familiar face. My eyes do not deceive me, it is Victor, walking away from the market, a basket full of provisions. This opportunity is too good to let it slip through my fingers. I quickly tap my contactless card onto the card reader and say goodbye to Magalie rather abruptly.

'I'll be back soon,' I say, already a few strides away. 'We'll chat more then!'

Magalie looks a bit startled and says something, but I am already too far away to hear her. Her voice is drowned out by the ambient chit chat of the market. Stealthily, I weave between idle shoppers and market stalls. Victor is about a hundred meters ahead of me, and it is difficult to keep track of his movements because of how busy the market is. On a few instances, I almost lose sight of him until I see his blonde head emerge above the crowd. I am lucky that he is tall and that his hair is so distinctively light. I accelerate until I am right behind him. Gingerly, I take hold of his arm. He turns around sharply, a polite smile on his face which rapidly fades away when he realises it is me. We stand facing each other next to the '*Saucisson Corse*' stall, forcing shoppers to circle around us. An elderly lady shoots us an outraged look. How dare we stop in the middle of everyone's way like this? Quickly, we both move to the side, closer to the *saucissons*, and unintentionally, to each other.

'Hi, Anne,' Victor greets me. He sounds resigned, he clearly does not want to talk to me, but he has accepted that this conversation is inevitable. I wonder if he already knows what I want to talk to him about.

'Hello, Victor. Listen, I've been wanting to speak to you. But I didn't want to go over to your place. I want to stay discreet. Do you have a minute?'

'Sure, might as well,' he replies gesturing to the full canvas basket he is carrying. 'Can't take too long though, I've got some oysters in there, I need to put them in the fridge asap.'

'Don't worry,' I say, 'I won't be taking too much of your time.' I gesture to our right, in the general direction of Royan's park. It is located right next to the market, but it is not visible from where we are standing. Most importantly, it is not a particularly nice nor very busy place, we are unlikely to run into any of our respective family members there. 'Let's go to the park. I'm sure there's a free bench somewhere.'

'Fine. After you,' he says.

I lead the way, my stride purposeful. The quicker I get this conversation over with, the better. I do not like hashing over the past. Especially a past I have worked so hard to forget. A past I have not spoken about for so long, it has genuinely started to feel like it never happened. Finally, we find a shaded bench by the pond. We sit far away from each other.

'I haven't been able to stop thinking...' I dive straight in. 'After what happened last night...'

'I have been thinking about the same thing,' replies Victor.

'What do you mean? What do you think that same thing is?' I want to make sure we are not talking about two completely unrelated things. Although I know deep down, there are very little chances of that.

'About Alex. I mean, I have always wondered... We never spoke about it outright, but we both know we were thinking the same thing when you found out you were pregnant.'

'You mean that he could potentially be yours?'

'Yes. You found out you were pregnant a month or so after you and Thomas started seeing each other again.'

'A month after we last slept with each other.'

'Exactly. I mean, there's always been a small chance that he was mine.

195

But it never really mattered. We were all friends, we spent all our time together with our families, I got to see him all the time. That was enough, I didn't need to know if he was mine or Thomas's. It never really mattered.'

'Until last night.'

'Until last night,' he repeats gravely.

'If Alex is yours...' I start hesitantly.

'That means that Diana would be his half-sister.'

'And they slept together. Victor, listen to me.' I lean towards him urgently and grab his arm. I squeeze hard so he understands how serious I am. He flinches and tries to pull away from me. I lean in even closer.

'Nobody can ever find out. It's more important now than ever before. Do you understand me? And it's not about protecting ourselves any more. It's about protecting Alex and Diana. If they find out... What they might potentially have done... I don't know... It would be pretty traumatic...'

'I think it's already been quite traumatic for Diana. She just found out that the boy she lost her virginity to, used to have an affair with her mum...'

Suddenly, I feel guilty. In my rush to speak to him, I never once stopped to consider how Victor might be taking the news of his wife cheating on him. 'I'm sorry about Louise, by the way,' I say to Victor apologetically. 'That was inconsiderate of me, I should have asked you how you were doing.'

'I suppose it's karma in a way, isn't it?' Victor smiles bitterly. 'What goes round comes around. I cheated first, the only difference is that no one knows about it.' He pauses. 'Don't worry, I'll keep our secret, just like you, I don't want anybody to know about this. I mean, we've done a bloody good job keeping the truth from everybody for the past twenty years, I don't see why that should change now. It happened so long ago that unless one of us talks, there is no way anybody could ever find out.'

'Thank you, Victor. I just had to make sure we were on the same page about this.'

We fall into a charged silence. Tentatively, I say, 'I didn't realise you and Louise were going through a rough patch.'

'*Um,* listen, Anne, no offence, but you are probably one of the last people I want to talk about my marital problems with. Let's just agree to bury the fact that our children might potentially have had sex with their half-sibling and forget we ever had this discussion. To be honest, after last night, I doubt we'll be seeing much of each other again...'

Abruptly, Victor gets up, grabs his shopping basket and gives me a curt nod before walking off. I watch his silhouette disappear in the crowd of shoppers drifting in and out of the market. As I sit there, I cannot help but cast my memories back twenty years ago, when Thomas and I were broken up and I started spending way too much time with Louise and Victor.

CHAPTER 31
DURHAM, 2000

Anne

Anne and Thomas had broken up three weeks ago and Anne was starting to get used to him not being around her flat all the time any more. The first week, she questioned her decision every day, especially when she spent time with Louise and Victor. Being single whilst living with a couple was not easy. Little by little, she got used to his absence. She did not crave his presence as much as she used to and to her surprise, Louise and Victor, who originally only reminded her of what she had lost, became a welcomed distraction. She was aware that they did their very best to keep her busy and distracted, and she appreciated their efforts. She had no doubt they would have rather spent some evenings alone as a couple instead of having dinner and watching a show with her, but they never made her feel like a third wheel. She felt like she had gotten to know Victor very well in the last few weeks and she enjoyed their new friendship.

It was a sweltering summer evening. Anne was at home alone and all the windows were open in the hope of a refreshing breeze. Unfortunately, the air was still and Anne was lying on the living room couch, too hot to move. She was fanning herself with a magazine and flicking between channels on the television. She could not find a show that caught her interest. It was at times like this that she could not help but question her decision to leave Thomas. She was bored and lonely, and she knew that if they were still together, she would be doing something more fulfilling with her time, maybe cooking a nice meal or drinking a cool glass of rosé in nice company. She decided she should have some rosé anyways, and maybe some ice cream. She had a tube in the freezer and nobody left to impress. Anne was halfway through pouring herself a (very) large glass of wine when the doorbell rang. She was confused for a second and wondered if Louise had forgotten her keys. It would not be the first time. Consequently, she was surprised to find Victor standing on her front porch.

'Oh, hello, Victor! Louise isn't home yet.'

'I know, she told me she was going to be home late from work today, I just thought I'd come over and wait for her here,' he replied, stepping into the flat and giving her a big hug. Anne was not wearing much because of the heat and she suddenly felt very self-conscious of her bare skin against Victor's. She pulled back quickly and invited him into the kitchen.

'I was just pouring myself some wine; do you want some? I'd offer you a beer, but we do not have any,' she said.

'Oh, don't worry, wine would be lovely, I need a cool and refreshing drink. Do you have anything to eat?' he inquired. 'I'm famished.'

'I've got some crips and some olives. Could make a salad or something, anything that doesn't require any cooking. I can't bear the thought of turning the oven or stove on just now. It's already warm enough.'

'That sounds good, let's have a drink first and some crips and then we can sort out dinner.'

'Perfect. Let's go into the garden, it's not much cooler than inside the house, but it's nice,' replied Anne.

The two of them clang their glasses against each other and for a little while, they talked about everything and anything. The wine went down quickly and before they realised it, they had finished the bottle. Thankfully, Anne had another one waiting in the fridge. Eventually, as the night fell and the temperature got cooler, Anne and Victor went back inside the house and cooked dinner together. The alcohol had built an appetite and they prepared large bowls of pasta laden with cheddar cheese and tomato sauce. They ate their food perched on the breakfast bar with some more wine. Anne's loneliness was long forgotten about, this was the most fun she had had in a long time. The conversation flowed more freely when it was just the two of them without Louise. Victor did not feel the need to fall into the boyfriend role and that made him cheekier. She enjoyed it, and for a second, she wondered if what Victor and she were doing could be described as flirting, but she dismissed the idea straightaway. She was not going to start feeling guilty about having fun with her best friend's boyfriend, that was ridiculous.

'So, how have you been feeling recently? Since the breakup? You still believe you made the right decision for yourself?' asked Victor between two mouthfuls of pasta.

'I guess we had to bring Thomas up at some point, didn't we?' replied Anne. She felt her mood plummeting and drained her glass of wine in the hope of getting back to her previous, carefree self. 'Yeah, I know I've made the right choice... We had different ideas about the future and if we tried to make it work, I think we would only have been delaying the inevitable. It's hard though, you know, it's not like I wasn't into him anymore.' For some reason, Anne couldn't bring herself to admit she loved Thomas in front of Victor. She wasn't too sure why, but it felt too intimate to discuss those types of feelings with him. 'Just need to get used to being single. You know, lots of fish in the sea, just need to get out there again. Which I will, I know… In due time.'

'I'm sure you'll have no problems getting boys interested in you,' said Victor. He didn't quite meet her eye as he said those words.

Anne felt herself blush, but couldn't resist the temptation to prod.

'Oh really, you think I won't? And why is that do you think?'

'You're pretty and funny and smart. If I was single, I'd want to get to know you.' They locked eyes for a second and Anne knew a line had just been crossed. She suddenly felt drawn to Victor, a feeling she had never experienced up until that final comment. How quickly a few words can change the dynamic between two people, Anne thought to herself. The noise of the front door opening and closing, followed by a quick pair of footsteps along the corridor, broke the spell between them. Anne felt strangely relieved and disappointed. Relieved they had not had the chance to say anything else that was compromising. Disappointed she no longer had Victor all to herself. She wondered if she would still feel the same way about him once the wine had worn off the next morning. She doubted she would and found the thought quite comforting. 'Oh my god!' exclaimed Louise as she stormed into the kitchen. She let herself fall heavily on the last available chair and reached for a glass and the wine bottle. 'Jesus, you guys have put a massive dent into this one,' she moaned.

'You're back late,' replied Victor. He got up to get her a new bottle and poured her a glass after kissing her on the forehead. Anne looked away.

'Gosh, thank you, honey, you are such a sweety pie,' said Louise gratefully.

'How was work?' inquired Anne. Sweety pie? She wanted to gag.

'I've just had the worst shift ever,' replied Louise.

She had started working as a waitress in a restaurant after they finished their exams to keep herself busy until the start of her master's degree. It was her first time working as a waitress, and her first job full stop, and she was finding it hard to adjust to the realities of the hospitality industry. Anne doubted she was a very good waitress. Louise came from a well brought up family and she was not the type of person who was cut out for long, physical and dirty jobs such as working in a restaurant. But Louise was not the type of person to quit at the first hurdle and she strongly believed that with time, she would get used to the late-night shifts, demanding customers and gross cleaning duties after closing time. So far, however, she dreaded going to work every day and always came back complaining about her shift.

'Oh no!' exclaimed Victor. 'What happened?'

'So, I was carrying this huge tray stacked with different drinks, I had a few wine glasses, some water and some tea.'

'You can balance all of that?' asked Anne, surprised.

'Well, kind of, I usually hold the rims of the wine glasses with my free hand,' replied Louise. 'But I am getting more confident. Usually, the less I think about what I am doing, the easier it is to carry stuff around.'

'Anyways,' cut Victor, 'continue your story. What were you about to say?' He wrapped an arm protectively around Louise's shoulder.

She looked surprised and so did Anne. Victor and Louise were not usually ones for public displays of affection, and they had been particularly careful when it was just the three of them since Anne broke up with Thomas. Anne could not help but wonder if Victor was trying to make a point.

'Right, yes, sorry, I got sidetracked,' continued Louise. 'So, I was carrying this huge tray and slaloming between tables to get to the terrace outside. The tray was so big and full, it was blocking off my view, I had no idea where I was going. And it was heavy, so I guess I was rushing a bit, I was worried my arm might give way under the weight... Anyway, I couldn't see my feet, I was halfway through the restaurant, clearly struggling and all of a sudden, I stumbled on something. My foot got caught on an object lying on the floor, I missed a step or two and I went flying across the room in slow motion.'

'Oh, my goodness!' exclaimed Victor. 'Did you fall?'

Anne thought that he was a little over-invested in the whole story. So far, nothing extraordinary had happened in her opinion. Waiters trip and fall all the time. The rubbish ones, at least. The venom of her own thoughts surprised Anne. It was not very nice to think of her best friend in such a condescending way. Was she jealous? But of what? Surely not of Victor paying her attention?

'Oh god, thankfully not, that would have been even worse. No, I managed to catch myself in time but obviously as I stumbled to regain my balance, I lost control of what I was carrying. The wines went flying

hand.

'Sorry, I honestly though you and Louise had left. I couldn't hear you any more. That's why I screamed, I wasn't expecting to see anybody.'

'Louise left for work and I'll be gone in a minute, I just needed a drink before heading out to the pub.'

'Ah, I see.'

'So, were you eavesdropping on Louise and me?'

'What? Why would you say that?'

'Well, you said you couldn't hear us anymore.'

'I mean, I wasn't eavesdropping, noise just travels around here.'

'Fair enough,' Victor replied.

Anne hesitated for a moment. 'Sounded like you were having an argument though.'

'Yeah… I don't really want to talk about it, to be honest.'

'Sorry, I didn't mean to pry.'

'Don't worry about it.' They stood in silence for a few awkward seconds. 'So,' continued Victor, keen to break the tension, 'what are you up to tonight?'

'Oh, well nothing much, no plans, but I want to get out of the house. Have a few drinks. If I stay home, I'm going to feel miserable and sorry for myself.' Anne regretted her answer instantly. It made her sound pathetic.

'Why don't you come out with us?' suggested Victor. 'We can have a beer here together and head out?'

'Really?' Anne hesitated. 'Do you think that is a good idea?'

'What do you mean? We're mates. Mates go out to the pub together with other mates.'

'I suppose you are right.' Anne paused for a second, considering her options. She was not doing anything wrong by going to the pub with Victor. She was not putting herself in a risky situation, some of his friends would be around. And it would be lovely to spend some time with him again. 'You know what, sod it. I'll come. Can you give me twenty minutes, though? I need to get changed.'

'No problem. Do you want a beer while you are getting ready?'

'Of course.'

Victor opened the fridge and reached for a beer which he opened using another bottle.

'Sorry, I just bought those an hour ago. They're still a bit warm.'

'Don't worry about it. Anyways, I'll go and get ready, I won't be too long.'

'Take your time, there's no rush.'

Anne tried not to think too much into her outfit choice. She grabbed a comfy pair of jeans and a nice top and applied some light blush, mascara and lip balm. She did not want Victor to think she cared about what she looked like in front of him.

They walked to the pub and spent the evening with three of Victor's friends; Allan, Keith and Dylan. It was a student venue with dim lighting, sticky surfaces and cheap pints. The five of them were sat in a booth in the far-right corner of the pub and Anne felt this was the most fun she had had since the breakup. Being around a group of boys was very different from going out with girls. They never talked about anything serious and were not worried about making fools of themselves.

Dylan, a rugby lad Anne soon found out, loved a drinking game and kept coming up with countless different ways to get the rest of the group to down their pints. Victor had to keep whispering in her ear to explain the rules of Dylan's games to her. For a while, they were only allowed to drink with their left hand. Then, the aim of the game was to drop a 10p coin into another person's drinks without them noticing. If the coin was thrown into your drink, you had to down it. Anne managed to avoid that but she forgot about the left-hand rule and ended up having to down her drink anyways. Quickly, she lost count of how many pints she had been drinking. Everyone kept buying rounds and if was hard to keep track with all the games and downed drinks. Their table was littered with empty glasses and they were definitely one of the loudest groups in the pub.

Once in a while, Dylan would speak so loudly his voice would drown out the lyrics of the cheesy music playing in the background. By the time it got to nine p.m. and Anne stood up for the first time to find the loo, she felt a lot more drunk than she had expected to be. She swayed slightly on her feet and had to concentrate to walk straight. Finding the toilet was an ordeal and waiting in the queue excruciating. She had consumed a significant volume of liquid and she was desperate for a wee. However, she made friends with a girl in the queue and their drunken chitchat distracted her from her bursting bladder for a while. By the time a cubicle was finally free, this stranger had become Anne's new best friend and they had made plans to find each other in the pub and get both of their friendship groups together.

Anne had forgotten all about that promise by the time she sat back down next to Victor. Somehow, Dylan had found a way to get his top off during the short time she was gone and was shouting something indistinct to nobody in particular. His speech was getting more and more slurry and incoherent. Victor smiled apologetically at Anne.

'I can imagine that is not exactly what you had in mind...' he shouted at her over the music and Dylan's voice.

'What do you mean?' she shouted back. 'I'm having a great time! Oops!' exclaimed Anne as she accidentally knocked over her drink. It had been almost full and beer spilt all over the table.

'Oh shit, I'm so sorry!' exclaimed Anne. In her attempt to stop the amber liquid from dripping all over Victor, she leaned over too quickly and lost her balance. She landed awkwardly against him and her hands brushed against something bumpy along his leg. Anne went bright red. 'Oh my god, I didn't mean to do that!' Now she was absolutely mortified.

To add to her embarrassment, Dylan started shouting, 'Ohhhh, Anne's drunk, Anne is druuuunkkk! Anne's spilt the pintttt! One pint down, Anne!' Thankfully, he did not say anything about the inappropriate touching. He must not have seen it, thank goodness, thought Anne. Dylan continued with his baritone voice, 'Oh we like... to drink with Anne,' he started singing, 'oh we like to drink with Anne!'

Allan and Keith decide to join in and together, they bellowed in unison, 'Oh we like to drink with Anne! Oh, we like to drink with Anne.' Naturally, they ended the song by downing their pints.

'Sorry, sorry, sorry,' muttered Anne, not knowing where to look. Certainly not down there. She was scared of doing something inappropriate again and therefore, she held her arms rigidly along the sides of her body, helplessly watching as the beer spread further and further around the table and started trickling on the floor.

Victor nudged her. 'Hey, let's get out of the booth before it falls on our lap.'

'Sure, OK,' she replied docilely, unable to meet his eye.

'Let me get you another one,' said Victor, 'to replace the one you just spilt everywhere,' he added humorously.

Anne felt like she was able to look at him again and smiled gratefully. He was going to pretend like nothing happened and she was more than happy to play along.

'You know what, actually, I'll have a little break for now,' she replied. 'I might have a glass of water instead.' She swayed on her feet again and for the second time of the evening, wondered how she had gotten so drunk. On the bright side, alcohol had helped dissipate her embarrassment pretty quickly, so there were some positives. And she was too drunk to think about Thomas and to worry about the consequences of going out drinking with her best friend's boyfriend. She was floating in a bubble of insouciance and she enjoyed the feeling immensely.

Maybe I should do this more often, she thought to herself.

'Oopsila!' she exclaimed as she tripped onto an invisible obstacle on the floor. She regained her balance by latching onto Victor's arm. She giggled. 'Yep, definitely a glass of water for me! Nooo beer!'

Victor laughed. 'Jesus, I don't think I've ever seen you this sloshed before!'

'I feel great! I feel fabulous!' Anne turned around to face him and said very seriously, 'You're quite handsome, you know.' The alcohol was breaking down her inhibitions and she felt like giving into her impulses. 'Very handsome. Like Don Juan... Well, maybe not like Don Juan. He is handsome handsome. Like godly handsome. But you are more normal handsome. Not bad looking.'

Victor laughed. 'We've gone from handsome to not bad looking very fast.' He was choosing not to take her seriously. He was using humour as a barrier against their unspoken (and illicit) attraction to each other.

Anne shrugged and flashed Victor a cheeky smile. She leaned closer to him and playfully poked the tip of his nose with her index finger. 'Handsome and cute. Very cute!' She then twirled around and glanced around her. 'Where is the dance floor?' she demanded bossily. 'I feel like dancing.' The latest pop hit started blasting through the speakers. She shrieked, 'I love that song! Come on, let's go. We need to dance.' She grabbed Victor's hand and pulled him to the back of the pub where a makeshift dance floor had been set up with a small DJ booth, a few throb lights and a glistening disco ball. The area was sparsely crowded; however, Anne still managed to walk straight through a small group of friends dancing in a circle and she accidentally stood on one of the girls' feet. 'Ooooppsss, sorry!' she apologised nonchalantly.

The girl threw her a death stare and Victor, who was being dragged purposefully in her wake, held up his free hand and mouthed, 'Sorry,' on her behalf.

Once they had walked a safe distance away from the group, Anne turned around and let go of Victor's hand. She closed her eyes and started swaying to the rhythm of the music. She raised her arms up in the air and moved her hips side to side. She was not thinking of anything or anybody any more, she was just losing herself in the music. She had not felt this free and this comfortable in her skin in ages. She did not care one bit what she might look like and what other people might think of her dancing. She was having fun and that was all that mattered. She twirled around on herself, eyes still closed and arms still raised in the air and lost her balance slightly. She opened her eyes, stumbled to regain her footing and caught Victor staring at her. He had a lustful look on his face. All of a sudden, Anne felt self-conscious. What was she doing, dancing around flirtatiously with her flatmate's boyfriend? This was not the kind of behaviour she condoned.

'I think I need a big glass of water,' she said to Victor.

'Sure,' he replied to her. His voice was rasp and charged. 'Let's go to the bar.' He put his hand lightly on her hip and guided her towards the front of the pub. Anne's skin prickled under his touch. She was surprised by Victor's audacity, she knew she should extricate herself from his grip, but she could not bring herself to break physical contact. She had never felt this highly aware of someone touching her before.

'Oh, there you are!' exclaimed Allan, suddenly appearing in front of them. 'We'd been wondering where you guys had gone.' Victor dropped his hand swiftly and discreetly. A wave of disappointment swept over Anne.

'Just getting Anne some water,' he replied casually, 'taking a break from the pints for a minute or two.'

'Fair. Listen, Dylan's been kicked out...'

'No way!' exclaimed Anne. 'Why?'

'Well, he tried to start a fight with the lads sat sitting at the table next to us...'

'What? Why?' inquired Anne.

'God knows why,' replied Victor, 'he just does that sometimes. Drinking makes him very aggressive.'

'So, we're going to head to McGullies instead,' finished Allan. McGullies was the only Irish pub in Durham. 'Are you guys coming with us?'

Victor looked at Anne to see how she felt. She shook her head faintly and said, 'You guys go without me. It's time for me to go to bed.'

'I'll walk you home,' said Victor.

'What, no, don't be ridiculous, I'll be fine. It's really not far. You go have fun with your mates. You're probably ready for some lads only time now,' she added jokingly.

'No, you've had quite a bit to drink,' added Victor firmly. 'I'll walk you home.'

'Don't be silly,' Anne protested, 'I can get a cab!'

Victor turned to Allan. 'I just want to make sure she gets home OK and then I'll come and join you guys at McGullies. Hopefully, Dylan doesn't get kicked out of there too by the time I get back.'

Allan looked at Victor doubtfully. 'She could just get a cab, you know.'

'I know,' Victor replied, 'but I just need to be sure she gets back OK.'

Allan bored his eyes into Victor's. 'OK. Whatever you want, mate… I'll see you later, I guess.'

'I won't be long.'

Allan walked off in one direction, Victor and Anne in the other. After few meters, Allan stopped in his tracks and turned around. He watched Victor and Anne as they stumbled along the cobbled streets of central Durham together. Victor had put his arm around Anne's waist and she was leaning heavily against him, one hand on his shoulder. She looked unsteady and no doubt, Victor's only intention was to make sure she did not trip or fall over onto the road. Nevertheless, they looked very intimate, their bodies pressed slightly too close and too comfortably against each other. Allan raised an eyebrow, he was glad Thomas was not there to see this. Unaware of his friend's judgemental stare, Victor gripped Anne's waist a little tighter than necessary. She was drunk, but still perfectly in control of her movements. However, Victor doubted such a perfect yet innocent opportunity to hold Anne so close to him would present itself again, and he was intent on making the most of it. From an outsider's perspective, he was not doing anything wrong. He reassured himself that only he knew his intentions were questionable and that he was consequently betraying both Louise and Thomas. But thankfully, no one would ever know what he was thinking at this exact moment in time and he would get away with it.

It was a warm and cloudless summer night, and the faint glow of the stars shimmered in the ink blue sky. Victor and Anne's solitary footsteps echoed ominously along the winding and steep streets of Durham. Neither of them felt like talking, they did not want to break the spell of this illicit moment together. Eventually, far too soon for both of them, they reached the intersection between The Avenue and Sutton Street. They clambered up the punishing incline of The Avenue, Victor holding onto Anne even tighter to keep her from falling, and finally, they arrived in front of Louise and Anne's house. All the lights were out. Victor checked his watch. It was shy of eleven p.m., quite early still. Louise was most certainly still at work. Anne fished for her keys in her small blue clutch. Victor knew he did not have any reason to keep hold of her any more, and reluctantly let go of her waist. The walk had cleared his head and the guilt that the alcohol had previously pushed to the very back of his mind was slowly creeping back to the forefront of his consciousness. He took a step back. Unfortunately for him, Anne was still just as drunk as she had been twenty minutes earlier at the pub. She turned around after finding her keys and stumbled clumsily into him. Victor had no choice but to press his body against hers to prevent them both from falling down the stairs. Their faces were inches away from each other.

'Thank you,' whispered Anne. Victor could feel her breath on his face, her breasts against his chest. One of her legs was lodged right next to his crotch and he hoped she could not feel his mounting erection. Anne carried on, 'I had a lot of fun. The most fun since... You know.'

'I had a lot of fun too,' he replied hoarsely.

'Are you and Louise all right?'

The question surprised Victor. 'Why do you ask?'

'Because you were arguing earlier.'

'*Ehm*, yes, things are a bit tense right now. Which is why I needed tonight. You to distract me...'

They stood inches away from each other for a few seconds. Both of them yearned to break the minuscule distance that separated them from each other, but both of them were held back by the consequences that would ensue from their actions. Eventually, simultaneously relieved and disappointed, they broke apart. Nothing had happened, they were still blameless.

'Good night then,' whispered Anne.

'Good night, Anne,' replied Victor.

She turned her key into the keyhole, opened the door and disappeared into the house. Victor stood there for a second, then climbed down the stairs, exhaling hard to catch his breath, running his hands through his hair in confusion. He needed a drink to process what had just happened so he turned back the way he had just come from.

CHAPTER 33
DURHAM, 2000

Anne

Anne was walking on the narrow footpath that snaked along the Wear. The vegetation that bordered the river was overgrown, and Anne regularly had to duck under leaves and branches. It was another sunny summer day in Durham and Anne wished she could have spent it differently rather than trudging across town to her ex's flat. But some of his belongings had been lying around her house for weeks now and she was keen to get rid of anything that reminded her of their relationship. She wished she had remembered to give Thomas his things back when he dropped her stuff off weeks ago, but their interaction had been so awkward she had completely forgotten about it.

Anne arrived at the bottom of a brick staircase that led back up from the river to the main road. She walked up the stairs slowly, she was in no rush to get to Thomas's. She did not feel ready to see him. Unfortunately, sooner than she would have wished for, Anne found herself walking down New Elvet Road and taking a right onto Church Street. Thomas and Victor's flat, which stood out from the neighbouring buildings with its blue painted walls and yellow door, was now only a short distance down the road. Bracing herself for an awkward and potentially teary conversation, Anne rang the doorbell. Expecting Thomas to open the door, she could not hide her surprise when she found herself standing in front of Victor instead. *Maybe Thomas is avoiding me?* thought Anne to herself. *After all, he seemed pretty upset the last time we hooked up* after *Victor's birthday party. Maybe he hasn't forgiven me for not wanting to get back together after that.*

'Oh, hello! Sorry, I wasn't expecting you to be home,' said Anne. She could feel herself blushing. Victor and Anne hadn't seen each other since that drunken night at the pub three days ago. Anne had woken up with a splitting headache and a deep sense of shame. She was embarrassed when she thought about how she behaved towards Victor and she could not believe what a poor friend she had been to Louise that night. She was determined to do better in the future and consequently had pushed her crush on Victor to the very periphery of her mind. She would not let herself talk to him nor think about him. The former was relatively easy, Louise and Victor were still arguing so she had not seen much of him at the house. The latter had proven itself to be... slightly trickier.

'Hi there,' replied Victor, flashing her a coy smile.

Anne hesitated. '*Ehm*... I'm here to see Thomas.' She gestured at the carrier bag she was holding. 'I brought back some of the stuff he left at mine.'

'Oh yes, he told me about that...' Victor paused. 'He asked me to say something came up and he had to leave urgently so he asked me to collect his stuff for him.' Victor paused and added truthfully, 'But the reality is, he didn't feel quite ready to see you. I just thought I'd tell you the truth. He's still hurting pretty bad.'

Anne looked at the ground. Victor's words made her feel guilty. She did not know what to say. Victor noticed her unease. 'Gosh, sorry, I didn't say that to make you feel bad. I just couldn't lie to you. Anyway, come in.'

'Thank you. I'm sorry you've ended up in the middle of all of this.'

'It's OK. The two of you are my friends. I just want both of you to feel better.'

Anne could not help but notice he called her his 'friend'. She wondered if that was Victor's way of dismissing what had happened between them a few nights ago.

'I won't take up too much of your time. I'll just drop this off and go.'

'Don't be ridiculous, there's no rush. Stay for a cup of coffee at least. You've come all this way after all.'

Anne hesitated. 'What if Thomas comes back? Surely that would defeat the whole purpose.'

'I don't think he'll be back anytime soon.'

Anne raised her eyebrows interrogatively. 'He's gone to spend the day in Newcastle with Allan, Dylan and Keith. I'm going to meet up with them later. We're all going to a gig tonight.'

'Surely you would have wanted to go with them?'

'They're going to the pub beforehand. I'm not too bothered, to be honest. I was only going to join them for the concert anyway, so this really isn't any trouble.'

'Still. I think Thomas should take care of his own business instead of asking you to handle the situation for him. That's not very fair on you. Surely there are other things you would want to be doing right now rather than staying home waiting for me to come over to drop off a few things.'

'I really don't mind, to be honest,' Victor replied. He added shyly, 'I offered to help.'

This comment startled Anne. She was not used to Victor being coy around her. She was not sure how to interpret his behaviour.

'Oh really?' she replied. 'That's nice of you.'

'Come on, come in and have a cup of coffee. Or would you prefer some tea?'

'Coffee sounds great,' replied Anne as she stepped over the threshold of the front door.

'Where should I put Thomas's stuff?' she asked holding up her Sainsbury's carrier bag.

'Just leave it at the bottom of the stairs,' Victor replied over his shoulder.

Anne dropped off the bag where indicated, then made her way into the kitchen and sat on one of the wooden chairs around the kitchen table. She watched Victor as he boiled the kettle. He had his back to her. His shoulders were broad and she enjoyed watching his biceps move under the fabric of his t-shirt. Victor turned around and Anne quickly averted her gaze. She hoped he had not caught her staring.

'You like yours black, don't you?' he inquired.

'Yes, no sugar, no milk.'

'Yes, that's what black means,' he replied teasingly.

Anne laughed. He knew she could take his banter. They sat opposite each other, their drinks too hot to sip from just yet. Anne blew into her mug to cool hers down. She watched as the dark liquid's surface rippled under her breath. When she looked up, Victor's eyes were boring into hers. She felt herself blush.

'I've been wanting to apologise to you,' she finally said. She had been hesitating about bringing up this topic of conversation ever since she entered the flat. But she could not resist opening the pandora box. She was curious to find out what would come out of it.

'What for?' asked Victor, confused.

'For the other night...' He didn't seem to understand what she was referring to, so she added more explicitly, 'When I went out with you and the boys. I got very drunk. Thank you for taking care of me and making sure I got home safe.' Victor remained silent and Anne felt the urge to fill in the gap in conversation. 'I also want to apologise for some of the things I said to you. That was the alcohol talking. Really not appropriate of me, I don't know what I was thinking. I didn't mean any of these things. I just wanted you to know all of that.'

'That's a shame,' Victor finally replied.

'What do you mean?' Anne felt her heartbeat accelerating.

'It's a shame you didn't mean any of the things you said to me.'

There was a long pause. Without realising, Anne and Victor had leaned towards each other over the table. The air was charged with anticipation.

Without much conviction, Anne objected, 'I'm not sure we should be talking like that. You're dating my best friend. I used to date yours.'

'I know. I don't think this is a good idea either.'

Despite their best intentions, Anne and Victor kept edging closer and closer to each other. Their morals and loyalties stood no chance against their sexual impulses and the attraction that had been growing between them for the past few weeks. Finally, their mouths were just inches away from each other, almost touching. They stayed like this for a few seconds, a short space of time that seemed to stretch for an eternity. As long as they stayed like this, almost touching but not quite, they could still go back. Nothing would have really happened. The moment they bridged that gap, harm would be done and they might as well go all the way. They were both debating these two options, aware of the one they should pursue, whilst knowing deep down which would eventually prevail. A small part of Anne and Victor hoped the other one would make the sensible choice and turn away. It had to be the other one, because they knew that they did not have the strength to do it themselves.

Victor stood up. Relieved, but mostly disappointed, Anne leaned away from him. He reached his hand out and grabbed the back of her neck. Pleasure flooded her body and she knew this was what she had wanted all along. They kissed. It was a long kiss, lustful and passionate, weeks of missed kissing crammed into one moment. He led her into his bedroom. For a second, Anne reflected that it was strange for her to walk past Thomas's bedroom, a bedroom she had been into countless number of times, and into Victor's, an unknown territory up until now. He stripped her from her clothes, she took off his t-shirt, unbuckled his belt. They had sex once, it was quick and intense, then once more, taking their time, lingering over each other's bodies. Later, when Anne was getting dressed to leave and

I asked. 'It's not like you and I are ever going to be a thing.' I had whispered that last bit even though Thomas looked sound asleep on his bed.

Victor motioned me to leave the room and he silently closed the door behind us.

'You would never do that to Louise either,' he said to me. We were standing in the narrow corridor of his flat, only centimetres away from each other. We were a bit drunk, angry and lustful. A dangerous combination. We had hot sex, a tangle of limbs on Victor's bed. I had to bite his shoulder to stay quiet. I doubted anything could wake Thomas up in the state he was in, but I did not want to take any risks. It was the last time it happened. I felt too ashamed to go back and lie down next to Thomas after that, so I went home. The nice thing to do would have been to stay with Thomas and make sure he did not choke on his own vomit whilst asleep, and then to help him nurse his hangover the next morning. But I did not have the courage to face him.

Guilt racked at me for weeks. I spent many hours debating if I should come clean to Louise and Thomas. But the reality was, since Thomas and I had started seeing each other again, the four of us were the happiest we had been in a long time. As happy as we used to be. I could not bring myself to ruin it. Eventually, I convinced myself that coming clean would be more painful for Louise and Thomas than silencing the truth. I was keeping a destructive secret from them, but I was doing it for their own benefit. At least, that is what I told myself.

That month, my period was late. I did not think much of it, but nevertheless decided to take a pregnancy test. I had not been very diligent about taking the pill ever since Thomas and I broke up.

I could not believe it when I found out I was pregnant. These things did not happen to girls like me. It was incomprehensible. Of course, I could not say anything about not knowing who the father was. I convinced myself that it had to be Thomas's and decided to take the baby as a sign that we were meant to be together. I remember the look on Victor's face when Thomas told him I was expecting. That we were going to keep it. A flicker of fear. He realised there was a possibility it could be his.

But he also understood that he would never know for sure. We never spoke about it. It is a secret we both buried so deep inside us, after a while I was able to convince myself that Victor and I never happened. There was no one to keep the memory alive with me, not even Victor himself, and therefore, it gradually lost its grip on reality. Alex was born and I continued to ignore the fact that I was not sure who his father was. Victor continued to ignore the possibility that it could be his. We got on with our lives, these doubts never made a difference, and slowly, I forgot about that whole chapter of my life. It had happened a long time ago, and it ended up having so little impact on my life, I began to think it was no longer relevant. Until last night.

CHAPTER 35
SUMMER 2022

Willow

The sun is already setting by the time we board the ferry back over to Royan. We are going to get back to the villa quite late, but I have a feeling that was Dad and Mum's intention.

The four of us left at the break of dawn this morning, and unfortunately, I have not been able to speak to Katie since last night. She was already asleep by the time we came back from Mario's yesterday evening and I did not want to wake her up. I feel bad about not speaking to her, although it is not my fault. She must be going through a difficult time and as her friend (I am not sure if I can call myself her girlfriend – we never discussed that) I should be there to support her. By eight a.m., we were in the queue to the ferry. We did not have to wait a very long time to get on, we had left so early there were only a handful of cars in front of us. If we had left a few hours later, we would have ended up being stuck in a two- or three-hour-long queue along Royan's coastal roads before we would have been able to cross the estuary. Dad parked the car in the lower levels of the boat and we ate a *croissant* on the outside deck. I was glad I took a jumper with me; despite it being the middle of summer, the sea breeze felt icy against my bare legs. Once we got to Soulac, we drove inland along the D2, also called 'Route des Châteaux' or 'The Wine Route'. Mum and Dad stopped at a few *châteaux,* one of the owners even gave us a tour of his estate, and they bought a few cases of red wine to bring back to London at the end of the holiday. Mum and Dad were having a fabulous time, but Leo and I were pretty bored. Thankfully, they felt sorry for us so they eventually drove back to the beach and took us out to a *créperie* for lunch. I had a *galette jambon, fromage* as a main and a *crêpe banane, chocolat* for dessert. It was the best part of my day.

Finally, we turn into the little side street that leads to the villa's garage. Dad turns the ignition off and with a sigh of relief, I step out of the car. I reach my arms over my head and stretch my stiff back. If Mum and Dad planned to make a discreet entry, they failed. We get accosted by Anne as soon as we step foot through the front door. She is standing at the bottom of the staircase and I cannot help but wonder if she has been waiting for us all this time. She looks tired and dishevelled; her hair is hanging limply around her face and she is rubbing the bridge of her nose between her thumb and index as if nursing a headache. As soon as she sees us, however, she snaps up straighter and forces a shaky smile across her face.

'You are back! How was Soulac?' she asks over-enthusiastically.

'It was lovely, thank you,' Mum replies.

I am surprised by the formality of her tone. They sound like two strangers exchanging pleasantries instead of two old friends catching up about their day.

'I am glad you are back,' Anne soldiers on. 'We were just about to have dinner, I am going to order some pizzas. What should I get for the four of you?'

Mum and Dad look at each other uncomfortably. I know they were hoping to escape dinner with the Daltons but given Anne's tone, I do not think we have much of a choice. Mum ends up ordering the same pizzas we had yesterday; pepperoni, vegetarian, ham and mushroom and four cheeses and forty-five minutes later, Katie, Alex, Thomas, Anne, Leo, Mum, Dad and I are sitting in strained silence around the kitchen table. I feel very uncomfortable and I do not know where to look. Thomas looks murderous, Anne a bit demented, Alex like he is about to throw something out the window and Katie like she is about to throw up. I tried to shoot her a comforting smile when I sat in the chair next to hers but I am not sure she saw me. The safest thing to do now is stare at my plate, I decide. I am debating if I could get away with discreetly squeezing Katie's hand under the table to let her know that I am there for her without anybody noticing when Thomas's angry voice suddenly makes me jump out of my seat.

'I can't take this awkward silence any longer!' he exclaims. 'How long are we going to sit here for without saying anything?'

'If you have something to say, just say it,' replies Alex defiantly.

I cringe inwardly. I do not want to be caught in the middle of their screaming match. This has nothing to do with me. Mum attempts to say something about leaving to give them some privacy but once again, Anne is not having any of it. She says something about organising a family trip to l'île d'Aix which sounds like a ridiculous idea to me, but I am not really listening to her any more. Katie has just buried her head in her hands and I am worried about her. Deciding I do not care if anybody notices, I reach over and lay a hand on her thigh to comfort her.

She whispers, 'Let's get out of here. I don't think I can stand being in the same room as all of them for a second longer.'

I look up but it does not seem like anybody is paying us any attention. Anne, Thomas and Alex are too busy shouting at each other and Mum, Dad and Leo are doing their very best to ignore the screaming match that is unfolding next to them by talking about the weather. I catch Mum's eye and nod towards Katie, then the garden. She understands what I am trying to say and gives me a discreet thumbs up.

I lean closer to Katie and whisper, 'Let's go outside.' I do not think Katie's parents notice us leaving.

Five minutes later, we have found shelter behind our favourite set of bushes at the back of the garden. The evening breeze has brought some freshness to the air and even though it is still warm, it definitely feels a little bit cooler than it did a few hours ago. I welcome this milder temperature with a sigh of relief. I am tired of constantly breaking into a sweat as soon as I step outside. Katie sits heavily on a tree trunk and I wrap my arm around her shoulder. She leans into me and I kiss the top of her forehead. I am being a lot more forward than I am used to, but right now I care more about Katie's wellbeing than about my insecurities.

'I am so happy you are here,' she says to me. 'What an absolute nightmare.'

'I cannot believe any of this is happening,' I agree with her.

'I feel so bad about Diana...' Katie continues. 'I wonder if what happened with Alex is part of the reason she stopped being friends with me.'

I stop to think about that. The thought never crossed my mind. 'It's hard to say,' I reply cautiously. 'I mean, what happened between them has absolutely nothing to do with you, so it doesn't seem fair for Diana to cut you off as a reason. But I understand she might have found it hard to be around you because you might remind her of him... And that would probably not have been very helpful if she had wanted to forget about the whole situation.'

'This is just so messed up!' exclaims Katie, shaking her head left and right. 'I just wanted to have a fun, amazing summer and spend as much time as possible with you! We have been here one day and already summer is ruined.'

'Don't say that,' I try to reassure her. I grab her by the shoulders and force her to look at me. 'You and I can still have the amazing summer we planned on having. Fuck Alex and Louise and Diana. Fuck that shit, none of it has anything to do with us. They can deal with their drama and you and I will just stay away from them as much as possible and have fun.'

'You think so?' she asks vulnerably.

'A hundred per cent,' I answer.

Katie leans into me and we kiss more passionately than we ever have before. In this moment in time, I am convinced that whatever happens with her family and the Munroes, her and I will be OK.

CHAPTER 36
SUMMER 2022

Katie

I munch on my pizza slice, eyes glued to the glass of water in front of me. The dining room is dead silent. Mum and Dad have both been out for most of the day and nobody could be bothered to cook. So we are eating pizzas from Mario's. That is not normal. Mum and Dad usually love to cook fresh meat, vegetables and seafood bought from the market. They say we need to make the most of the local produce we cannot get in London. But tonight is not a normal night. I quickly glance at Willow and catch her eye. She looks as uncomfortable as I feel. Liliane and Sasha tried to get out of having dinner with us. They said they were happy to give us some family time to work through what happened last night. But Mum was not having any of it. She insisted they have dinner at the villa. She said she wanted things to feel normal. Unfortunately for her, this dinner is anything but normal. None of the eight of us are talking and everybody is either resolutely staring in every possible direction apart from Alex's or casting him furtive glances. I almost feel sorry for my brother, but then I remember what he did and I figure he deserves of bit of naming and shaming.

The Brandsons left the villa at the break of dawn. They caught the ferry over to Soulac and were not back until an hour ago. Mum ambushed them as soon as they got back and almost marched the four of them into the dining room. Clearly, they are trying to avoid us and I cannot blame them, although I am disappointed I have not been able to hang out with Willow at all today. Even though we have both been home alone all day, Alex and I have barely spoken a word to each other. I do not know what to say to him and frankly, I am not ready to talk to him yet. Right now, I cannot believe that the person sitting opposite me is my brother. His actions have transformed him into a stranger. The person I have known for the past seventeen years would never have done anything like that. Sleeping with one of my classmates... And then with her mother... But then, maybe I did not know Alex as well as I thought I did. As far as brothers and sisters go, we have always gotten on. But I guess we have never exactly been close. I quickly shoot a furtive glance in Alex's direction. He is staring obstinately at his plate, avoiding all eye contact. I catch Mum also watching him on the sly.

Last night's events hang heavily over the dinner table, yet nobody is brave enough to bring them up. I look at Dad. Behind him, through the sliding windows, I can still see empty glasses of wine, half-eaten bowl of crips and tipped over chairs lying messily in the garden from last night. Nobody has gotten around to tidying that yet. Dad is munching ferociously on his slice of *pizza reine*. His gaze keeps shifting between Mum and Alex, his eyes darting back and forth at an unnatural speed. Alex does not meet his eye. Mum cannot hold his gaze. I can tell Dad has a lot on his mind. A lot he is burning to say. For some reason, he is keeping all of his thoughts bottled up inside him. That is unusual. Dad is an expressive kind of guy; what he thinks, he says. No passive aggressiveness, no snide remarks couched into polite conversation. He does not do well with subtlety, he is very direct. Very un-British in a way. Mum says he has more of a French temperament, which is ironic, because out of all of us, Dad is definitely the one with the worst French. Suddenly, Dad slams his fists on the kitchen table. Willow and I jump, Liliane and Sasha drop their cutlery, Leo gasps and Mum squeals and knocks over her glass of water. Even Alex looks up for a moment. Dad's temper outburst catches all of us by surprise.

'I can't take this awkward silence any longer!' Dad exclaims. 'How long are we going to sit here for without saying anything?'

'If you have something to say, just say it,' replies Alex defiantly.

'Maybe we should give ourselves a little bit of time,' intervenes Mum, forever the peace keeper. 'Think over what we want to say to each other before we discuss last night's events.' She looks at Dad pointedly as she says that last sentence.

'I think we should go—' Liliane starts, but she is immediately interrupted.

'How do you want me not to think and talk about what happened last night?' bellows Dad angrily. He gestures at the garden behind him. 'This whole place is a living reminder of what happened. Of the secret your son has been keeping from this family.'

'You are right, what we need is a change of scenery,' exclaims Mum enthusiastically. 'Somewhere we can reconnect as a family and not think about the Munroes.'

I can tell from the look on Dad's face that this is not at all what he had in mind. Thankfully, Willow rescues me from this nonsensical conversation and we escape into the garden.

CHAPTER 37
SUMMER 2022

Anne

I walk along the white, gravely path that stretches in front of me. On my right, the green, blue water of the Atlantic Ocean. On my left, low and spiky bushes, their leaves either a faded green or a scorched yellow from the blazing sunlight. I can see small beads of sweat trickling down my husband's back in front of me. He is walking angrily, at a steady speed, the three of us clambering to keep up behind him. He did not want to come here, and he has made every step of our journey to l'île d'Aix, the island of Aix, as unpleasant as he could possibly manage.

We left the house early this morning, before eight a.m. Thomas did not enjoy having to get up this early on holiday.

'Why on earth is this stupid thing making so much noise?' he bellowed as my phone alarm went off this morning. It was seven fiftee a.m. and it felt like we were back in London about to start a working day instead of on holiday. I scrambled to turn it off. In my haste, I dropped my phone from my bedside table and as I struggled to retrieve it from underneath the bed, the alarm gradually got louder and louder, much to Thomas's fury. Nothing I could say after that managed to calm him down.

'I thought we'd try and get the nine a.m. ferry to the island this morning,' I explained calmly, finally finding my phone and turning the alarm off with a decisive tap on the screen. 'And it's a thirty-minute drive to La Tremblade, let's say thirty-five minutes if we account for a stop at the *boulangerie* to get *croissants* and *chocolatines* for the boat ride. So, really, we need to leave the house by eight a.m. at the latest.'

La Tremblade is a small fishing port situated on the estuary of the Seudre and twice a day during the summer, at very specific times, you can catch a ferry that takes you to a lovely yet minuscule island called l'île d'Aix. L'île d'Aix is situated in between the much larger islands of l'île de Ré and l'île d'Orléon. Thomas, the kids and I have been to this island countless number of times, and it remains one of our favourite family excursions. The island is truly minuscule, three kilometres long and 0.6

kilometres large and home to 232 inhabitants, a local waitress once informed me. It takes about two hours to walk around the entire island. I hoped that this trip, far away from the theatre where all our family drama unfolded two nights ago, might take our minds away from the sordid revelations we had been privy too. I hoped it would allow us to rekindle as a family and allow Thomas, Katie and I to find it in ourselves to forgive Alex. Unfortunately, Thomas does not seem to be in the mindset to forgive anyone just yet. On the contrary, it seems like his anger is growing more and more vicious with time. It worries me.

When I told Thomas about my plans this morning, my optimism about our day's trip was met by a grumpy grunt. Thomas turned away from me and pulled the bed covers up to his nose with a forceful tug. The sentiment was clear. He did not want to go. I sighed. Clearly, Thomas had decided to behave like a child. There was not much reasoning and rationalising to be done with him. Unsure how I would get him out of bed, I went to check on Alex and Katie. Unsurprisingly, they were both also still in bed, woken up by my alarm, but just as unenthusiastic as their father. A flash of anger surged through me. Was I the only one who wanted to keep this family together?

'Get up, the lot of you!' I shouted.

Many grunts, sets of teeth ground against each other and multiple sighs later, the four of us were in the car. The journey to La Tremblade was not a pleasant feat either. Of course, Thomas wanted to drive which I knew was not a good idea. He was angry and frustrated and when he gets behind the wheel in a mood like that, nothing good ever comes out of it. I tried to dissuade him from driving, I suggested I should take the wheel, but he shot me one angry look and I knew it was safer to back off. Of course, me suggesting he should not be driving added an extra layer of anger and resentment on top of his destructive mood. He refused to use the GPS.

'I know where I am going!' he shouted as I bent over to activate the small device. 'We've driven this way thousands of times, I don't need that stupid thing, I'm not an idiot!'

'I know you are not, honey,' I tried to reason with him calmly.

I could see Alex rolling his eyes at his father from the back seat and prayed Thomas would not notice. He did not need another reason to be angry at his son.

'I just thought it might show us about a shortcut we don't know about.'

'Of course, I am angry, but I choose to be angry towards Louise before I get angry at our own son. She could have stopped this.'

'Well, I choose to be angry at you,' replies Thomas for the first time, turning away from the horizon and looking me straight in the eye.

I move back, surprised and confused.

'At me?' I don't understand. 'Why?'

'Because of the secrets *you* kept.'

Dread courses through my veins. It obliterates everything around me. I cannot hear, see nor think about anything else but the words that are about to come out of my husband's mouth. Terrified, I barely bring myself to ask, 'What secrets?' My question comes out as an inaudible whisper.

'The fact that you are not sure who Alex's father is.' Rage has distorted Thomas's features, he looks at me with an emotion that looks close to hatred. He almost takes pleasure in watching my face crumble as he says the following words, 'The secret you have kept for over twenty years and which means that Alex might be Diana's half-brother.'

A loud gasp tears me away from the icy look in my husband's eyes. Both of us turn around, looking for the origin of the sound. To my greatest horror, Alex is standing within ear's reach from us, his face white with shock.

Distressed, he whispers, 'No... No...' he pleads at me, 'Mum, please tell me that is not true.'

CHAPTER 38
SUMMER 2022

Thomas

Anne has decided to play happy family and I just cannot go along with the deception. For the past two days, I have been struggling with the potential implications of the secrets uncovered during our disastrous *apéritif*. I made my peace with Anne sleeping with my best friend years ago. I decided I did not want to give up on our relationship because of a 'mistake' as I liked to think about it. I have no doubt Anne regrets what she has done. I trust that these regrets, no doubt compounded by a healthy level of shame, have injected her with a strong sense of duty, of dedication towards our marriage and family. She has been nothing but a faithful and loving wife and consequently, I moved on a long time ago. But today, this secret, this betrayal, has suddenly become relevant again.

I have tried to remove myself from the situation, to calm down. I wanted to make sure I would not do, or say, anything rash. But every time I see Alex now, I see a stranger, and I cannot help but wonder if he is mine. I have not wrestled with these thoughts in years. I cannot believe they are back at the forefront of my mind, I feel like I have taken a step back. Of course, when Alex was a toddler, when he first started to express an interest for the F1, when I saw him play with Victor, I could not help but wonder. But Victor had his own children and eventually, none of it seemed important any more. Time had gone by and our lives had remained unchanged by the events that took place that summer when we were still students. I forgot. I think all three of us forgot. And now, Louise and Diana have forced us to remember.

This whole day on the island has been painful. I cannot believe Anne is willing to pretend she never slept with Victor. I thought she would come clean to me straight after we found out our son had slept with Diana and Louise. But she did not. Her determination to bury her head in the sand, to believe that only the Munroes are affected by this twisted love triangle, sickens me. In the past two days, a deep-rooted anger towards my wife has been growing inside me. An anger I suspect I have always harboured in the depths of my heart and soul, a rage I managed to convince myself had disappeared for years, and which has finally broken free from its chains, more powerful and destructive than ever before. I have been trying to tame the beast, to contain it for the past two days but now, standing on the bow of the ferry, staring at the blue horizon ahead of me, on our way back from our disastrous family trip on the island, I know I am fighting a losing battle. My anger has rubbed off on Katie, Alex and Anne, and now, all four of us are sitting alone miserably in four different corners of the boat.

I sigh. What do I do next? Do I reveal to Anne that I know about her and Victor? About who our son might be or not be? Or do I keep quiet one more time? I cast my mind back to when Allan told me about his suspicions. What reasons prompted me to keep quiet twenty years ago? Do these reasons still stand?

It was a rainy summer afternoon. I was hanging out in Allan's flat, we were mindlessly watching something on the telly, probably drinking some beers. Allan was bored, I was gloomy. I could not get my mind off Anne and doing nothing did not agree with me. I needed to keep my mind and body busy in order to keep my spirits up. I think Allan probably had enough of my constant brooding.

'You need to stop thinking about that girl, man,' he eventually said to me. 'I really don't think she is worth the trouble to be completely honest with you.'

'She is worth it, man,' I replied, slightly annoyed at being called out for being a miserable, heartbroken, wet wipe still pining after his ex-girlfriend weeks after she had broken up with him.

'I really don't think she is,' he insisted. I could not help but notice his tone, he sounded a bit off.

'What do you mean by that?' I asked, sitting up.

Allan looked at me uncomfortably. Now I was truly intrigued. Something was not quite right. I prodded.

'Come on, out with it. There's something you are not telling me, I can tell. What is it? What do you know?'

'Well, I don't know anything for sure,' he replied. 'It's more of a suspicion, probably nothing.' He paused. 'I shouldn't have said anything, I feel like a shit friend for bringing anything up.'

'A shit friend to who?' I asked. Once again, Allan did not say anything, so I insisted, 'You would be a shit friend to me if you thought you knew something important about Anne and didn't tell me about it.'

Finally, Allan caved. 'Fine. It's about the other night. We all went out; Dylan, Keith, Victor, Anne and I.'

'Where was I?'

'That's the night your parents came to visit, you were having dinner with them.'

'Oh right, I see,' I replied. 'Anyway, carry on.'

'We all went to the pub, Dylan got pretty fucked, the usual. Anne got pretty pissed too. Nothing really happened but her and Victor... They looked pretty cosy. Lost them for a bit of the evening as well, no idea where they went or what they were doing. Keith and I were taking care of Dylan, he got kicked out of the pub so I went back inside to let Anne and Victor know we were going somewhere else. It was weird. I got the feeling I was interrupting them. Anyway.' Allan sighed. 'As I said, Anne was super drunk and decided to go home. So, Victor walked her back. I'm not sure why he didn't just get her a cab, I thought it was a bit odd at the time but didn't think too much into it. It's just... It took him a very long time to walk her home and then come back.' Allan scratched the back of his neck. 'I remember Keith joking about it, asking him what he had been up to for the last hour, hinting he was going after your sloppy seconds. Victor looked pissed, I thought he was being overly defensive about it. Clearly, Keith was just joking around. You know, you two living together, being best mates and all... Keith didn't actually believe Victor would try anything with Anne. But I don't know. Victor's reaction got me thinking... Maybe he did. So, that's what I mean by she's not worth it. What if she's shacking up with your best mate?'

Allan looked up at me, clearly worried about my reaction. I sat there motionless, staring at him in shock, a sinking feeling in my stomach. I thought, *He is insane. He is completely paranoid, making up stories from nothing. There is no actual evidence to support what he is implying. That Victor and Anne have had a one-night stand. This whole story, it's all based on how Allan thinks Victor should have reacted instead of how he did react. It's all bullshit.*

'That's insane,' I finally replied. 'I know Victor and Anne. They are decent people. I trust them. They would never do anything like this. Of course, Victor was defensive. It's completely tasteless from Keith to imply he would do something like that to his best mate.' Saying it out loud made me feel better. I knew I was right to defend Anne and Victor. They would never do this to me.

That would be too cruel.

'Of course, you are right,' replied Allan with his hands up in the air. He was clearly uncomfortable and desperate to drop the subject. 'I told you it was nothing, that I shouldn't say anything because it was just a ridiculous speculation. Forget I said anything. As you said, Victor's a sound guy.'

'And Anne's not like that either,' I added. 'She wouldn't stoop that low. She's got more class than that.'

'Of course, of course,' Allan nodded.

Allan and I never spoke about it again, but our conversation shook me. Even when Anne and I started dating again, I could not shake that tiny shred of doubt from my mind. Every time Victor and Anne spoke to each other, laughed at each other's jokes, jealousy soared through my veins and rushed up to my brain, impairing my thoughts, clouding my judgement. The more time I spent with them, the more insecure I got and my jealousy culminated the night of our final university formal.

Victor and Anne were sat next to each other on the long dinner table. I could not help but dissect their every move, read into every one of their interactions. I started seeing signs of filtration where there were none, I imagined hands brushing against each other, knees leaning into one another underneath the table, gazes being held for little bit too long. Eventually, I could not stand my paranoia for any longer, so I got paralytically drunk. I vaguely remember the end of the meal, the pub, some singing and Victor and Anne carrying me back home. After that, I blacked out for a few hours.

When I woke up, I was lying diagonally across my bed, all my clothes on, the duvet underneath me, only my shoes had been taken off. I wondered where Anne and Victor had gone, as my last memory was of me leaning heavily against both of their shoulders. I thought they might have gone back to the pub, which I understood from Victor, but which angered me from Anne. Surely, she should have stayed with me to check I was OK. That I would not throw up and choke on my own vomit in my sleep. I got up to go to the loo, I desperately needed to pee and some painkillers, all that beer had definitely gotten the better of me. I do not think Anne and Victor even noticed that they had left the bedroom door slightly ajar. That unfortunately, when I walked back from the bathroom, the gap between the door and the wall gave me an unmissable view of the floor by Thomas's bed. I recognised the orange dress Anne had been wearing that night. It was hard to miss. So bright and flashy. I knew then that Allan had been right all along. Thankfully, I was too hungover, or probably still too drunk, for the reality of what I had just seen to really sink in. I went straight to bed, and it is only the next morning, when I woke up with a soaring headache, that I truly felt sorry for myself. I lay there for hours, wondering what I should do. I knew I had to break up things off with Anne. Whatever we were to each other, it had to end. I just felt too awful to take action. I put it off. One day, two days, a week. We all moved out of Durham during that time, so it was easy to avoid Anne and Victor. I went back home for a few days before moving to London. I still did not tell a soul. I suppose I felt ashamed. Ashamed that I meant so little to the two people I thought of as my closest friends. I was in denial but I was still determined to break up with Anne at some point. I just wanted to make sure I could do it discreetly, so that nobody would find out about what Anne and Victor had done to me. I could not cope with the shame.

Then one day, I received an alarming text from Anne. She said she had something important to tell me. According to her, it could not wait. So, I told her to come over. She arrived just before dinnertime. As I mentally prepared myself to rip the bandage, to finally tell her it was all over, Anne told me she was pregnant. I could not believe it. Immediately, I understood that it could be Victor's as well as my own. I had a choice. Accept this child and trust my instinct that by telling me about her pregnancy first, Anne had chosen me over Victor. Or leave her to deal with the child on her own. I made my choice. I learned to live with it. I learned to forget about it.

But the truth has finally caught up with us and I realise that I am ready for Anne to know. To know that I see her for who she is. A liar. A cheat. That this image she has of ourselves as a happy, successful couple has only ever been a charade. A charade that only continued to exist because I decided it could. And now, I am ready for the deception to end. I do not hear Alex creeping up behind us. I did not want him to find out. Despite my mixed feelings towards him, I still think of him as my son. It was my instinct to protect him. I failed.

CHAPTER 39
9 MONTHS LATER
LONDON, 6 MAY 2023

Alex

I am running along an empty corridor. Suddenly, doors, all of different colours – blue, red, purple, yellow – appear around me along the walls I am racing past. I cannot decide if I should keep running, or if I should find out what lies behind one of them. Out of nowhere, a loud, masculine voice echoes, 'Fly little canary, fly, fly out of your cage.' Are these walls my prison? Finally, I come to a decision, I am going to open the yellow door. Yellow like a canary. I stop and reach for the handle. My hand gropes the empty air, how am I meant to get in? I lean against the yellow panel, which suddenly gives way underneath my weight. I fall forwards and as I brace myself to hit the hard, tiled floor, I keep falling. I fall and fall and fall. Suddenly, my whole body is submerged under ice-cold water. I have landed in a gigantic pool. The water is fluorescent green. The lifeguard blows into his whistle with all his might.

'Get out of there!' he yells at me, 'No one is allowed in the water!'

What kind of swimming pool does not allow people in the water, I wonder. As I come back up to the surface, I try to explain to the lifeguard that I did not mean to get in the water. I accidentally fell in. But he will not listen to what I have to say. He keeps blowing and blowing and blowing into his whistle, piercing through my temples with its strident shriek.

I wake up with a jolt. My morning alarm is blearing next to me on my bedside table. Its red, angry light is flashing 6:45 a.m. With a groan, I roll over and grab my phone to turn it off. I greet the silence with a sigh of relief. It is Monday morning, and last night, I promised myself I would get up early to go to the gym before work. I get up, put on some clothes, rub my sleepy eyes and make myself a quick coffee. Headphones in, I walk fifteen minutes to the gym. Like most Monday mornings, it is relatively busy, I have to wait five minutes before I find an empty squat rack. I wonder if the people around me are hardcore fitness freaks or if, like me, they are starting their week with a gym session in order to make up for all the drinking and partying they did over the weekend.

I start off with four sets of ten front squats, increasing the weight by 5kg for each set, followed by four sets of bent over rows. I am sweaty. It is the same routine every week. I always start the week off strong, I have three 'good days'; Monday, Tuesday and Wednesday. I get myself into a healthy routine, I work out, I eat well, I am productive. I feel good about myself, like I am winning at life. Then comes Thursday, the tiredness of the week starts to settle in, I cannot motivate myself to wake up early to go to the gym anymore. Thursday is also work drinks day. I get drunk with the guys from work, and I spend Friday hungover at my desk. I feel better by Friday evening but then it is the weekend and it is hard not to have plans when you live in London. Especially plans that do not revolve around alcohol. On Saturdays, I usually go to the pub with some uni friends or visit some mates in Clapham.

Recently, I have started going out clubbing more regularly, like I used to when I was a student. I usually have coke, or MD. I do not seek out drugs, they are just easily accessible. One of my friends will have some on them and they will want to share. Unsurprisingly, as a result of my Saturday antiques, Sundays are a pretty bleak and lonely affair. I usually end up nursing a hangover and a comedown on the couch, watching TV and picking at a takeaway pizza. My spirits are typically pretty low at that point, I feel exhausted and sorry for myself. I am almost excited for Monday morning, I cannot wait to get back into a healthy routine, to sort myself out. Every Sunday, I promise myself to break the vicious circle. I will set myself challenges, such as not to drink for a whole week, or only limit myself to one pint a night.

Sometimes, I am successful for a few weeks. But eventually, there comes a time when I feel that I 'deserve' to 'treat' myself because I have been very 'good'. That is when I go out on a full-blown bender. They usually involve a lot of tequila (especially if it is a Thursday) and occasionally, a blackout. I finish my workout with a ten-minute ab session.

I am out of the gym thirty-five minutes later. I walk home, absently scrolling on my social media feed. A photo of Katie pops up. I frown. She looks so different from what I remember. She is wearing all black – a tight skirt, a crop top and some black fishnets – and her arms are wrapped around two girls I do not recognise. They are in a dark room illuminated by flashlights and behind them, I can see a thick crowd of people facing a stage. My frown deepens. It looks like a night club. What is Katie doing in a nightclub? Her 18th birthday is still a few months away. The three of them are wearing sunglasses and sporting a beatific smile. I recognise that look. I am pretty sure Katie was high when that photo was taken. I scroll down to the caption, *'Nothing like night out with the gals to forget all about your worries #outout #girlz #clubbing #Neonnoir'*. My little sister was at Neon Noir this weekend, one of the biggest nightclubs in London. I wonder how she managed to pull that off without Mum and Dad finding out. If we were still talking, I would probably send them a screenshot of her latest post and tell them they need to have a chat with her. But we do not talk any more. We haven't since last summer. And the likelihood is, Katie would not be going on wild nights out if it had not been for last summer either. Apparently, we are both coping with the events that unfolded nine months ago in the same manner. Excessive partying and drugs. Thank goodness she does not know about Mum and Victor. About the other secret as I like to call it. The darker one. God knows what she would do to cope with that.

I flew back to London as soon as I possibly could after overhearing Mum and Dad's conversation on the ferry back from l'île d'Aix. Mum tried to talk me out of it, to have a conversation, but I shut her down. I wanted to scream at her, to throw something at her, but I did none of that. Katie was in the room next door and I wanted to bury this secret as much as Mum did. It was too shameful for anybody else to find out. But it was the final straw. Finding out about Mum and Victor, and Dad admitting that he always knew about it, made me realise how sick and twisted my family was. If I wanted to live a normal, healthy life filled with wholesome relationships, I had to get out of there.

I am financially independent, I have a job, a flat in Brixton, my own life separate from them, so the separation has not been too hard. Mum tried to reach out a couple of times, but I blocked her number, blocked her on social media, ignored her emails. Eventually, she gave up. I have completely segregated myself from my deceitful parents and tried to forget about my perverse, potentially deviant actions. Unfortunately, I am still waiting for the happy life I have been aspiring to materialise itself. Too often still, I am sucked into a spiral of self-destruction which stems from self-loathing and a desire to punish myself. At least, that is what my therapist has been saying. I started seeing Doctor Jacobs when I could not bring myself to get out of bed, even to go to work, a few months ago. Patrick, my boss, forced me to use the company's private health insurance to see a counsellor because he suspected I was suffering from depression. I would not have gone to see Doctor Jacobs if he had not forced me to. I suppose I am thankful for it now. I suppose I feel a little bit better than I did nine months ago. But sometimes, it is hard to know for sure. With all the pills and booze and medication…

CHAPTER 40
9 MONTHS LATER
LONDON, 6 MAY 2023

Victor

'Diana, Marco!' I bellow from the kitchen. 'It's eight fifteen, you need to have breakfast now or you are going to be late.'

I hear a pair of hurried footsteps racing down the stairs and my daughter storms through the door. I cannot help but scrutinise what she is wearing.

'Dear god, Diana, what is that on your face?'

Her eyelashes are caked with mascara and her lips are covered with a shiny layer of lip gloss. But when I see what she is wearing, her makeup becomes the least of my worries.

'There is no way in hell this skirt is appropriate school uniform length.' I cannot help but squirm at my daughter's bare thighs. She cannot leave the house like that. She would be a gust of wind away from flashing everyone around her. Diana rolls her eyes.

'Jee, good morning to you too, Dad,' she snaps at me.

'I am serious, young lady,' I continue, 'you need to change into something else. This is indecent.' I hate the thought of my little girl's body being exposed for everyone to see. She is too young to present herself as an object of sexual desire.

'This is nothing,' she replies, 'you should see what some other girls wear to school.'

'I don't care what other girls do, they are not my daughter. I want you to get changed. Now!'

'Oh my god, what is your problem?' Diana is now shouting. 'You have been on my back for months. Whatever I do is never good enough for you. I dress too provocatively, I don't work hard enough at school, I spend too much time with my friends, I give you too much attitude. Ever since you left Mum, you have been an absolute nightmare. I almost miss having her around!'

CHAPTER 42
9 MONTHS LATER
LONDON, 6 MAY 2023

Diana

I run to the bus stop and catch the bus into town in the nick of time. It is crowded with girls wearing the same stripy, black and blue blazer as I am. However, I do not recognise any of my friends so I sit on my own at the back of the bus until I get to the common. I walk through the green towards Lady Cecilia's front entrance and I almost jump out of my skin when I feel someone grabbing me from behind.

'Diana, I've been calling your name for ages!' my friend Rebecca exclaims as I spin around.

I take my earphones out and apologise.

'Sorry, Rebs, I didn't hear you over the music.' As a matter of fact, I had the volume cranked up so loud I could barely hear myself think, so it does not surprise me that I did not hear her approach. I was hoping the sound of my favourite singer's voice would help me drown out the fight I have just had with Dad, but I have not stopped thinking about him since I left the house. I hate myself for being so cruel to him. I blame myself for tearing our family apart and I am taking my anger out on him. It is not fair but I cannot help myself.

Rebecca and I walk into the school's main building and head to our first lesson. We have Maths, Spanish and our last lesson before lunch break is English. As per usual, we sit at the back of the classroom. Willow is already there when we walk through the door. She is sitting with her friend Tabatha and she is laughing at something she just said. Katie walks in the classroom just before the bell rings. She strides towards the last available chair and slouches into it with a heavy sigh. She keeps her head down and Willow turns her body around slightly so that she is facing in the opposite direction of where Katie is sitting. Willow looks in my general direction and we both advert our gazes, narrowly avoiding eye contact.

I have not spoken to either of them since the beginning of the new school year and thankfully, English is the only class we have together. Katie and Willow remained friends for a little while when we came back from Royan last summer, but they rapidly drifted apart when Katie started rebelling and hanging out with a wilder crew. I do not think Willow wanted anything to do with Katie's late-night partying and underage drinking (not that I would know for sure; after all, I have not spoken to her in months). Willow looks happy though, she is head girl and apparently, she is dating Luke, one of the hottest boys on Chelsea's School for Boys' lacrosse team. Good for her, I suppose. Not that I care about Luke. Or any other boy as it matters. On the contrary, I definitely do not want anything to do with boys anymore.

Miss Longbridge's shrill voice snaps me out of my reverie. We are studying classical English literature this term. Quickly, I open my notepad and grab my battered English book out of my backpack. I would not say I am the kind of person who loves to go to school and study, but at the moment, I welcome any distraction from my disastrous personal life with open arms. I focus on Miss Longbridge's description of nineteenth century Britain and soon enough, I lose myself in the past, a blissful world in which the Alexes and deceitful mums of the world do not exist.

CHAPTER 43
9 MONTHS LATER
LONDON, 6 MAY 2023

Katie

It is a relief when the school bell finally rings for lunch time. I pack my English books into my bag and follow my classmates out the door, impatient to get away from Miss Longbridge. She is the most boring teacher ever. I thought English was going to be an interesting subject. If I had known how dull my teacher was going to be, I would have chosen to study something else instead. I follow the stream of girls along the corridors. We are all heading towards the lunch hall. I spot Lucy and Hariette, who are wearing the same dark makeup and rolled up skirts as I am and weave my way through the crowd towards their table. I sit down and grab my packed lunch from my black backpack. I disregard the sandwich, too stodgy, and nibble on some carrot sticks instead. Lucy is scrolling on her phone and shows me the photo she is currently looking at, which happens to be my latest Instagram post.

'Love that photo,' she comments, 'your boobs look huge in it!'

I smile as if that is the greatest compliment a girl could ever wish for.

'Thanks, girl,' I reply. 'Last Saturday was fun!'

'So fun,' adds Harriette. 'Those fake ids your brother got us, Lucy, worked like a charm! I still can't believe we got into Neon Noir.'

'I know, it's insane,' replies Lucy. 'We definitely need to do this again.'

'Oh, oh,' says Harriette, interrupting our conversation. 'Mrs Keller incoming…'

All of us roll our eyes and try and keep our heads down. At least once a week, one of the three of us gets a telling off by the head teacher for wearing makeup and short skirts to school.

Unfortunately for me, today is not my lucky day.

'Miss Dalton!' Mrs Keller's voice pierces through the air and I have no choice but to look up at her. I make sure I stare at her with as much contempt and annoyance as I possibly dare. I want her to know I find her irritating, but I do not want to antagonise her too much either. The last thing I need is to get expelled from school. Things between Mum and Dad are already tense enough, I do not need to give them another reason to argue.

'Yes, Mrs Keller?'

'You know very well students at Lady Cecilia are not allowed to wear make up at school. Nor nail polish.' I glance down at my red nails, I painted them this weekend before we went out and they are already pretty chipped.

'I forgot,' I reply without too much conviction.

'Well, thankfully, I have makeup and nail polish remover in my office,' the head teacher replies to me. 'Follow me please, Miss Dalton, you need to get all that stuff off your face now.'

Mrs Keller stands next to our table until I get up. She turns around and I make sure I roll my eyes at my friends before I follow her out the lunch hall. As I walk through the rows of tables, I accidentally catch Willow's eye. She is sitting with her new and improved group of friends and I cannot help the surge of jealousy that boils through me. Rapidly, we both avert our gazes.

I think about Willow all the way to Mrs Keller's office and how our relationship slowly deteriorated over time. It all started when her parents decided to leave Royan early last summer. That was a very difficult time for me, I needed Willow to get through everything that was happening with my family and through no fault of her own, she abandoned me when I was most vulnerable. So, I started looking for distractions elsewhere, which came in the surprising form of Nora and Tala, Diana's holiday friends. We ran into each other on the beach, they asked me why Diana had left Royan and I said something unconvincing about her deciding to attend summer school to prepare for Six Form. I am sure they knew I was not being honest. I am a pretty poor liar, especially when I am put on the spot, but thankfully they did not press me on the issue. I could not exactly tell them the truth, which was that Diana's dad had decided to leave their mum and taken her and Marco back with him to London because he had found out she had cheated on him with my brother.

We started hanging out pretty regularly after that. Tala, Nora and I do not have much in common, they are pretty boy crazed which is definitely something I cannot relate to, but they love to go out and get drunk, and that was something I was more than happy to go along with. For Tala's sake, I even pretended to find Bastien cute, she is the kind of girl who loves to hear that she is getting with the boy that everybody else fancies. I definitely did not feel comfortable enough around these girls to tell them I am gay. I still have not told my parents about it, and with everything that is going on, I do not think I am going to be telling them anytime soon.

When I started clubbing in Royan, it was like a revelation. I had finally found a way for all my worries, anxieties and insecurities to disappear for hours on end. Finally, there were moments in life where I found a little peace and quiet inside my head. It was a relief and I was not going to give that up just because summer was over. So, I came back to London, changed up my style and made new friends. Superficial friends with whom I share shallow interests but friends who have the same intrinsic desire to get fucked up as I have.

Willow did not like the changes she was seeing in me. She tried to reason with me, she stuck by me at the start of the school year hoping I would grow out of my underage drinking and clubbing phase. She even made an effort to try and get to know Harriette and Lucy. But she stopped trying after she accompanied us to this random flat party in February. Harriette, Lucy and I got blackout drunk on vodka and according to Willow, she spent most of the night holding my hair back whilst I was throwing up in the bathtub. Harriette had already laid claims on the toilet and Lucy had to settle for the sink. I do not remember any of this, but apparently, I was awful to her. Willow told me all about it the next day over the phone. She was crying. She told me how I called her names and outed her in a game of spin the bottle. Apparently, I made a comment about Dean, whom the bottle was pointing at after she had spun it, not being her type. That he needed bigger boobs for her to want to kiss him. Willow never spoke to me after that. She broke up with me at the end of that phone call and I have avoided her ever since. Every time I see her, I feel unbearably guilty. I cannot deal with that emotion, so it is easier if I avoid it, and by extension Willow. I cannot help but wonder if that is the reason why she is dating that stupid lacrosse boy. I outed her before she was ready, she did not know how to deal with people's reactions and as a result, she is dating some random guy to deflect people's attention.

'There you go, Miss Dalton,' Mrs Keller's voice snaps me out of my reverie. She hands me a pack of makeup remover wipes. 'Now take off all that paint you have smeared across your face and then we will deal with those nails of yours. I know I have nail polish remover somewhere in here,' she says as she rummages through the drawers of her desk.

I sigh, this day is going from bad to worse. I cannot wait for the weekend.

CHAPTER 44
9 MONTHS LATER
LONDON, 6 MAY 2023

Sasha

'Lili, I'm home,' I shout from the landing as I close the door.

'Sasha? Is that you?' the voice of my wife bellows back at me from the depth of the house.

'It's me!' I reply. 'Where are you?' I ask as I take off my shoes and shrug my jacket off my shoulders.

'In the conservatory,' she replies. I head towards the back of the house, following the sound of her voice. 'You're early,' she says with a big smile as I wrap my arms around her and kiss her on the cheek.

'I know, I just didn't feel like staying at school late today.' I point at the big shopping bag dangling heavily from my left hand. 'But unfortunately, that does not mean that the working day is over. I have so much marking to catch up on. How's your day been, honey?' I ask as I sit down at the table opposite her, taking a huge pile of yellow English books out of my carrier bag and dropping them with a heavy thump in front of me. Begrudgingly, I grab the book at the top of the pile and glance at the name. Sebastian. I sigh painfully. His handwriting is so messy, marking his work is like trying to decipher a secret code. This is going to take me forever.

'It's been OK,' replies Liliane. 'The Stanley wedding is in two weeks now so I am finalising a few details. And I've had a nightmare with the catering staff for that corporate charity event, so spent most of the day sorting that out.'

I nod sympathetically. Liliane's phone buzzes.

'Just got a message from Leo,' she informs me. 'He's asking if Marco can come over for dinner after football training.'

'That shouldn't be a problem,' I reply.

Marco has been spending a lot of time at ours lately. Home life must not be very fun for him because of his parents' recent separation so I understand his need for escapism. Liliane feels very sorry for Marco and

Diana and as a result, she has been going out of her way to make Marco feel welcome in our home. If Willow and Diana were still on speaking terms, I am sure she would also be trying to have her around as much as possible. I understand where Liliane is coming from. I also feel sorry for those two kids. Their family situation is beyond messed up, but thankfully they do not know the whole extent of it. Unfortunately, Liliane and I do.

I remember it like it was yesterday. Liliane and I had broached the topic of leaving Royan early with Anne and Thomas to give them some privacy and space to work through their issues. But they would not hear anything about it. I think as long as we were still there, they could hold on to the illusion that things were more or less normal. The situation was pretty awkward for Liliane and I. On the one hand, we really wanted to drive back to London, it just felt too uncomfortable staying in their home with everything going on, especially once Alex left. His departure made the huge rift that had just torn their family apart even more tangible. On the other hand, we did not want to upset our friends any more than they already were. So we stayed put for about a week or so until one evening when Liliane and I accidentally overheard Anne and Thomas in the garden. We did not mean to, we were on our way out to Cédric's for a nightcap and we did not realise they were standing under the trees next to the front gate until we were within earshot. They were so absorbed in their conversation, they never noticed we were there.

'... I can't even look at you right now, you disgust me so much,' I remember Thomas saying.

Liliane and I froze. This was clearly an intense conversation and we did not want to interrupt them. We silently agreed to retreat back to the villa; after all, there was a well-stacked bar in the kitchen we could just help ourselves from. But Anne's response stopped us dead in our tracks.

'Why are you suddenly disgusted with me now? You found out about Victor and me twenty years ago and you decided to let it go. It's too late to be disgusted now. You had the chance to leave me when you found out I was pregnant and knew there was only a 50/50 chance it would be yours. You made your bed and now you need to lie in it.'

To this day, I still remember the look of pure horror on my wife's face. I am sure my expression was exactly the same. We immediately understood the implications of the conversation we had just overheard. Alex could be Victor's son. This would make him Diana's half-brother. And Louise's stepson. That was one degree of messed up too much for us. We could not pretend everything was fine for a second longer.

The next day, our bags were packed and we left the villa. Anne and Thomas did not try to stop us. They knew Royan was no longer the paradisiacal place it used to be. Even the kids did not protest our sudden departure too vehemently. I have a feeling they were secretly pleased to put some distance between themselves and the drama that had unfolded here a week ago. Of course, Liliane and I never said anything to the children. For the first few months we were back in London, we talked about the state of our old friends' marriages at length in hushed voices before going to bed. But after a while, life continued its course, we slipped back into our usual routine and we slowly started to forget about Anne, Thomas, Victor, Louise, Alex and Diana. Whatever was going on between them, it really did not concern us anymore. We had cut ties with them and as a result, their problems were no longer our concern. Of course, we have been trying our best to welcome Marco into our home whenever we can. After all, he is only a child and has nothing to do with any of it. And it is Liliane and my duty to preserve his innocence.

CHAPTER 45
9 MONTHS LATER
LONDON, 6 MAY 2023

Willow

I get off the bus and Luke follows closely behind me. He slides his hand into mine and together we turn into Eden Road. It is a ten-minute walk to my house from here and Luke has gotten into a habit of walking me home most days after school. I cannot help but find it mildly irritating and overbearing. I know I should not be feeling that way. If it were Katie walking me home, I would find it adorable and considerate. But Katie and I are no longer on speaking terms and since that horrible party where she outed me in front of half of the school, I have been working hard to put the rumours that I like girls to bed.

I am slightly disappointed in myself. I know I should not feel ashamed about being gay. I know it is not fair to use Luke and toy with his feelings for ulterior motives. I want to be open and proud about my sexual orientation. That night, even though I was angry at Katie for insinuating I liked girls in a game of spin the bottle, I was ready to admit to the truth. For a short moment, I almost felt relieved Katie had said something. I was ready for all the secrecy to end. But as I was hunting for some kitchen towels and cleaning spray to wipe all of Katie's vomit from the bathtub, I overheard a couple of Year thirteen girls gossiping about me.

'Do you think it's true?' one of the girls asked her friends.

'I wouldn't be surprised if she were actually gay,' replied another one. 'My little sister is in her year and I remember her telling me about some creep checking out all the other girls in the changing rooms during PE. Hundred per cent sure that's her.'

'*Eww*, gross, what a perv!' they all screamed in chorus.

'I mean, she's not the prettiest, is she?' another girl added. 'Maybe it's best if she prefers girls... It's not like plenty of boys will be lining up for her...'

I am sure they continued making fun of me for a while, but I left the room before I could hear anything else. I know those were a bunch of mean girls and that everybody was not going to react like them. I knew there were lots of children at Lady Cecilia who were inclusive and open-minded and who would have absolutely no issue with me being gay. Hell, there were lots of other girls at school who were out of the closet. But that night, I realised that the moment I decided to come out, I would inevitably become a topic of gossip and some girls would have nasty things to say about me. And I was not ready for that. I still am not ready for that. Which is why I am dating Luke. Which is why I do not speak to Katie any more. She betrayed me and on top of her recent destructive behaviour and having to keep that horrible secret about her brother from her, it became impossible to hold on to our friendship.

Nobody knows I know about Alex. I am aware Mum and Dad have been trying hard to keep this a secret from Leo and I, but they are not the most discreet people. I overheard them one evening whispering about it in the living room. I was on my way to the kitchen, I could not sleep and I fancied a cup of herbal tea. They did not hear me walk past the living room door and they did not hear me walk away. They were too absorbed in their conversation, wondering if Alex and Diana knew they were potentially half siblings or if Victor, Anne and Louise had managed to keep it a secret from them. I remember them saying they did not think Katie, Alex, Diana and Marco knew anything about the incestuous love triangle that linked both of their families together and that it was important it stayed that way. I was shocked. Naturally, I never said anything to Katie. She is already out of control, drinking and going out all the time even though she is only seventeen. This would tip her over the edge.

Luke and I suddenly arrive in front of our front door. He traps me in a tight embrace and presses his lips against mine. I can feel his tongue darting into my mouth and his body pressing against mine. I try to respond as convincingly as I can. We are girlfriend and boyfriend after all, this is normal, this is what couples do. We break apart and he gives me a big smile. Once again, he says something about his parents being away this weekend and having the house to himself. I know what he is hinting at. And I do not know how many more flimsy excuses about my busy schedule he is going to accept before he starts suspecting something. I smile back at him and tell him that sounds nice.

I close the door behind me and lean against the frame in relief. Leo's muddy football gear is littered all across the floor of the entrance hall. I take off my shoes and follow the voices into the kitchen. Marco and Leo are wolfing down a huge bowl of cereal and telling Mum all about their practice session. Dinner is almost ready but I know those two will still be hungry